"What began inside my mind and in front of my computer ended in the winter woods eighty miles north of St. Petersburg and encompassed my own initiation into pre-Christian European magic."

—Kenneth Johnson

In Eastern Europe and European Russia, the spiritual world of primordial hunters is still alive, even though their hearth-fires are long cold. Until now, few scholars were even aware that a magical tradition still existed in the land now inhabited by Slavic peoples.

Author Kenneth Johnson presents his true-life experiences with the living practitioners of a magical discipline extending back into pre-Christian times. Johnson traveled to Russia and studied with several Slavic sorcerers, one of whom took him under his wing and put him through extensive training in Pagan Earth Magic.

Slavic Sorcery serves as a course in the mythology and lore of the Slavic peoples, covering the seasonal festivals, cosmology, the gods, the Otherworld spirits, beliefs about the ancestors, and authentic shamanic practices. Journey through the Earth's power centers—groves of trees, bald mountains, rivers, fountains and stream banks—and discover the life-force that has animated and vitalized the Slavic peoples for more than a thousand years.

About the Author

Kenneth Johnson holds a degree in Comparative Religions with an emphasis on the study of mythology. He is the author of *Jaguar Wisdom* (Llewellyn, 1997) and *North Star Road* (Llewellyn, 1996), co-author of *The Silver Wheel* (Llewellyn, 1995) and *The Grail Castle* (Llewellyn, 1995) with Marguerite Elsbeth, and *Mythic Astrology* (with Ariel Guttman, Llewellyn, 1993). Born in southern California, he has lived in Los Angeles, Amsterdam, London, and New Mexico, and currently resides in Santa Cruz, California.

To Write the Author

If you wish to contact the author or would like more information about this book, please write to the author in care of Llewellyn Worldwide and we will forward your request. Both the author and the publisher appreciate hearing from you and learning of your enjoyment of this book and how it has helped you. Llewellyn Worldwide cannot guarantee that every letter written to the author can be answered, but all will be forwarded. Please write to:

Kenneth Johnson
c/o Llewellyn Worldwide
P.O. Box 64383, Dept. K374-3
St. Paul, MN 55164-0383
U.S.A.

SLAVIC SORCERY

SHAMANIC JOURNEY OF INITIATION

KENNETH JOHNSON

Foreword by
Igor Kungurtsev & Olga Luchakova

1998
Llewellyn Publications
St. Paul, Minnesota 55164-0383, U.S.A.

Cover design: Anne-Marie Garrison
Cover art and interior illustrations: Helen Michaels
Photographs: Kenneth Johnson
Book editing and design: Astrid Sandell

Library of Congress Cataloging-in-Publication Data
Johnson, Kenneth, 1952-
    Slavic sorcery : shamanic journey of initiation / Kenneth Johnson ;
foreword by Igor Kungurtsev & Olga Luchakova.
        p.   cm.
    Includes bibliographical references.
    ISBN 1-56718-374-3 (pbk.)
    1. Shamanism—Russia. 2. Shamanism—Europe, Eastern. I. Title.
BL2370.S5J64 1998
299'.18—dc21   97-32118
                                                                  CIP

PUBLISHER'S NOTE:
Llewellyn Worldwide does not participate in, endorse, or have any authority or responsibility concerning private business transactions between our authors and the public.
    All mail addressed to the author is forwarded but the publisher cannot, unless specifically instructed by the author, give out an address or phone number.

Printed in U.S.A.

Llewellyn Publications
A Division of Llewellyn Worldwide, Ltd.
P.O. Box 64383, Dept. 374-3
St. Paul, MN 55164-0383, U.S.A.

Also by Kenneth Johnson

Jaguar Wisdom: Mayan Calendar Magic, 1997

North Star Road, 1996

The Silver Wheel: Female Myths and Mysteries in the Celtic Tradition
(with Marguerite Elsbeth), 1996

The Grail Castle: Male Myths and Mysteries in the Celtic Tradition
(with Marguerite Elsbeth), 1995

Mythic Astrology: Archetypal Powers in the Horoscope (with Ariel
Guttman), 1993

Forthcoming by Kenneth Johnson

Witchcraft and the Shamanic Journey (revised edition of *North Star Road*)

CONTENTS

	Foreword	ix
	Preface	xi
one	Ancestors	1
two	Darkness and Light	19
three	Magical Healing	47
four	Icons and Archetypes	71
five	Earth Magic: The Green Hills	101
six	Earth Magic: The Magic of Trees	123
seven	Otherworld Spirits	141
eight	Earth Magic: Wintersong	167
nine	Healing the World Tree	181
	Resource Directory	199
	Glossary	201
	Bibliography	211
	Index	213

FOREWORD

The book you are about to read is unique and, undoubtedly, one of the first to be published on this topic in the West. Although a body of literature analyzing Slavic folklore and fairytales does exist, the reader will here enjoy, for the first time, a personal account of the author's actual apprenticeship with modern successors of the ancient Slavic sorcerers.

Slavic sorcery and its healing arts should not be confused with Siberian shamanism. In their beliefs and practices, the Slavic wizards more closely resembled the ancient Druids of Western Europe than Siberian medicine men. But the most amazing fact, and one which is unknown even to experts in mythology, is that the tradition of Slavic sorcery is alive today. It survived the Christianization of Russia by Vladimir of Kiev. It defied the Westernization introduced by Czar Peter the Great. And it preserved itself by going underground during the Communist regime.

So it was not at all illogical that Ken Johnson should go to Russia in search of a living tradition which disappeared long ago in Western Europe. Prior to that, he had done significant research on Slavic history, mythology, and folklore—all of which is reflected in the book. In fact, one of the features that makes his book unique is the alternation of mythological research with the accounts of field experience—a structure that provides an historical perspective and places the material on a serious anthropological basis, while avoiding the pitfalls inherent in both Castaneda's phenomenalism and in more abstract anthropological reductionism.

The sorcerer's world is a subtle one. Without direct experience, it may easily be misinterpreted, especially when the interpretation stems from an essentially cerebral Western culture. We especially appreciate Ken's talent and efforts in entering into the world of Slavic sorcery and subsequently describing its esoteric practices without distortion. We have studied with many mystics in Russia and it is our pleasure to confirm that the author's understanding of the traditional methods and their experiential results is accurate.

Ken Johnson has done a great service to Western readers in presenting this book on a largely unknown subject, a book that reads like a fascinating mystery and adventure (which it is!) and yet remains anthropologically sound.

Igor Kungurtsev
Olga Luchakova, Ph.D.
Adjunct Professors
Institute of Transpersonal Psychology
Palo Alto, California
John F. Kennedy University
Orinda, California

PREFACE

This book began simply as an attempt to convey something of Pagan Slavic mythology and lore; it evolved into something quite different. Early in my research, I interviewed Drs. Igor Kungurtsev and Olga Luchakova of the California Institute for Integral Studies in San Francisco, authors of an article (in *Gnosis* Magazine) that dealt with the Russian "spiritual underground," including the practices of traditional sorcerers whose art clearly extended back into Pagan times. I imagined that such traditional practitioners must be remote and difficult to access; consequently, I was amazed when Igor and Olga told me: "If you can manage to get yourself over to Russia, we can arrange for you to meet and study with some of the sorcerers."

From that moment on, the book became a deeply personal rather than a merely intellectual matter, a chronicle of my own inner journey into Pagan sorcery as well as an exploration of folklore and myth. What began inside my mind and in front of my computer ended in the winter woods eighty miles north of St. Petersburg and encompassed my own initiation into pre-Christian European magic.

Olga has warned me against attempting too sharp a distinction between practices that are identifiably pre-Christian and those that have entered the Slavic sorcery tradition from other sources—notably Eastern Orthodox mysticism and magical Buddhism. I have tried to make such a distinction anyway; in so doing I may have done a disservice to some of my teachers, especially Vladimir Antonov, whose personal vision includes Taoism, Hinduism, and mystical Christianity as well as traditional Pagan Sorcery.

I owe a great debt to all the people who helped me while I was in St. Petersburg. The names and addresses of the healers and magicians with whom I worked can be found in the Resource Directory at the end of this book. Unlike Castaneda's Don Juan, they are relatively accessible and, in most cases, eager to teach. I would also like to thank the healer Galina Vaver, who cleansed my inner centers; Dr. Ina Kirtchik, at whose home I stayed during my sojourn in Russia; Dmitri Vinogradov and Arina Kol'tsova, who served as translators while I worked with Dr. Polyakov and Natasha Sviridova respectively; and Gennady Ivanov, who helped me make several valuable connections. Most of all, my deepest thanks to Igor and Olga, without whom this book simply would not have been possible.

Kenneth Johnson
Santa Cruz, California
October 1997

ONE

ANCESTORS

THE MAN IN THE CHARCOAL-GRAY SUIT moved through the corridors of the Hermitage Museum with an almost manic vigor, as if leading a horde of Cossacks into battle. The tall young woman who accompanied him managed to keep pace, but I lagged somewhat behind.

He came to an abrupt halt in a room filled with paintings by Rubens. "With Rubens, you see, the energy is not at all peaceful. He scatters everything in every direction. I will show you. It is like this."

He fumbled frantically in the pockets of his suit, muttering a great deal and coming up empty-handed. The young woman reached into her bag and handed him a scrap of paper. He fumbled in his pockets again, and again the woman reached into her bag, this time handing him a pen.

Dr. Vadim Polyakov, President of the Association of Applied Parapsychology at St. Petersburg Technical University, planted himself in the center of the room, gazing at a large canvas—a typical Rubenesque hash of fat ladies and cherubs—and muttering. The old woman who sat in a corner guarding the room (every room in Russian museums is guarded by old women) glared at him with icy ferocity but said nothing.

Polyakov held the pen in his left hand, suspended over the piece of paper held in his right.

"I concentrate my attention," he chanted. "And...."

His left hand began to shake, creating an intense-looking squiggle on the scrap of paper.

"You see," he said, rather proudly, "that's Rubens."

I looked. I didn't see Rubens. I could see that Polyakov was responding to the quality of psychic energy he perceived in the painting, and that he was reproducing it on paper by allowing his hand to respond automatically to the "vibrations." But I didn't see Rubens.

"Rubens," he went on, "was out of harmony because he had a physical problem. But where? Let us see." He turned the scrap of paper over. He furiously crossed out some jottings which Arina, his companion, must have made and proceeded to sketch the outline of a human form.

"Like this, see. I concentrate my attention, and...."

Again, the wild squiggling. This time, however, he produced a thick blob of ink on the outline's thigh.

"Rubens had a problem in his thigh. It gave him great pain. He was out of harmony." He took one more look at the canvas, his eyes narrowing to tiny slits as he ran his long, thin fingers over his sparse hair. Then he shook his head disapprovingly.

"His energy was not good," he pronounced. "Let us go." We continued to storm the Hermitage. I was beginning to wonder why.

This wasn't exactly what I was looking for. I had contacted Dr. Polyakov because, as a parapsychologist, he had worked extensively with folk healers from the villages of Russia. The spiritual philosophy and, especially, the magical practices of these rural magicians were what I had come to Russia to study. Polyakov, however, kept insisting that village healers were "too primitive," and that he had improved upon their techniques in his laboratory. He insisted that it could all be done more efficiently on a computer. He told me he would show me.

But New Age computer programs could be had, in abundance, back home in the United States. What I wanted was "the primitive." So I was a bit disappointed. I had to agree with him about Rubens, though. I had never liked all those cherubs and fat ladies.

As we made our way through the Hermitage, Polyakov continued to trash the accepted canons of Western art criticism. According to his doctrine of the psychic energy present in paintings, "good" paintings were those embodying perfect and regular geometric patterns while at the same time giving forth an aura that was either moderately "warm" or a little bit "cool"—but never downright "hot" or "cold." He favored painters like Camille Corot and Claude Lorrain, whose pastoral calm strikes many critics as somewhat dull. On the other hand, he thoroughly disapproved of Vincent Van Gogh, whom he regarded as an embodiment of chaos, and Wassily Kandinsky, whom he dismissed with an imperious wave of his hand, not even deigning to look. Even Leonardo da Vinci, in his opinion, was a little bit nervous and off-center. The medieval Russian icons, with their quiet, meditative faces surrounded by Byzantine gold, were his idea of artistic perfection.

After about an hour, it became apparent to me that his judgments were based on a system of cosmic dualities not unlike the Chinese yin and yang. Here, at last, was something I might find useful, for the old Slavic Paganism had included a similar dualism.

"I have an appointment at the office," announced Polyakov quite suddenly. Our time was up. He shook my hand, invited me to call him at the office, and—still followed by Arina—stalked off at the same hurried pace that had characterized our whole tour of the Hermitage.

After Polyakov and Arina had gone, I toured the museum at my own, somewhat slower, pace. I had to agree with Polyakov again—the icons were more interesting to me than the seventeenth and eighteenth century pieces, or even the moderns.

In the late afternoon, I started home. I was scheduled to meet Vladimir Antonov that evening, another potential contact in my search for those remnants of pre-Christian Europe that, I had been assured, still survived in Russia.

I decided to change some money first. I strolled from the Hermitage to the Square of Arts, past the statue of the poet Pushkin, who died in 1837, but whose monument is still strewn, every day, with bouquets of flowers left by admiring Russians. Beyond lay the Grand Hotel Europa and, across the street, the Commercial Bank. The American Express office was housed in the Europa, but, at the moment, was refusing to serve any customers who didn't carry American Express traveler's checks or an American Express credit card, so I had to go elsewhere. I crossed the street to the Commercial Bank and joined the line outside. For some reason I was never able to understand, the bank seemed to be terrified of its customers. The doors were kept locked. Customers were admitted one at a time by an armed guard, who then locked the doors once again. Each time a customer entered or left the building, the door was unlocked and then locked all over again.

The line stretched down the steps and onto the street. I was going to have to wait for a while.

I pulled my coat in closer against the late afternoon chill and studied the faces of the people in line. Only a few of them were tourists or foreigners—October is not exactly the peak month for tourism in St. Petersburg. Most of them were Russians who, for one reason or another, had been paid in "hard" (i.e., Western) currency, and wanted to change their money at a decent rate. Ordinary people.

IN MY IMAGINATION, I transport the people in the bank line to another time and place. I bend the line into a circle, conjure the autumn into spring, and summon music from the twilight air...

To the sounds of flutes and drums they gather, the villagers, garbed in leather leggings and woolen tunics. The women wear garlands of flowers in their cornsilk hair. Here, at the foot of the sacred hill, the meadows are riotous with spring flowers and the droning of bees, and it is here that the ceremony will take place. The old wise woman prophecies the coming year and its harvest. The people dance in a ring, their faces turned toward the light of the sun that, once again, has brought an end to winter.

And now the village elder arrives to imprint his sacred kiss upon the blossoming earth. A mystic wildness seizes the people of the village; they dance, they leap, intoxicated and transported with mead and sex.

Night falls. The maiden who has been chosen as bride of the harvest god Yarilo bows to his image carved in wood. And as the elders, dressed in bear skins, watch impassively, the girl begins to dance in the center of the ring, faster and faster, spinning in a wild ecstasy, a mystical abandon....

Until, at last, she dies, the sacrificial bride of Yarilo.

That, at least, is the picture of the ancient Slavic world captured in Igor Stravinsky's ballet *The Rites of Spring*. The ballet was in fact a kind of collaboration between four men: Stravinsky wrote the music; Nicholas Roerich wrote the scenario; Nijinksy choreographed the original production; and Sergei Diaghilev produced it.

In a way, these four men constitute a kind of group portrait of the Slavic magical spirit: Stravinsky, the scholarly humanist whose music shocked the world; Diaghilev, the fanatical impresario for whom art was a kind of religion; Nijinsky, the legendary "holy fool" whose dancing was believed to embody genuine feats of levitation and who, possessed by the archetype of Dionysus, ended his life in a mental institution; and Roerich, the gifted painter who began as a student of Pagan Slavic Earth Magic and finished as a universal mystic, wandering the steppes of Central Asia in quest of the fabled city of Shambhala.

Though Roerich ended his scenario with a scene of human sacrifice, he himself had a deep love for the ancient ways of the Slavic people; he had worked as an archaeologist in the Russian dirt, and had visually recreated the Pagan Slavic lifeway in some of his early paintings. In *The Rites of Spring*, he evoked a world that harks back to some of the most ancient spiritual concepts in the European mind.

THE LANDS NOW inhabited by Slavic peoples include almost all of Eastern Europe and European Russia, a truly vast geographical region larger than Western Europe. Some of the magical and mythological themes common throughout this immense landscape are incredibly ancient. The grassy steppes of the Ukraine were a favorite haunt of Ice Age hunters, and some of the oldest habitations constructed by humans —huts made of mammoth bones and covered with skins—have been found there.

The spiritual world of these primordial hunters is still alive, even though their hearth-fires are long cold. The mammoth hunters worshipped a goddess who is sometimes depicted as large-bodied and naked, sometimes slender and clothed in animal skins. Linked with both the hearth-fire and with animals, the goddess figurines of the mammoth hunters are decorated with abstract markings such as chevrons, meanders, lozenges, and parallel lines.[1] This deity and her abstract symbols still survive in many shapes and forms, notably in the folk arts and handicrafts of Slavic women such as *pich* or stove decorations, women's clothing, and embroidered ritual towels.

Around 7000 B.C.E., agriculture began to make its way into Eastern Europe, inaugurating a way of life that left indelible traces on the folk practices and mythologies of the region. Today, only large mounds of earth mark the location of villages that flourished for thousands of years; but beneath those mounds lies a wealth of pottery, jewelry, and figurines which attest to the grace and charm of that long-ago era. The ring dance, captured in Stravinsky's ballet, also appears on the pottery of these ancient villages, and it is this epoch which has attracted the attention of so many contemporary worshippers of the Goddess. They see in the Neolithic cultures of ancient Europe a social model and ideal relevant to their own lives. Whether or not the European Neolithic was the kind of earthly paradise that feminist historians such as Riane Eisler[2] have imagined is highly debatable, but it was a vivid and colorful era marked by a high level of artistic achievement and striking religious imagery.

A few figurines of male deities survive from this period, suggesting that the Lord of the Wildwood and the Young Harvest God were the principal masculine divinities of that era, but it is the Goddess who, in myriad aspects and forms, dominates the spiritual world of the European Neolithic. She appears in the guise of a bird (usually a mallard duck) as creatrix of the universe and Mistress of the Waters of Heaven, while as a Snake Mother she watches over every village and house. She is the Mistress of Animals who haunts the wild places, as well as the birth-giving mother who, in the shape of a bear, nurtures and nourishes all her children. She is the fertile Earth Mother, pregnant and heavy with child. In the end, she is the White Lady of Death, the bone mother whose animal totem is the owl, and who slays us only to resurrect us.[3]

Around 4300 B.C.E., a new people emerged from the steppes. According to the dominant archaeological paradigm, these pastoral nomads spoke a language that scholars call Proto-Indo-European; and although many eminent Vedic scholars disagree, this hypothetical language is regarded as the ancestor of most of our present-day European languages as well as of Sanskrit and Persian. Armed with new and improved weapons, they moved westward into the heartland of Neolithic Europe. By about 3500 B.C.E., the old Goddess cultures had disappeared, replaced by the Indo-European lifeway.

Whether rightly or wrongly, feminist scholars regard the Indo-European movement into Europe as the great historical watershed or dividing line between matriarchy and patriarchy (and thus, in terms of radical feminism, between good and evil). They characterize the Indo-Europeans as a harsh and warlike people who, over the course of about 1500 years, invaded Europe, eradicating the Goddess-centered cultures of the Neolithic—which, by way of contrast, they characterize as peaceful and spiritual.

In fact there is little archaeological evidence to support the notion of a violent military conquest at the end of the Neolithic. Indo-European cultural traits increase throughout Europe very gradually, over a period of more than a thousand years. Though implements of war do tend to appear among the archaeological remains of the new cultures, there is nothing to suggest that the villages of Old Europe were burned to the ground, or that the Old Europeans of the Goddess cultures were massacred or slain. Rather, one gains the impression of a slow, continuous stream of nomads moving west into new country. As they proceeded upon their path, they may have occasionally entered into military conflict with the earlier people—though this does not necessarily mean that they were always victorious. More often, however, the Indo-Europeans seem to have made their way through compromise, inter-marriage, and through a merging of traditions. Hence the mythologies of Pagan Europe were, in reality, "composite" mythologies made up of two different traditions, two different lifeways and world-views—that of the Indo-Europeans, and that of the Goddess cultures who went before.[4]

The ruler of the new Indo-European heaven was a contemplative god who reflected much and acted little; his worldly manifestation lay in the sun and the daytime sky. Action was the province of the warlike Thunder God who rode through the sky in a great chariot with a thunderbolt hammer and who was the special deity of Indo-European warriors. The Underworld, home of the departed ancestors, lay beneath our world, a gloomy place ruled by a dark lord whose totem was a gigantic serpent and who was engaged in a perpetual struggle with the Thunder God.

While the Indo-Europeans were warriors and nomads, the Old Europeans of the Neolithic had been tillers of the soil, and it was in the guise of earth deities that their goddesses and gods survived. The Russian goddess Mokosh, "Moist Mother Earth," is a descendant of the pregnant vegetation mother of ancient times, while Lada, goddess of the spring, is reminiscent of an even older figure, the slender young goddess of the Ice Age. The forest spirit, or Leshy, of Russian folklore is almost certainly an aspect of the Neolithic Lord of the Wildwood, and Kupalo, whose feast was celebrated on the summer solstice, an incarnation of the Young Harvest God. Baba Yaga, the wild old crone who guards the Water of Life and Death, is none other than the White Lady of Death and Rebirth.

THE LINE MOVED slowly. Having waited in the street in front of the bank, I now stood on its steps, feeling out of place. Survival was the principal concern among the citizens here; if I had been able to converse with the people in line (I spoke no Russian at all), they would have found my reason for being here exotic to the point of craziness.

Unlike most Americans, I had never been raised in any identifiably "Christian" tradition. My parents attended a bland, colorless Protestant church with great reluctance, and only until I was five years old. At that point they told me: "God, Jesus, the afterlife? We don't have a clue what's out there. Believe whatever you like."

I was always curious. Having grown up in southern California during the 1950s and 60s, I became familiar with the spiritual traditions of India, China, and Japan earlier in life than most people—even then, California was a spiritual smorgasbord comprised of offerings from all around the globe. During my first years of college in the early 1970s, my friends and I would hitch-hike up to Los Angeles, going from one foundation or ashram to the next, collecting literature and conversation. I came to have a deep respect for those Asian traditions—but respect is not identity. I am not, by any stretch of the imagination, an ascetic; nor could I develop any affection for or sense of relationship with the religious imagery of the East, the serene (but to my mind rather cold) Buddhas or the fanged, multi-limbed deities of India. I have always been too cranky to submit to the regimen of any other mortal, whether drill sergeant or guru. And I hate being told what to eat.

It was only in college that I experienced a deep, life-altering contact with spiritual images and concepts that genuinely moved me. That experience took place through the study of mythology.

In the beginning, of course, mythology was simply "literature" to me, as it is to most of Western culture. The ancient gods and heroes, the elves and nymphs, the great World Tree that stood at the center of the old mythic universe—all these images captured my mind with an intensely emotional feeling, an inner resonance I recognized as "spiritual" in some fashion. Nevertheless, I didn't really think of mythology as a religion. Not at first.

I suppose that my own pilgrimage, over the years, was no different than that of many other people. The rebirth of Western mythology as spirituality in its own right was something that was "in the air," thanks to an increasing number of psychologists and artists who found their way to the work of Carl Jung and Joseph Campbell, and then to an appreciation of the vital spirit that informs the ancient myths. In time I came to realize that my own religious instincts were not really that difficult to define; they were simply Pagan.

However, "Pagan" is a term that is ambivalent and admits to no clear definition. Those who generally describe themselves as Pagans (or, more accurately, neo-Pagans) seem, at least to outward eyes, to be participants in a kind of costume party inspired by old movies, Renaissance Faires, and wild historical misunderstandings about European witchlore—frustrated office workers dancing round the port-a-potty by the light of the silvery moon.

What else can one expect from a tradition that has been reconstructed out of old books? To seek the ancient roots of the Western psyche is (to use the mythic term for it) a "night-sea journey," a quest undertaken in darkness, navigating by instinct alone. Because the pre-Christian religions of our ancestors died out hundreds of years ago, we no longer have the opportunity to sit at the feet of tribal elders and receive a living tradition. Books are our elders, and what we make of those books has become vicarious tradition.

Or so, at least, I had always believed. However, in the course of my own searching, writing, and studying, I had become aware that a considerable body of pre-Christian European practice survived here in Russia and in the other nations of the former Soviet Union.

By the time I emerged from the bank with a wallet full of roubles, the twilight was deepening. I didn't have a watch, but figured it was time to hurry back to the home of my hostess, Dr. Ina Kirtchik, to meet Vladimir Antonov. I crossed the Square of Arts. I knew I could veer left down the Yekaterinsky Canal, past the Church of the Resurrection, and then turn right again through a series of parks and gardens to the banks of the Neva, which would lead me home. But that was the long way around, so I decided to find a short-cut directly to the Neva.

I plunged into what soon proved to be a regular warren of streets. If I kept going in the right direction, I should emerge at any moment on the banks of the Neva.

Darkness fell quickly. The buildings loomed over me, brooding. It was true that my investigation (if that's what you want to call it) was only beginning, but I was already having reservations. One cannot simply stride into a Russian village, announce oneself, and ask to see the local *koldunya* or sorceress. To attempt to do so would be roughly equivalent to driving your Mercedes onto an impoverished Indian reservation and asking for the local medicine man, whom you expect to train you in the ways of magic. In other words, I would most likely meet with stony silence, or—in the case of Russia—something worse. The villages were full of ultra-nationalistic fervor, inspired by Zhirinovsky and his ilk, and an unwary foreign visitor might very well find himself thumped and left in a ditch by the local "good old boys."

I knew all this from the beginning, I told myself as I hurried, faster now, through increasingly unfamiliar streets. That was why I was relying on a medial world made available to me by Dr. Kirtchik's daughter Olga and her colleague Igor—a world midway between the ordinary urban Russian and the semi-Pagan villager, made up of parapsychologists like Polyakov who had studied and learned the means and methods of the village healers, or teachers like Antonov, a former college professor who had somehow acquired an extensive knowledge of the ancient Earth Magic.

Was I chasing a chimera? Polyakov admitted to having studied with the *kolduny*, but was inclined to dismiss them as "primitive," insisting on introducing me to his computer instead. I had not yet met with Antonov, but during a phone conversation he had regaled me with a great deal of Sanskrit and Theosophy and nothing at all which was identifiably indigenous.

Maybe I was crazy to think I could make even the slightest headway into the primordial world of the kolduny when I didn't even speak any Russian.

And if I wasn't crazy, I was, at the very least, lost. I could see that now....

It was dark, and the streetlights had not yet been turned on. I passed a road crew working late, tearing up the sidewalk in front of me and forcing me to veer through the street itself. I dodged a speeding car. All Russian drivers proceeded through the streets at breakneck speed, it seemed, and about half of them were intent on mowing down pedestrians—they seemed to be consciously taking aim. I looked back at the road crew and saw them outlined in the orange glare of their acetylene torches and work lamps. It was a scene reminiscent of all those *National Geographic*-style photos of the Soviet Union I used to see during my childhood: *These are our enemies, children, working in their big iron cities.*

It seemed that I had entered a whole other world now. I was no longer in elegant St. Petersburg, brisk with energy as it sought to regain its rightful place as one of Europe's great cities. Here, lost among these winding streets, I had stumbled into a dark Leningrad of the spirit, a region haunted by the ghost of its crazy namesake who still (yes, still!) lay under glass like an old pheasant in Moscow and who brooded over these streets, these streets filled with suspicious faces and towering buildings of gray concrete, the nightmare vision of a Stalinesque Eastern Europe which had been indelibly imprinted on the minds of all American children raised during the Cold War.

Where the hell was I, anyway? Where was the Neva? Feeling the sweat run down my face and start to freeze in the chilly October evening, I realized that I was no longer walking, but almost running. Almost anywhere else, people would be staring at me. But in Russia, as in New York, no one looked anyone else in the eye.

Then, suddenly, I emerged into bright lights. Here was the Nevksy Prospect, which was more or less the city's principal thoroughfare, and here was the Fontanka Canal. How did I get way over here?

In any case, this was an improvement. All the canals connected with the Neva River sooner or later, and by following the Fontanka I would reach the river at a very convenient spot not far from Ina's house. Of course I must be very late now. Things were not turning out very well, were they? I wondered if Antonov had given up and gone away by now. But if he were simply going to preach a lot of second-hand Hinduism (easy enough to come by in California or in my present New Mexico home), then what did it matter?

I reached the Neva and turned right, and soon I was on Shpalernaya Street. I took the stairs up to Ina's flat three at a time, and when I reached the warm, well-lit kitchen I was winded, breathing hard, and dripping with sweat.

Vladimir Antonov was sitting at the kitchen table. He stood up, looking like an old Russian bear in a sweater and flannel shirt. About fifty, he had sparse gray hair and a full gray beard reaching to the middle of his chest. He embraced me fiercely and kissed me on both cheeks.

After a bite to eat, Antonov herded me, still sweating, into the sitting room of Ina's flat. With us was a quiet woman who spoke no English and who had been introduced to me as Galina Vaver. I was to discover that she was Antonov's ex-wife and a rather celebrated psychic healer.

But for now, Vladimir was discoursing. He had asked me what I wanted to learn, and when I told him, he replied, "Of the old Pagan ways, nothing at all remains. But I will teach you Raja Yoga and Buddhi Yoga. I can see that you are in need of this."

Wonderful, I thought. Just wonderful.

VLADIMIR HAD SAID that nothing remained of the world-view of Slavic Paganism. He was wrong.

From 3000 B.C.E. on, Eastern Europe was home to a shifting array of cultures. It was from this restless matrix of peoples and tribes that the Slavs emerged.

Though the Slavs make their first appearance in history very late (about 500 C.E.), linguistic evidence suggests that the Slavic languages began to take shape almost a thousand years earlier. The original home-land of the Slavic peoples probably lay somewhere between the Vistula River and the Dnieper, in territory that is now part of Poland, Belarus, and Ukraine.[5] There are three distinct groups of Slavs: the Western Slavs who inhabit present-day Poland, Czech Republic, and Slovakia; the Southern Slavs of Bosnia, Serbia, Croatia, Slovenia, Macedon, and Bulgaria; and the Eastern Slavs of Russia, Belarus, and Ukraine. During the so-called Dark Ages, while the kingdoms of Western Europe were taking shape amidst the ruins of Rome, the Slavs continued to live much as European tribes had lived hundreds of years earlier. Their villages were ruled by local chieftains; patriarchal families were organized into clans, and the clans into tribes. Life was centered in the great forests and plains rather than in the comparatively sparse settlements. Subsistence depended on fishing, hunting, bee-keeping, cattle herding in the forest clearings and natural meadows, and farming. Houses were made of wood from the forests. The Slavs sold honey, beeswax, and skins to the merchants of Byzantium and the Viking North.

Scholars like to describe Slavic religion as "rustic"—gods and nature spirits were carved from wood, sometimes oak. (This practice can still be seen in the western Carpathians to the present day, where village sorcerers carve nature spirits out of wood for use in healing and exorcism rituals.) The creator or sky god common to all the Indo-European peoples appears in Slavic myth as Svarog; his son, Dazhbog, was the visible sun, and another god, called Svarovitch or "son of Svarog," was a god of the primal fire. A thunder god by the name of Perun was commonly worshipped in Slavic lands as well.

The ancient worship of the ancestors and the Neolithic nature spirits and ancestors survived among the Slavs in a more vital form than elsewhere in Pagan Europe. The Byzantine historian Procopius wrote that the Slavs "worship rivers, nymphs and other spirits, and make offerings to them all." A monkish chronicler of the Middle Ages, writing after the Slavs had been "officially" converted to Christianity, tells us that "these very people have begun to sacrifice to the Rod and to the Rodzhenitsye (deities of the ancestors), to Perun, their god, whereas formerly they sacrificed to vampires and *bereginy* [nymphs]."[6]

The holy places of this earth-centered religion were hilltops, groves of trees, and the banks of rivers. Elaborate temples were constructed only rarely. Comprised of large upraised platforms (up to 25 meters in diameter) in a round or oval shape, they typically contained an idol, pole, or column in the center. The platforms were surrounded by ditches or embankments and frequently encircled by pits used for ritual fires and sacrificial offerings of food, vegetation, and animals. Frequently, the entire structure was oriented towards the four directions.

Formal pantheons, in the Greek or Norse sense of the word, emerged only at the end of the Pagan period, and even then only at Kiev and on the Baltic island of Rugen. A powerful Pagan state, originally founded by Swedish Vikings, took shape in Kiev during the ninth century. During the 980s, Prince Vladimir of Kiev established an "official" Paganism out of the highly individualistic and heterogeneous spiritual practices of the Slavs. These gods of Kiev were not worshipped in a temple; rather, their stone and wooden idols stood on the top of a hill under the open sky, and Vladimir himself officiated as high priest. The pantheon was dominated by Perun the Thunder God, and included a sun god variously called Dazhbog or Chors, a god named Simargl who is probably the ancestor of the legendary Russian Firebird, and a god of the winds called Stribog. There was only one goddess—Mokosh, the Earth Mother.

Vladimir's pantheon, however, reigned for only a few years, for Vladimir converted to Eastern Orthodox Christianity in 988 and imposed his new faith on all of Russia. He decreed that the entire kingdom must accept Christianity, whether willingly or otherwise. The idol of Perun, with its silver head and golden moustache, was torn down and thrown into the Dnieper.

But that wasn't the end of it.

One very simple reason for the survival of ancient practices in Russia lies in the fact that the Russian Orthodox Church, unlike the Catholic and Protestant churches of the West, never organized mass persecutions for witchcraft. ("Witch burnings" that did occur were instigated primarily by the people themselves: if too many cows were dying unexplainably, an irate crowd of villagers was likely to lock the local "witch" in her barn and set it on fire.) Because of the relative leniency of the Orthodox Church, ancient traditions merely took on new forms rather than disappearing altogether.

Another reason for the survival of pre-Christian traditions in Russia lies in the nature of the Russian people themselves. The common people of Russia were often called "the black earth people" because of their closeness to the nurturing soil. These black earth people clung to their ancient beliefs as tenaciously as they clung to the earth itself. The Christian monks condemned them:

> On Saturday evening men and women come together, play and dance shamelessly and indulge in obscenities on the night of the Holy Resurrection, just as ungodly pagans celebrating the feast of Dionysos; men and women together, like horses, frolic and neigh and make obscenities....And now let them stop.[7]

But they didn't stop. For two hundred years after Vladimir's forcible conversion, Christianity was primarily the religion of the upper classes alone. Even among the aristocracy, women resisted the new dispensation, and their peasant sisters held to the old ways with such vigor that the priests branded them as "God-cursed hags." Vladimir even decreed that their children should be taken away from them and placed in special church schools to remove them from the pernicious Pagan influence of their mothers.

Early in his reign, Vladimir may have founded an "official" Pagan pantheon, comprised primarily of male deities and centered around Perun the Thunder God, but it was quite a different faith that prevailed among the "obscene" people of the black earth and the "God-cursed hags." It was the ancient, primordial worship of the ancestral spirit or Rod, the Rodzhenitsye or Mothers, and the myriad spirits of nature that survived, and in some respects continues to survive until the present day.

Russia has always remained semi-Pagan in spirit. While seasonal European folk festivals have always retained a great deal of pre-Christian practice and symbolism, the Russian seasonal festivals were so archaic that they actually bore the names of the old gods like Kupalo, Yarilo, or Kostroma until the end of the nineteenth century; the Neolithic ring dance that inspired Stravinksy was still performed at such festivals and peasant women dedicated magical rituals to Mokosh the Earth Mother until the eve of the 1917 Revolution.

Not only did the ancient faith survive, but so did its priests. The term for a priest of the old Pagan religion was *volkhv*, and the village sorcerers of old Russia were sometimes known as *volkhvy* until well into the nineteenth century, although *koldun* and *kolduny* are probably more common at present. The magical healers or sorcerers of today are the direct descendants of the volkhvy of ancient times. The general populace has continued to consult them for such services as healing and divination, even though the koldun or koldunya is an ambivalent figure, favored by some, feared by others, but generally respected by all.

Nor did seventy-five years of Communism succeed in eradicating the village healers and magicians. In the early 1970s, L. I. Min'ko complained in the journal *Soviet Anthropology and Archaeology* that magical healing was still endemic among the peasant population near Minsk.[8] Another twenty years of growing intellectual ferment and chaos likewise failed to put an end to the old Slavic folk magic; in fact, magical healing has become increasingly popular as Russia careens uncertainly toward democracy.

Something of ancient Europe was still alive in the hinterlands of Russia, and this was the tradition with which I hoped to make contact.

A FEW DAYS after my meeting with Antonov, I spoke on the phone with Ina's daughter, Olga Luchakova; she and her colleague, Igor Kungurtsev, had been instrumental in arranging my trip.

"Don't pay that much attention to what Vladimir says," she told me. "Raja Yoga and Buddhi Yoga are just terms he likes to use. Although he knows something of Eastern philosophy, his own practices have very little to do with yoga. In reality, his techniques are completely indigenous, a form of old Slavic Earth Magic."

This I could understand. No tradition, however archaic, can remain completely static or frozen in time; the world has become a very small place. The language of Eastern metaphysics has become a kind of universal spiritual language—terms such as "karma" or "chakras" or "kundalini" are understood virtually everywhere on the planet, and one could expect that present-day practitioners of the Slavic magical arts should also express themselves and their concepts in such universally comprehensible terms. As a matter of fact, it would be unusual if they didn't.

The next morning the phone rang early. It was Vladimir.

"I will send Galina over to you; she will cleanse your chakras so that you and I can work together. And also, you must stop eating meat or drinking any alcohol."

One of the reasons I have never followed an Eastern path is because I am temperamentally ornery and I don't like being told what to do. Now here was Vladimir, acting like some guru in a turban and telling me that he expected me to foreswear the tasty sausages Ina had been feeding me, as well as the companionable shot of vodka that came afterwards.

Vladimir called Ina to the phone and began explaining to her, in great detail, precisely what to feed me. I went to the kitchen to get a cup of coffee.

I *hate* being told what to eat.

Endnotes

1. Joanna Hubbs, *Mother Russia: The Feminine Myth in Russian Culture.* (Bloomington: Indiana University Press, 1989), 4-5.

2. See *The Chalice and the Blade: Our History, Our Future* (San Francisco: Harper and Row, 1987).

3. See the works of Marija Gimbutas: *The Goddesses and Gods of Old Europe: 6500–3500 BC, Myths and Cult Images* (Berkeley and Los Angeles: University of California Press, 1982); *The Language of the Goddess* (San Francisco: Harper and Row, 1989); and *The Civilization of the Goddess: The World of Old Europe* (San Francisco: Harper and Row, 1991).

4. Gimbutas, cited in Ralph Metzner, *The Well of Remembrance: Rediscovering the Earth Wisdom Myths of Northern Europe.* (Boston and London: Shambhala, 1994).

5. J. P. Mallory, *In Search of the Indo-Europeans: Language, Archaeology and Myth.* (London: Thames and Hudson, 1994), 76-81.

6. Quoted in A. Gieysztor, "Slavic Countries: Folk-Lore of the Forests," in *Larousse World Mythology*, ed. Pierre Grimal. (London: Hamlyn, 1965), 402-3.

7. Quoted in Robert Wallace, *The Rise of Russia.* (New York: Time-Life Books, 1967), 33.

8. L. I. Min'ko, "Magic Curing," trans. by Wm. Mandel in *Soviet Anthropology and Archaeology*, Vol 12 No. 1 (Summer 1973), Vol. 12 No. 2 (Fall 1973), and Vol. 12 No. 3 (Winter 1973–4).

TWO

DARKNESS AND LIGHT

THE WITCH BABA YAGA IS NOT merely an old woman bent on eating children; she is also a great serpent. This ancient reptile—or some say it is her son, also a snake—lies coiled round the Water of Life and Death, which all great heroes seek.

Some of them may win it from her by strength or by trickery; most receive it as a gift, for Baba Yaga, like the wild forces of nature, with whom she is one, may sometimes be kind.

If a hero pours this Water of Life and Death upon the corpse of one slain, that corpse shall rise to life again.

It is said, moreover, that the Water of Life and Death is in fact *a dual treasure, for there are two waters. If a corpse lies in pieces, one may sprinkle it with the Water of Death and the pieces shall surely come back together. And if the corpse, reconstituted, is thereafter sprinkled with the Water of Life, it shall be reborn....*

"THIS," SAID NATASHA matter-of-factly, "is the Water of Death."

Natasha Sviridova placed the basin of water on the table. Yet another individual who had been recommended to me as "deeply immersed" in the tradition of Slavic sorcery (as well as possessing impressive credentials as a professor at a technological institute), Natasha had arrived at Ina's house with a big purse full of mystic diagrams, a dowsing rod, and jars of home-made raspberry jam. In the course of our conversation, she had been trying to make a point about the cosmic polarities that lie at the very foundation of Slavic magic (the same polarities that had governed Polyakov's critique of paintings at the Hermitage) and had gone into the kitchen, returning with the water.

"By itself," she explained, "all water partakes of the negative, or minus, polarity. So ordinary water is the Water of Death. When water is to be used for healing, it must be transformed into the Water of Life. Its polarity must be changed."

"And how is that accomplished?"

She looked at me as if I were very stupid, indeed. "Like this," she said, and picked up her dowsing rod, a simple implement made of wire bent in the shape of an L, with a sleeve covering the shorter end so that the rod could swing more easily. Natasha called it her "arrow."

Holding the sleeve of the dowsing rod in her right hand, she approached the basin of water. She held the rod over the water; it swung to the left.

Then she extended both her hands over the water and closed her eyes. She whispered a prayer. The dowsing rod swung to the right.

Natasha opened her eyes. "There. Now this water has a positive energy. It is plus, not minus. Now it is the Water of Life."

After Natasha had packed her diagrams and her dowsing rod back into her bag and departed, I went into the kitchen and filled another basin of water. I held my trusty old pendulum over it and watched it swing counter-clockwise, the direction I used for "no" or "negative."

Natasha Sviridova changes the negative polarity of the Water of Death to the positive Water of Life in order to use it for healing. A technique for performing this transformation is detailed on page 30.

Then I went back into the sitting room, where Natasha's basin of water still sat upon the table. I held my pendulum over that one too. It immediately began to swing in a big, graceful clockwise circle.

HOLY LAKES, SPRINGS, rivers, and wells were everywhere in the ancient Slavic world, and were inhabited by water spirits such as the Vodyanoi and the Rusalki. Places of prayer and sacrifice were often found near sacred springs, and some of the great heroes of Slavic legend appear, once upon a time, to have been river gods—the magical hero Volkh Vseslavich, for example, is associated with the river Volga, and where the knightly Dunai Ivanovich fell dead, a river sprang forth and became known as the Danube.

This veneration of rivers and springs is not limited to the Slavic countries. A Celtic goddess Sequana gave her name to the river over which she ruled; today we call it the Seine. Similarly, the Boyne River in Ireland is named for the goddess Boann. The god Nodens was the patron deity of the Severn River, and the healing springs of Aquae Sulis (present-day Bath in England) were sacred to the goddess Brigid. Even today, the landscapes of England and Ireland are dotted with "holy wells," places where healing is sought and decorated with the images of saints who, for the most, are simply reconstituted Pagan gods.

In Slavic sorcery, water has always been regarded as a great healer. Here is an old charm[1] called "Begging Pardon of the Waters": its purpose is to heal oneself through the spiritual agency of the water.

Begging Pardon of the Waters

Approach a natural source of water, such as a spring, well, river, or lake. Throw a piece of bread into the water, and, using your own words, ritually greet the water three times. Then pronounce the following words, once again repeating them three times:

I come to you, little Water Mother,
Repentant and with bowed head.
Forgive me, pardon me,
And you too, you ancestors
And forefathers of the water!

Beyond its healing powers, water is a simulacrum for the human body itself. Natasha said that "we can assesss each other's energy patterns on the psychic level by virtue of the fact that our bodies are mostly water." Later, when I was finally able to speak at some length with Dr. Polyakov, he put it slightly differently: "We are able to feel each other's emotions, whether favorable or otherwise, because our bodies are ninety percent water; water symbolizes the emotions and it is the water within us which forms the medium of emotional communication."

Russian sorcerers have a deep reverence for the powers of water, especially cold water; they like to bathe in it, even in the dead of winter. This practice has filtered down to the popular level, and many Russians enthusiastically praise the benefits of ice-water bathing.

In the 1930s, a peasant by the name of Porphyry Ivanov underwent a spontaneous mystical experience that, in time, made him a well-known spiritual teacher, though in fact he may be most accurately regarded as a master of the Slavic sorcery tradition. Combating cancer with positive affirmations, imprisoned by the Soviets and given large doses of anti-psychotic drugs, which he overcame with his will-power,

Ivanov roamed through Russia barefoot and dressed only in his shorts in summer and winter alike. Tall and powerfully built, he sported long white hair and a full white beard. Bathing in ice-cold water was one of his favorite practices, a method for obtaining magical power. His influence on Russian magic has been great, and in part accounts for the present popularity of ice-water bathing.

During Word War II, the Nazis occupied Ivanov's home village. The Germans decided to test Ivanov's power. They cut a hole in the ice, tossed him in, and forced him to remain naked in the freezing water for nearly four hours. Then they drove him around on a motorcycle for another two hours. He never even became ill.[2]

In fact, Ivanov's feats are characteristic of the most esoterically minded Russian sorcerers. The traditional Russian sauna is as much a Pagan rite as it is an aid to good health—in fact the sauna and the Russian bathhouse of medieval times are part of the great "circumpolar" tradition of the sweat lodge, as are the sweat ceremonies of Native Americans. After a sauna, the sorcerers often plunged into icy water; those who were particularly adept with this practice could use their "inner heat" to warm the water and melt the surrounding ice.

As Igor and Olga have pointed out,[3] this is reminiscent of the Tibetan practice called *tumo*, in which the yogi produces an inner fire that melts the Himalayan snows surrounding his meditation spot. Indeed, Ivanov taught special methods of concentration—including deep relaxation and the cultivation of inner joy—which allow one to enter cold water without stress or tension. As Olga puts it: "We think the cold water will be a shock to the body, but it isn't. In reality, it is a shock to the mind, and by changing the mind we can change our response. When entering cold water—the optimum temperature is just a little above 10 degrees celsius—one must imagine that the water is literally boiling."

To merge one's inner heat with one's icy surroundings is to mix Fire and Water. Fire and Water may be considered as elemental symbols of a fundamental duality of existence—a duality that underlies Pagan Slavic thought and explains why there are, in reality, two kinds of water: the Water of Life and the Water of Death.

A medieval Russian creation story tells us that in the beginning there was only the great ocean, which was everywhere, but without boundaries, without order. Then came that mystical creature who remains a popular figure in Russian art and folklore to this very day—the Firebird. It was she who laid the egg of life in the primal chaos; when it hatched, all things were born. From the egg of life came purpose, and order—Heaven, Earth, and the Underworld, the circling stars, and the four directions.[4]

This creation story has its roots in the oldest European thought, and is far older than the Slavic peoples or their languages. It comes to us, still fresh, from pottery found in what is now the Ukraine and dating back to the Neolithic. Here, on this most ancient European pottery, the cosmic egg, symbol of all generated life, appears over and over again in connection with a water bird (often a mallard duck and usually female), which represents the creative power of the universe. In the original myth, perhaps, all was water in the beginning. From the water came forth the Goddess in the form of a bird. As a bird, she laid the cosmic egg. As a snake, she entwined herself around it. When it hatched, the world began. Light and Darkness, the upper waters and the lower, were made separate. All was placed in order.[5]

But chaos remains with us, everywhere, on the boundaries of our reality, for it is the ground of all being. This fundamental dualism is inherent in traditional Slavic magic: Chaos and Order. The entire human cosmos and the three worlds express themselves through this dualism. The unknown wilderness of forests and swamps contrasts with the orderly world of village life. The chaos of the Underworld contrasts with the order of the heavens; the dark half of the year, centered around the winter solstice, contrasts with the lighter half, dominated by the summer festivals.

This dualism was sometimes personified as a pair of gods: Belobog (the White God) and Chernobog (the Black God). Belobog is the god of light and day, Chernobog of shadows and night. Thus the sorcerers said: "There are two gods, one above and the other below." In the folklore of Belarus (White Russia), Belobog appears as Belun, an old man with a white beard, dressed in white. He is only seen during the daytime. His actions are benevolent: he aids lost travelers and helps unfortunate peasants with their farmwork.[6]

Despite the seeming identification of "white" with light and order, or "black" with darkness and chaos, we should not make the mistake

"There is grace in Nature...." Contemporary Russian sorcerers point out that the grace of nature partakes of both cosmic polarities in the old Slavic world view.

of assuming (as many scholars have) that the Pagan Slavs equated these opposites with "good" and "evil" respectively. To make such an assumption would be to think entirely in Christian terms.[7] For example, even though the wilderness was identified with night, winter, chaos, and the Black God, it was not necessarily an evil place. In fact, the Hutsul people of the Carpathians believed, at least until the early part of this century, that the cities "stink till you choke, that there is no water there," and that the houses "are set one on top of another,"[8] while the present-day Russian sorcerers say: "There is grace in Nature."

But they also say "There is Nature even in the city." Herein lies the subtlety and wholeness of the dualistic concept: the eternal cosmic polarities of Light and Darkness are interwoven with each other in the colorful tapestry of animate life, interpenetrating and interdependent.

It is clear, then, that these Slavic dualities represent the same magical dynamism of opposites that is embodied in the Chinese concept of yin and yang, or in the alchemical opposites of Sun and Moon. Scholars have argued that this dualism must have entered the Slavic myth system from parts farther east—perhaps from Zoroastrian Iran, as the Russian language has a number of provocative affinities with Old Persian. However,

"And there is Nature even in the city...." Russian sorcerers are firm that nature is everywhere. This belief reflects the ultimate unity of the dualistic concept; the eternal polarities of light and darkness are forever interwoven.

Zoroastrian dualism itself is rooted in much older soil, for the tribal cattle-herders who spoke "Proto-Indo-European"—the root language that gave birth to English, Russian, Persian, Sanskrit, and so many others—seem to have believed in a similar dualism. Though any reconstruction of their myths must be hypothetical, they appear to have taught that there were two divine twins at the dawn of time. One sacrificed the other; the survivor became the Sky God, while the sacrificed twin became the Lord of the Underworld. Hence Sky and Earth were in eternal opposition. Linguistic evidence suggests that the shamans of that long-ago era faced east when they prayed, thus placing the south upon their right hand and the north upon their left; words associated with "right" and "south" tend to have a positive context, while "left" and "north" tend to have a negative one.[9] So we need not postulate a Persian origin for Pagan Slavic dualism—it may well have been there since the beginning.

In fact, this doctrine of polarities goes beyond Western culture altogether. The most obvious example, already mentioned, is that of the Chinese yin and yang. As I have tried to show, ancient Slavic dualism was just as subtle as the Chinese concept, and cannot be reduced to a mindless "good" and "bad." Darkness and Light, Chaos and Order, were interdependent—one could not exist without the other.

It is tempting to simply dispense with the whole business by saying that Pagan Slavic dualism is identical to the Chinese doctrine of polarities, and indeed there are many present-day Russian practitioners of sorcery who would do precisely that. As I said earlier, the language of Eastern metaphysics has become a universal language, comprehensible anywhere; but the indigenous Slavic dualism has its own richness and associations worth considering in more detail.

"People who operate primarily on the plus polarity have the attributes of kindness, vitality, and creativity," says Natasha. "They operate on an open system, not a closed one. In order to operate this way, you must have sensitivity, empathy, and the ability to exchange information with the world surrounding you. Those who function primarily through the minus polarity are angry, egotistical, dull, and engaged in profound struggles with their inner conflicts. That is a closed system."

Porphyry Ivanov would have agreed with Natasha; he taught his disciples to cultivate joy and loving kindness towards all living entities. Dr. Polyakov, however, had a slightly different view of the cosmic polarities.

I went to visit him at his place of business, the St. Petersburg Technical University Association of Applied Parapsychology, which was located in a suite of rooms in a turn-of-the-century courtyard just off the Mayakovskogo. Polyakov sat at his desk, still scribbling furiously on pieces of paper as he ignored the telephones and the two receptionists who answered them.

"I myself use terms such as plus and minus, or yang and yin. But in the villages they speak of Sun and Moon, Sky and Earth. They speak of White and Black, Good and Evil, Heaven and Hell, Male and Female. Everything partakes of one of these two categories.

"Each polarity is necessary unto the other. Healing consists of a state of balance between the two. Most people are not balanced; the yin polarity is more comfortable for most people."

This was quite different from what Natasha had said. Was Polyakov suggesting that most people were comfortable with anger, negativity, and conflict?

In fact, Polyakov's entire concept of the polarities and their attributes was a bit different than Natasha's. "The masculine polarity is hot, and its color is red, whereas the feminine polarity is cold and white. The masculine polarity's motion is swift, whereas the feminine polarity moves slowly. The quartz crystals which are so popular in the West these days—they are masculine. Their energy is swift and hot. Seashells, on the other hand, are essentially feminine. And this is what most people find comfortable—cool and slow and white. The hot, fast, red energy of the masculine polarity is much more difficult for most people to work with. But true healing lies in a balance between the two."

The ancient dualism of Fire and Water, then, was alive in Polyakov's thought, for his masculine polarity had all the attributes of Fire, and his female polarity those of Water. To charge a bowl of water so as to change its essentially feminine polarity was to introduce Fire into the Water.

Water, as a primary metaphor of the negative polarity, has "coldness" as an attribute, and this explains why the Slavic sorcery tradition insists upon the use of cold water, whether for healing or for bathing. Coldness is linked indissolubly with all things dark, lunar, feminine, and moist.

To introduce Fire into the Water changes everything; it is no longer the Water of Death, but the Water of Life. Herein lie some of the oldest concepts of the world's mythologies.

In Babylonian mythology, the primal waters of Chaos are guarded by a female dragon named Tiamat—an ancestress of the serpentine Baba Yaga. The dragon is slain by Marduk, who, as a Thunder God, wields the lightning, the power of Fire, and who, in slaying Tiamat, brings Order into the Waters of Chaos. Similarly, the Vedic Thunder God Indra slays the dragon Vritra, whose death results in the release of seven streams of water that renew the earth. Sri Aurobindo and other esoteric interpreters of the *Rig Veda* (the ancient collection of hymns that contains the story of Indra and Vritra) affirm that the seven streams of water are the seven chakras, and that Indra's magical lightning is the kundalini force which sparks the chakras into action by liberating these Waters of Life or primordial energies. The same concept was retained in medieval alchemy—the alchemical dragon guards the "water" from which the universal elixir of life may be extracted, though initially this "water" is a deadly poison.

Water of Life, Water of Death...though as Natasha said: "Water of Death is also valuable water, good water." The elixir and the poison are one.

The concept that the Water of Life and Death bestows immortality upon human beings is likewise most ancient. As far back as ancient Sumer, it was said that the goddess Inanna, after her visit to the Underworld, was resurrected by the Water of Life and Death poured forth upon her body by the other gods.

Polyakov never told me exactly how to transform the Water of Death into Water of Life. Natasha made use of an Orthodox Prayer; it begins "O Heavenly King, the Comforter." As we shall see, Slavic sorcerers pray to specific Orthodox saints for specific purposes, and the saints themselves may often be identified with Pagan gods who once ruled over the same aspect of human life. Natasha's prayer invokes what she termed "the Holy Spirit," moving like a current of energy through her hands, to enter the water. The Holy Spirit, then, would seem to refer to the positive polarity of cosmic energy, the yang or masculine force. We may remember that the Apostles, when filled with the Holy Spirit at Pentecost, were said to have "tongues of flame" upon them (Acts 2:2-4).

In some Christian traditions, however, the Holy Spirit is (or was, before the Council of Nicaea) perceived as a feminine potency, and symbolized by a bird—the dove which descended upon Christ's head when he took his own cold-water dip in the Jordan. Whether masculine or feminine, the Holy Spirit always refers to the creative aspect of the infinite—and in Hindu Tantra, as well as in certain schools of the Kabbalah, it is the feminine rather than the masculine polarity which is dynamic and creative. This mingling of polarities finds apt expression in Russian folklore in the figure of the magical Firebird—the bird itself is typically female, but it is associated with fire and hence with the creative or masculine polarity.

On page 30, then, is another method that I have found effective for charging water with positive energy. This technique is based upon the identity of the Holy Spirit with the creative Fire.

Creating the Water of Life

Hold both your hands over a bowl of cold water. Close
your eyes and breathe in. As you breathe, imagine that your
hands are filled with fire. See them glowing with red,
brighter and brighter with every breath you take. Use all
your powers of imagination and try to feel the heat in your
hands. Then literally breathe the energy out of your hands
and into the water. The change should be measurable with
a pendulum.

THE ATTENTIVE READER—especially the attentive female reader—will by
this time have noticed a not-so-subtle sexism implied in these polarities:

(+) = Masculine	(-) = Feminine
Fire	Water
Order	Chaos
Sky	Earth
Sun	Moon
Red	White
Hot	Cold
Fast	Slow
Crystals	Seashells
Heaven	Hell
Good	Evil
Belobog	Chernobog
(The White God)	(The Black God)

Polyakov's attribution of "red" to the masculine polarity and
"white" to the feminine polarity is one found in Hindu Tantra,[10] but in
the villages it is the masculine polarity which is typically regarded as
white and the feminine as black. The female polarity also has such
charming attributes as "evil" and "hell."

As we have seen, the more ancient concept of dualism implies an
interdependence rather than opposition; the two principles are complementary rather than hostile to each other. The demonization of the

feminine principle is, more than likely, one of Christianity's regrettable consequences. Christian dualism is absolute rather than complementary; there is God and there is the Devil, and healing most certainly does not consist of balance or equilibrium between the two.

Natasha introduced me to Andrei and Alla Goroshosky, a couple who run the Center for Inner Harmony. Their methods of healing and harmonizing the personality, like those of so many others, owe a certain debt to traditional Slavic magic, though any American New Ager would find himself comfortable amid Andrei and Alla's collection of crystals, soft synthesizer music, and "channeled" paintings of gentle, Otherworldly scenes. Nevertheless, they are well acquainted with the ancient polarities and deeply concerned over the demonization of the feminine principle.

Alla showed me a picture, painted by Andrei, which depicted a spiral of energy rising from the Underworld and ascending to Heaven. This, she explained, had been a vision on Andrei's part.

"The feminine principle is being healed. It is rising out of Hell and will unite with the masculine principle. There will be unity between the two, and in that unity is balance. This will happen. This is the task of the future."

American women would certainly agree; the ancient denigration of the feminine principle will hopefully become a pile of detritus on the garbage heap of history. However, American feminists might thoroughly disagree with Andrei, Alla, and many other Russians concerning just how that unity is to be accomplished.

"Women have to act like women and men have to act like men," Alla affirmed quite simply.

During the Soviet era, women were encouraged to break free of existing female stereotypes—to become doctors and physicists, to drive tractors and work on construction sites. Soviet propaganda posters featured an ideal Soviet woman with the physique of a football player, dressed in overalls, her hair concealed behind a workman's bandana, a monkey wrench in her hand and her face shining with the sweat of hard labor. This Russian version of Rosie the Riveter was one of the first images to be discarded by the Russians themselves when the Soviet regime began to crumble. After seventy-five years of enforced drabness, Russian women are now anxious to dress to the hilt, wear make-up, and in general cultivate "traditional" feminine behavior such as flaunting, flouncing, and flirting. The men, they say, should quit drinking, quit lazing around, and get back to work.

This, according to Russian women, is how the polarities should be harmonized.

In any event, it is not terribly difficult to reconstruct the ancient dualities as they must once have been understood:

(+) = Masculine	(-) = Feminine
Fire	Water
Order	Chaos
Sky	Earth
Sun	Moon
White	Black
Day	Night
Summer	Winter
Hot	Cold
Upper World	Underworld
Civilization	Wildness

As we have seen, these polarities interpenetrate; there is grace in nature and there is nature in the city. Not only do they interpenetrate spatially or conceptually, they also interpenetrate in time.

POLYAKOV STOOD UP at his desk and placed his hand close to his stomach.

"The energy is down here now, you see. I am operating on the minus polarity. Now...."

He closed his eyes, waited, then moved his hand to the top of his head.

"And now it has shifted. Now I am a plus. Everyone shifts polarities on the average of about once every ten seconds."

Tantric Hinduism contains similar teachings regarding the flow of polarities in time. Life itself is a flow of internal seasons, the energies of Fire and Air (masculine) alternating with those of Earth and Water (feminine); a great deal of the theory behind Ayurveda or Yogic medicine is based upon this concept. In Tantra, this alternation is literally as subtle as breathing; one's breath may be predominantly through the right nostril (solar breath) or left nostril (lunar breath) at various times during the day. One form of yogic breathing calls for a conscious harmonizing of masculine and feminine energies through alternate nostril breathing.

In the Slavic tradition, the cosmic polarities shift naturally at particular times of the year. The followers of Porphyry Ivanov, for example, ritually immerse themselves in icy lakes and streams during the dead of winter—on the Orthodox Feast of the Baptism of Christ (January 17/18). On this night, they say, the waters are filled with the Holy Spirit, which, as we have seen, is a metaphor for the creative power of the yang polarity.

Natasha says, "All water on the planet is constantly shifting from Chaos to Order and back again. This is a natural process. But we may also affect that process ourselves. When one bathes in cold water after praying, one may shift its polarity from minus to plus. On certain Orthodox holidays, the water will naturally shift from minus to plus, and at such times it is not necessary even to pray. The waters are simply charged with the positive polarity. This occurs most especially on the night of the Baptism of Christ, but also on Easter."

Despite its seemingly Christian rationale, the belief that water shifts its polarity at particular times of the year is a very ancient idea, and one based upon the Pagan perception of time as a shifting tapestry of Darkness and Light. This seasonal drama is itself founded on the Pagan Slavic picture of the cosmos—a vision rich with some of humankind's oldest spiritual concepts. These concepts are an important part of the world-view of shamanism, the magical discipline which lies at the root of so many Pagan European as well as Native American religions, and which almost certainly dates back to the Ice Age.

SHAMANIC PEOPLES THE world over affirm that the North Star is the central axis or pivot of the sky, the point around which all else—including planets and stars—ultimately revolves.

The North Star is only a celestial metaphor for what we may term the cosmic center of being—the inner point of stillness around which life and consciousness revolve. We take our spiritual sustenance directly from this center, for though the human world is in constant motion, the center is unwavering.

Tribal and traditional peoples regard themselves as dwelling at the center of the universe. Wherever they go, the center of the universe goes with them. Wherever they pitch their tent, the center of the universe is there; for indeed it is everywhere, and we always dwell within it.

This universal center can be expressed through an infinite number of metaphors. Not only is it the North Star—the pivot of the sky—it is also a straight line or path leading from the world to the top of the sky. This lifeline to Heaven or road to the North Star may be perceived as a great pillar or column, a world mountain, or a celestial river. For our purposes, the most important image of this North Star road is the World Tree.

Shamanism, at least in its classic Siberian and European forms, postulates a cosmos with three levels or worlds: Heaven, Earth, and the Underworld. The World Tree, as both the center of this cosmos and the road thereto, has its deep roots in the Underworld and its highest branches in Heaven, while its trunk passes through this middle world or Earth upon which we live. The great tree at the center of all things mediates between the worlds, and forms a pathway from one to the other.

The World Tree is a common theme in the folklore of the Slavic countries. It is said to stand in the midst of the great primal ocean which is the origin of all things; it has been there since before there was Heaven and Earth. Different stories mention different kinds of trees, though one of the most common is the oak. It also constitutes a favorite motif in folk art, especially domestic handicrafts such as pich or stove decorations, women's clothing, and embroidered ritual towels.[11]

Heaven or the Upper World may be found at the topmost branches of the World Tree; and in those celestial branches, according to Slavic folklore, lives a bird, variously said to be a falcon, a nightingale, a pair of doves, or a magical cockerel. Earth is the middle level, the one at which all of us live and dwell and have our being; it is home to all the majesty of field and forest as well as the locus of all our domestic comforts and joys. The imagery associated with this middle level is usually circular; on a Pagan Slavic idol found at the Polish village of Zbruch, Earth is symbolized by a ring of dancers, all holding hands—the concept is one of a human community linked together in a sacred circle of harmony. The image of human interaction as a dance is an ancient one indeed, and is found among the Goddess cultures of the Neolithic (as well as in Stravinsky's ballet). Among Slavic countryfolk, such a dance was called a *khorovod* and was performed during all the major festivals of the Pagan or traditional year. The word khorovod is linked with the name Khors, a Russian sun god; the dance, therefore, may be seen on one level as a celebration of the circling sun which gives us the gift of life.

At the roots of the World Tree lies the Underworld, the home of the dead. According to Russian folklore, these roots are perpetually being gnawed away by animals such as the serpent and the beaver. This legend is reminiscent of Norse myth, wherein the roots of the World Tree are consumed by an Underworld serpent or dragon. The Baltic, Slavic, and Norse peoples all shared a common picture of the Underworld as a dark place inhabited by a primal serpent.

Hence the alternation of Darkness and Light is exemplified in the structure of the World Tree, for the Underworld is a place of Darkness, and the Upper World a world of Light. Our world is the point of equilibrium between the two, the point of balance which Polyakov defines as true healing.

Both the sun and moon are said to circle around the top of the World Tree, and these luminaries govern the light and dark halves of each day respectively. The World Tree, then, is also the center or point of origin for the four cardinal directions, as the symbolism of the four directions has its origin in the daily path of the sun, which rises in the east, reaches its zenith at noon, sets in the west, and reaches nadir at midnight.

In order to diagram this flow of Darkness and Light properly, we must follow the practice of astrologers and Chinese mapmakers (rather than Western cartographers) by placing south at the top of our map.

In this daily round, a diagram of which appears on page 36, we clearly see the alternation of Darkness and Light. At dawn, the two polarities are in a state of balance, with the Light or Dayforce beginning to grow stronger. The Light reaches its apex at midday, symbolic of the powers of the Upper World, and then begins to decline. At sunset, the two polarities once again stand in balance, while at midnight the Darkness or Underworld has reached its own climactic moment. The sun is the logical ruler of the Dayforce, while the moon aptly symbolizes the Nightforce.

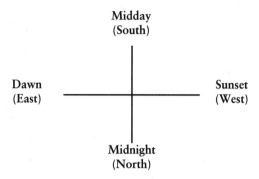

This diagram illustrates the flow of Darkness and Light as a daily cycle which corresponds with the four cardinal directions.

By the same token, the seasons move from spring (east) to summer (south) to autumn (west) and then to winter (north), tracing the progress of the solar force throughout the year. On the spring equinox, the days and nights are equal, while the summer solstice, the longest day of the year, represents the triumph of Light, the Upper World, and the solar force. At the autumn equinox the polarities are once again in balance, and at the winter solstice the days are short, Darkness reigns supreme, and the Underworld predominates over the Upper World.

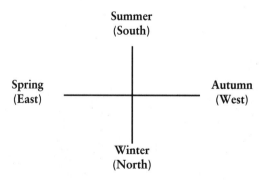

The seasons also trace the progress of the solar force throughout the year, as demonstrated by the above diagram. As in the flow of Darkness and Light, the seasons also correspond to the four directions.

Human life, as well as the day and the seasons, was governed by this flow, and resonated to a similar alternation of Darkness and Light, as shown in the diagram below.

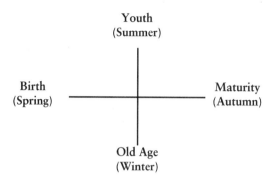

Youth
(Summer)

Birth
(Spring)

Maturity
(Autumn)

Old Age
(Winter)

Just as the times of the day and the seasons of the year both followed the same flow, so also do the stages of human life.

The cross (or, more properly, cross within a circle) that serves as metaphor or mandala for this cycle of Darkness and Light is found on the most ancient Neolithic pottery, dating from about 5000 B.C.E. and unearthed in what is now the Ukraine and Moldavia. The late Marija Gimbutas, who devoted most of her archaeological career to the religious iconography of that era, believed that it did in fact symbolize the cycle of time and the directions that we have outlined here.[12]

Thus the seasonal round was itself a myth, and one with a profound effect upon the cycles of human life. In order to remain in balance with the cosmos, the life of the community had to move in harmony with the cycle of the seasons, the alternation of Darkness and Light. Though influenced to some degree by Christianity, the folk festivals practiced by Slavic peasants up until the early part of the twentieth century still embodied the seasonal flow of the cosmic polarities.[13]

During the spring, the Darkness and Light stood in a state of perfect balance, but the Light was increasing and the festivals of the season celebrated that increase. A pre-Lenten carnival called the Maslenitsa, held on the Christian Shrovetide, was characterized by drinking, sexual license, and general gluttony. Sometimes the return of the light was celebrated by building bonfires or circling the village on horseback with a torch, or pushing a wheel that contained a pole with a flaming torch around the village. A feast was held at the local cemetery amid a mixture of mourning and laughter; food was left for the dead.

The festival of Stritennia or "meeting," a Christian holiday which peasants regard as "the meeting between winter and spring," likewise shows its Pagan origins clearly, for it was dedicated to the goddess Lada, the eternal Flower Maiden who was the incarnation of springtime and who, at that season, returned from the lush, evergreen land of Vyri in the far south or southeast, bringing with her the vegetation and the birds. During the Stritennia, pastries were baked in the shape of birds to welcome the returning spring.

In general, most of the Pagan festivities associated with the spring equinox were syncretized with Easter, which was celebrated with spring songs, games, and round dances. The sun "danced" at dawn; the entire family or community blessed their ritual food and exchanged gifts, such as Easter eggs ornamented with geometric, vegetative, animal, or other life-affirming symbols.

The polarities of Fire and Water figured strongly in Easter rites. "Live" fires were kept burning on Holy Thursday, which was a day of purification. People washed in water that was drawn before sunrise and fumigated themselves with juniper smoke. Rites for the increase of livestock were performed, and a special "increase food" called *kozuli* was baked. The dead were thought to come alive, or to return from Vyri to celebrate their own Easter on Holy Thursday. On Easter Sunday itself, the coloring, exchanging, and rolling of eggs was a central feature. The eggs were rolled along the ground in order to effect a magical transfer of the creative power of the egg to the earth.

Even before it reached its climax at the summer solstice, the growing tide of Light was honored as the summer grew. At the beginning of the season came the Green Holidays. Houses were decorated with vegetation, creating the proper conditions for the return of the ancestors, perhaps even drawing them into the house. The ancestors were greeted with food, singing, music and dance. At Whitsuntide the Rusalki, or female spirits of lakes and trees, left their winter homes in the waters and went into the woods and fields for the summer.

The principal rites of summer, and those which represented the apex of the tide of Light, the spiritual realm at the top of the World Tree, were held on the summer solstice (June 21) or, in Christian times, on St. John's Eve (June 23). Anciently, the summer solstice was known as the Feast of Kupalo, the god of vegetation, the life force, and of healing water (in some regions the vegetation god was known as Kostroma or Yarilo rather than Kupalo). The Feast of St. John the Baptist was the Christian holiday that came closest in time to the Pagan solstice. Hence St. John and Kupalo became syncretized—archetypally identical—and the solstice time itself was known as the Feast of Ivan-Kupalo, Ivan being the Russian form of our name "John." At this time the sun and the element of Fire triumphed altogether over the dark Underworld forces represented by winter. Again, the sun "danced," and the festivities, like those of the spring, were characterized by intoxication and sexual license.

Kupalo was represented by an idol made of straw and dressed in a woman's gown adorned with ribbons and necklaces. Sometimes the idol had wooden arms hung with floral garlands and other feminine ornaments. During the festival, it was placed under a sacred tree. The local women harnessed themselves to a wagon, went in procession to the forest, and chose a birch tree that was solemnly transported to the festival ground. The tree was stripped of its lower branches; the upper ones formed a crown around the top. The tree was then fixed in the ground and hung with garlands of flowers. No men were allowed to touch the sacred tree; all the rites were performed solely by women.

Like Water, Fire played a part in the rites of Kupalo. The holy fires lit during St. John's Eve possessed the power of purification. Kupalo's worshippers danced the khorovod or solar ring dance around the fires and jumped over them. A form of divination was associated with these midsummer fires as well. Young people met near the river and bathed until twilight, when the fire was kindled. Then two sweethearts joined hands and together jumped over the flames, hand in hand. If they could jump without loosening their hands, or if a spark followed them out of the flame, they would someday be married. Wheels of fire were sent rolling down the hills—this was a sad event, for it represented the fact that the season had turned, the sun at its apex was about to decline, and the days would begin to grow shorter.

On the morning of St. John's Day, people bathed in the rivers and washed themselves in "the dew of Kupalo," dew which had been gathered during the night of the festival. Girls went to the woods early in the morning to pick flowers and make wreaths used to divine their future loves; they then threw their crowns of flowers into the rivers.

At sunset, the funeral rites of the god began, symbolizing the turning of the year towards darkness. The idol of Kupalo was carried in procession to the local river and drowned, though sometimes it was burned in a sacred fire.

Of the four major turnings of the year, the autumnal equinox is the only one which seems not to have been celebrated by the ancient Slavs. Although no major festival marked the equinox, there were various rites and holidays related to the fields and field spirits, and to thankfulness for the earth's abundance. There may have been a holiday dedicated to the ancestral spirits known as the Rod and the Rodzhenitsye during what is now the Orthodox Feast of the Birth of the Mother of God.

During the harvest, particular attention focused on the first and last sheaves. The first sheaf was ceremonially brought into the house, threshed separately, blessed in the church, and mixed with seed grain. The last sheaf was subject to a special ceremony as well. It was believed that the invisible spirit of the harvest preceded the reapers and hid in the uncut grain; so when the last patch was reached, it was left uncut and decorated with a ribbon. The heads of the grain were bent to the ground and hospitality foods such as bread and salt offered to it. This was called "the curling of the beard"—sometimes said to be the beard of St. Elijah, or of the Underworld god Volos, or his Christian simulacrum St. Nicholas, or even of Christ. Finally the last sheaf was brought into the house, decorated with ribbons or flowers and dressed in women's clothing. It was placed in the entrance corner or under the household icon until October 1 (the Church holiday called Pokrov or the Feast of the Intercession of the Mother of God), when it was mixed with the cattle's feed.

Sometimes people rolled on the ground, as they also did in spring. During autumn, this was intended to take from the earth its fertile energy at a time when the vegetative and solar forces were beginning to separate, whereas in spring the custom was meant to return the energy to the earth.

With winter, the keeping of ritual fires and candlelight work began. The winter holidays, centered around the solstice, were primarily family celebrations dedicated to the ancestors. The year was in its deepest darkness now, and life itself was symbolically in the Underworld—it was an appropriate time for divination, sorcery, and the honoring of the family dead who dwelt in the Underworld. (Inasmuch as the polarities always intertwine and interpenetrate one with another, it is only right and fitting that the waters should resonate with the energy of Fire and Light during this darkest time of the year.) During the winter rites, new fires were ritually kindled and a twelve-course meal was eaten, featuring the ritual foods and products of the land and marked by invocations, prayers, and offerings made to the souls of dead relatives, the farm animals, the frost, and so forth.

In Russia, Christmas Eve was called Kuchiya—the day before New Year's was "Rich Kuchiya" because meat was eaten on that day, while the day before Twelfth Night was "Hungry Kuchiya" because lenten food was eaten. The word *kuchiya* itself refers to the food eaten on these special days—in Belarus it was a pudding made of barley groats and honey, and in the Ukraine of wheat groats, pounded poppy seeds, and honey. In Russia proper, kuchiya was a special porridge made of whole grains and pork. In fact, kuchiya was "food for the ancestors," for it was also eaten at funerals and on All Souls' Day.

Before supper the farmer walked about the house carrying the kuchiya, while the wife, having cleaned the room, spread hay over the table, then laid down a tablecloth and brought food to the table. After the father said grace, everyone sat down, and the head of the household went to a spot in the corner under the household icons. Here, he poured a cup of vodka, let a few drops fall on the cloth, drank the rest, and everyone else did the same. Part of the food was set aside for the dead. Finally, the kuchiya was served.

After supper, everyone rose except for the master of the house. He hid behind the pot of kuchiya and asked his wife whether she could see him. The wife always replied "Yes," to which the father's ritual answer was "I hope that you might not see me next year." This was believed to ensure a good harvest for the coming season—next year, the family affirmed, the harvest would be so great that the father would be invisible when he stood behind it.[14] After supper, many prophecies concerning the coming year were attempted. Finally, the hay placed under the kuchiya and table-cloth was given to the household animals. The fire was kept constantly burning. Very little work was done on this day.

Among the Serbs and Slovenes, this holiday was called "the Vigil." Before sunrise the head of the household or some other family member went out to the forest to seek a tree, which might be either oak, beech, or ash. When dinner was ready, he brought the tree into the room. He clucked like a hen while his children, standing behind him, cheeped like baby chickens. He carried the log into every corner of the room, saluting the other members of the house, who threw corn at him.

The log might be dressed in a new shirt or adorned with red silk, golden threads, flowers, and so on. When the fire was ritually kindled, the farmer spoke to the log, saying "Welcome! Come and eat your sup-per!" The log was a symbol of the household god or ancestral spirit as protector of the hearth, which had been ritually rekindled on that day (and indeed, in Russia it was often said that the ancestors resided in the flames of the hearthfire).

When the log was burning well, the farmer took a special bread in one hand and in the other a cup of wine. He walked toward the corn loft followed by the children, who made noises like domestic animals. A portion of the bread and wine were left on the window of the loft for the ancestors, and the rest was placed on a table in the room. The farmer filled a glove with kernels of wheat and a silver coin, then strewed the grain on the floor as if sowing. The children pecked at the wheat like chickens; the one who found the coin would have good luck. Straw was spread round the hearth and covered with sweets for every-one, and the farmer, hiding behind the heap of food, asked three times if the household could see him.

In Russia and other parts of the Slavic world, the rites of the Koli-ada were also taking place during the entire Christmas season. The word koliada itself may be derived from the Latin calendae, meaning "first day of the month," or it may be based upon the name of the springtime goddess Lada, who was said to "return" on the winter sol-stice, just as she was also said to return in the spring.[15] During the Koliada, as preserved until very recently by the Hutsuls of the Carpathians, costumed "visitors" in animal and spirit masks, por-trayed by children and representing the spirits of the dead, walked from house to house and sang carols (*koliadnyky* has the contemporary meaning of "carolers"). They performed ritual songs and theatrical skits which were accompanied by rhythmic movements, dances and gestures, invoked the deity Koliada (whether Lada or some other), offered greetings and wishes for a good harvest and abundant livestock, and, in turn, were presented with food and drink. Ritual foods were again eaten, and mock funerals were held in which someone pretended to be dead and was carried into the house with mixed laughter and lamentation. As with Christmas Eve, there was sometimes the lighting of a fire (in olden times, bonfires) at which departed ancestors were invited to come and warm themselves. Divinations were held at this time, primarily by young girls wishing to know if they would be married during the next year.

Thus the rhythms of human life and of the Earth itself merged into an elegant mandala of time and space which symbolized the flow of Darkness and Light that sustained the universe (see page 44).

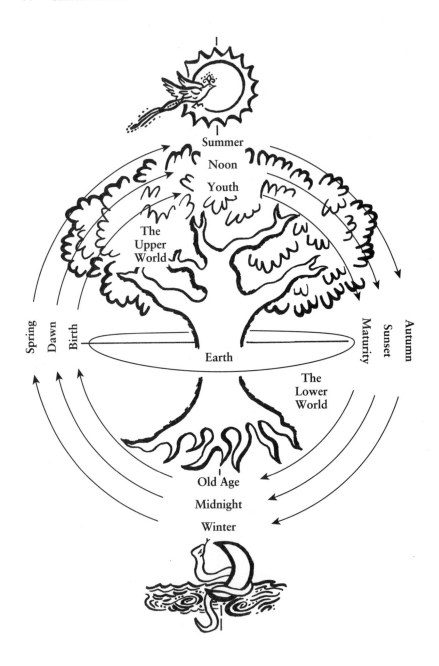

The Ancient Cosmos of the World Tree.

Endnotes

1. Quoted in G. Alexinsky, "Slavonic Mythology," in *New Larousse Encyclopedia of Mythology*. (London: Hamlyn Publishing, 1981), 296.

2. Igor Kungurtsev and Olga Luchakova, "The Unknown Russian Mysticism," in *Gnosis*, No. 31, Spring 1994, 25–6, and Vladimir Antonov, conversation with the author, October 1995.

3. In *Gnosis*, op. cit., and in conversation with the author, July 1995.

4. Adrian Ivakhiv, "The Cosmos of the Ancient Slavs," in *Gnosis*, No. 31, Spring 1994, 33–4.

5. Gimbutas, *Goddesses and Gods of Old Europe*, 102.

6. Alexinsky, "Slavonic Mythology," 283.

7. In fact, Russian villagers often do reduce the cosmic polarities to "good" and "bad," although this reduction argues for the influence of Orthodoxy on the more ancient concepts. I will have more to say about this a few pages farther on.

8. Stanislaw Vincenz, (translated by H. C. Stevens), *On the High Uplands: Sagas, Songs, Tales and Legends of the Carpathians*. (New York: Roy Publishers, n.d.), 35.

9. Mallory, *In Search of the Indo-Europeans*, 140–1.

10. In Tantra it is noted that the male produces a white fluid (semen) while the female produces a red fluid (menstrual blood); the polarities interact and interpenetrate with each other, as illustrated in the well-known Chinese yin-yang symbol.

11. Ivakhiv, "The Cosmos of the Ancient Slavs," 30.

12. Gimbutas, *Goddesses and Gods of Old Europe*, 89–91.

13. My portrait of the seasonal festivals was constructed from two principal sources: Ivakhiv, "Cosmos of the Ancient Slavs," 31–4; and Machal, Jan, "Slavic Mythology," in Grey, L. H., ed. *The Mythology of All Races, Vol. III* (New York, Cooper Square, 1964), 305–314.

14. This custom seems to have had a definite Pagan origin, for the Baltic Slavs on the isle of Rugen practiced a similar ritual. According to the Danish chronicler Saxo Grammaticus, the priest of the god Svantovit hid behind the piled harvest which had been gathered in the temple, playing the role of the family father while the assembled people of Rugen played the role of the wife. The questions and answers, as well as the purpose of the ritual (to ensure a good harvest) were, however, precisely the same.

15. In the Baltic countries, the sun is a goddess rather than a god; one wonders if Lada was originally a solar deity.

THREE

MAGICAL HEALING

I FINALLY SUCCUMBED TO DR. POLYAKOV'S attempts to show me his computer. The wondrous machine had its own room, just to the left of the main entryway. Polyakov had designed his own distinctive program, based on a computerization of his hand-trembling technique. When I made my visit, he was busy dowsing a desert landscape for potential deposits of precious metals.

This was all very fascinating in its own right, but I was more interested in the archaic than the high-tech. After watching several demonstrations of the program, I was about to take my leave when Polyakov was suddenly called away to the phone.

"This is one of his patients," Arina said. "A very sick man. He is coming here soon for a treatment."

I knew that Polyakov, after having studied the traditional kolduny for so many years as a parapsychologist, had developed his own practice as a healer, but I had not managed to learn just exactly what he did. I assumed, however, that his methods made abundant use of the computer's potentials.

I waited for a few minutes, staring at the landscape on the computer screen. One of the receptionists peered through the door of the computer room and said something to Arina in Russian.

"Come with me," Arina said, and quickly led me to the main office room where Polyakov kept his desk. At the moment, however, he was seated by the phone, in a chair that was usually occupied by one of the receptionists.

"His patient has suffered a relapse," Arina told me. "He is too sick to come in. Too much pain."

Polyakov was talking to his patient, apparently probing for details: Where was the pain? When did it start? and so on. Though I understood little or nothing, I noticed that, over the course of the conversation, Polaykov's tone began to change. It became rhythmic, almost a chant, with long, drawn-out syllables. Words and phrases were being repeated over and over again.

"He is healing him over the phone," Arina said cheerfully.

"What exactly is he doing?"

"Imprinting positive imagery."

Polyakov held up his hand; as before, it trembled wildly. He studied his hand for a moment, then closed his eyes. He rocked back and forth in his chair, eyes closed, speaking—or chanting—with ever greater intensity in those long, slow syllables.

At last, and apparently rather suddenly, he was finished.

I was about to ask him for his own explanation as to what he had been doing, but just then a young man of perhaps twenty-five appeared at the office door. He was walking with a cane.

"Ah," said Polyakov, "my next patient." He turned to me. "Would you like to watch?"

"If the patient doesn't mind."

The patient didn't mind. We left the building and walked in the rain through the courtyard, dodging puddles under a gray sky. We went into another doorway, entering an office that was also part of

Polyakov's domain. Within was a kind of scientific research room furnished with typewriters, papers awaiting filing, and a great deal of instrumentation that I didn't understand. In another part of the suite there was a back room, which the four of us entered.

The healing room contained a massage table, a chair, a desk, and a bookshelf filled with case records and account books. At the foot of the bookshelf was a hot plate. Behind the desk was another chair and on the desk itself a lamp, which gave out a weak pinkish light. There were icons on the walls.

"Heat the wax," Polyakov told Arina. She extracted a wafer of natural beeswax from a cupboard, dropped it into a saucepan, and turned on the hot plate. Polyakov removed his coat and took a seat behind the desk.

"So, there is a problem in your leg?"

"Yes," replied the young man. (That much, it seemed to me, was obvious enough, considering the cane.)

"Yes, yes," muttered Polyakov, "but exactly where? Let me see." He opened a medical atlas onto the desk and found the page with an anatomical diagram of the human leg. He stared at the young man.

"I concentrate my attention, and...."

Holding a pen, his hand began to tremble above the page. He looked down, then spoke to the patient, mentioning a few specific muscles and bones.

The patient agreed that this was where the problem was. It turned out that the "problem" was the result of an industrial accident and had never healed properly through conventional medicine.

Meanwhile the beeswax had melted down in the sauce pan. Arina left the room, returning quickly with a bowl of water, which she placed on the desk. Polyakov opened one of the desk drawers, brought out a vial of liquid, and sprinkled a few drops into the bowl.

"Holy water from the church," he explained.

He instructed the patient to sit upright in the chair. I drew closer, watching as Polyakov lifted the bowl of water in both hands. Arina removed the sauce pan from the hot plate and poured the melted beeswax slowly into the water.

"The whole art lies in finding the exact distance," Polyakov explained—or tried to, since I was not at all clear what he was talking about. He held the bowl close to the patient, his hands moving in a slow, drifting motion.

"Here, this is exactly right...." Polyakov proceeded to move the bowl in circles around the patient, always at the same distance from the body, and keeping to the general region of the waist, hips, thighs, and lower back.

"The water is the human body, and the beeswax...that is the human brain. All disease begins in the brain and must find its way out in the same manner. So you see, the beeswax draws the illness out, draws it out, draws it out...."

In the dim pink light, Polyakov circled the young man, chanting, drawing the illness out of the body and into the bowl of wax and water. At last he pronounced this part of the session complete. During the chant, he had become highly animated, and now paced restlessly around the chair and the desk. He fished the congealed wax out of the bowl and placed it on the desk.

"There," he said, pointing to a thick mass which had arisen from the surface of the wax. "That's the illness. Right there."

He studied the congealed glob, as if gleaning some sort of information from it. Then he told Arina to take it away.

"You can do this for yourself at home," he told the patient. "It is always better to heal oneself. Once a day is good. The trick is to find the right distance, how far from your body the water should be held. But you will figure it out. The water itself will show you; it will guide your hands.

"You will need a little bit of holy water and some wafers of beeswax. The holy water can be obtained at any church. The beeswax is available at a store just down the street from here; I will give you the address. When you are finished with the treatment, throw out the water, fill the bowl again, and 'charge' the new water. Take the wax you have just used and melt it down again in order to burn away all the negativity. Pour it into the new water, let it harden, and then place it in a plastic bag and tie it off. Store it in the refrigerator. You can use the same wafer over and over again every day if it is treating the same problem. After you are completely finished, you can dispose of it."

"How do you know when the treatment is completely finished?" I asked. But Polyakov was already onto a different subject.

"Now that we have drawn the illness out, we must replace it with positive imagery. This, too, is something which must be done over and over again, every day. This works, but it takes time."

Polyakov quickly loosened his tie, then flung it onto the desk. He stalked across the room for a moment or two, then turned to face the young man. He began to speak to the patient, quietly at first, but with growing speed and intensity. Again, his voice took on the rhythm of a chant. He was trying to speak in English for my benefit, but kept lapsing into Russian (for the benefit of the patient, of course, whose English was good but not perfect). I shall try my best to provide an English rendering of what he said, in terms of both content and style:

"Begin breathing very deeply, very slowly. Deeply, slowly, deeply, slowly....Yes....Yes. And as you breathe, visualize a stream of healing energy moving up and down your body. See and feel it, see and feel it, all the way up and down your body, from your feet to your head....And down again. Feet to head and down again....Yes. And the energy is there, warm in your leg, warm in your thigh.

"And in your mind you see a church, big and vast and filled with gold. All the beautiful ornaments, all the beautiful icons, all the beautiful singing....And your eyes gaze upward, upward, to the dome, and beyond, to the sky, filled with light, filled with gold.

"And the energy is traveling, yes still traveling, up and down your body, carrying the pain from your leg, warming your thigh and carrying the pain, up, up into the golden church and beyond...the energy traveling...watch it travel, yes, up and up and up into the dome and beyond, into the sky...."

The room had become noticeably warmer, and Polyakov ever more animated as he stood there chanting in the dim light. Suddenly he commanded the young man to strip down and climb onto the massage table.

Polyakov unbuttoned the top buttons of his shirt, rolled up his sleeves, and approached the table. He began to sweep his hands vigorously down the patient's body, beginning at the head. Every once in a while he shook his hands as if to cleanse them, intoning the words, "Burn it in the fire. Burn it in the fire."

When he reached the patient's thigh, Polyakov raised his hand above his head, pointed his three middle fingers, and brought them down sharply toward the thigh, giving out a screech that reminded me of an eagle on a hunt.

Quickly, he finished up by "sweeping" the young man's body down to the feet. Then he was done. The young man shook his hand, thanked him, and left.

"My next client is a businessman," said Polyakov, wiping his forehead with a rag. "I will use the beeswax to divine the future of his business. He will, of course, prefer complete privacy. But do come back."

I assured him that I would.

THOUGH POLYAKOV HIMSELF was an academician, his healing methods were drawn straight from the archaic practices of the village sorcerers with whom he had studied for so many years.

In the old Slavic world view, magic was everywhere. Occult power was attributed to herdsmen, millers, blacksmiths, beekeepers, carpenters, and stonemasons, as well as professional sorcerers. Herdsmen, who were frequently retarded, were regarded as "holy fools," as well as being often in the forest where the Leshy or Forest Lord lived. Millers were rumored to be friendly with the Vodyanoi or water spirits. (Despite all this, "the devil" is conspicuously absent from Slavic sorcery, and persecutions tended to be individual, never reaching the epidemic proportions they did in the West.)

According to traditional lore,[1] a sorcerer may be either "born" or "made." Unusual signs and omens at birth typically mark the "born" sorcerer—people born with a vestigial tail, for instance, are commonly regarded as the possessors of unusual powers. A "made" sorcerer, on the other hand, can obtain his or her powers in a variety of ways. For example, a Russian folktale tells the story of a woman who wished to inherit the power of a dying witch; she obtained the old woman's power by going to a bathhouse and passing three times through the jaws of a gigantic spirit frog.

Sorcerers have numerous spirit helpers, which are sometimes the spirits of the departed and sometimes animals. These spirit allies live in the forest, in abandoned buildings, barns, or—in the last century—in the traditional Slavic bathhouse. Some peasants believe that spirits cannot dwell in proximity to an icon—though many sorcerers, especially the healers, employ icons in their practice.

Magic is a force of Nature; it is not a moral quality, whether good or evil. All definitions of "white" and "black" magic depend upon the intent of the practitioner. Evil sorcerers specialize in "spoiling"—they blight marriages, health, livestock, the fertility of the land. In order to cast a spell upon a person, an evil sorcerer usually acquires an object belonging to the victim, such as a belt, collar, or lock of hair. Hair is regarded as especially dangerous, for it is often used in death spells, worked into clay or a wax likeness of the person, placed in a little coffin, then buried and covered with a rock.

Another powerful charm is the earth surrounding someone's footprints; earth gathered from around a footprint is often placed in a little bag and hung somewhere in the house. One may cast a spell by etching the victim's shadow on a wall. Food consumed by the intended victim—especially salt—can also be used, for a spell can be cast by adding a potion or powder (normally made from grasses and roots) to one's food or water, placing it in his proximity, or sprinkling it in his path.

The magical power used in the casting of spells may be transmitted by touching, blowing, pinching, or kissing. Special powders can be released into the wind; sometimes a spell can be carried simply by the wind alone. Written and spoken charms are both regarded as especially powerful; amulets are made by combining special roots or grasses with written charms.

The most common illness attributed to nineteenth-century sorcery was the "shrieking illness," a form of hysteria that primarily afflicted women and was characterized by howling, cursing and falling to the ground during the liturgy, in church processions, or in the presence of icons or other religious objects. The shrieking illness also included pain in the groin or heart, bloating of the stomach, or foaming at the mouth. This affliction was usually bestowed through food or drink, and was not limited to single individuals—indeed, whole wedding parties could be afflicted.

The fear of evil sorcery has given birth to various folk methods of psychic protection. For example, in addition to the usual "sign of the cross," sorcery may be contravened with milkweed collected on the Feast of St. Nicholas (May 9). Or, one might give the devil his due. In nineteenth century Russia, it was often said that one could ward against the "spoiling" of a wedding by inviting a sorcerer to the feast.

The "good" sorcerers were—and are—called *znakhary* or healers. There were also "guessers" (*gadalky*) who located lost objects, and "fortune-tellers" (*vorozheia*) who divined by any number of methods. Like their evil counterparts, healers or znakhary could also be "born" due to distinctive physical signs, like the vestigial tail. Good sorcerers are seldom known to drink or swear. Their houses are clean and smell of healthful herbs. They are always ready to help their neighbors—and better still, it is said that they don't charge as much as the black magicians.

Nevertheless, the "good" sorcerers sometimes use methods that are fairly intense. To find stolen goods, for example, a "guesser" or *odgatchik* might take a small sample from the kind of object stolen and attach it to the mouth of the stove; if a fur coat were stolen, this sample might be a little piece of sheepskin. Then, as the sheepskin began to warp and burn, the "guesser" might say something like: "May the unclean force cause the thief to writhe and shrivel, just as this sheepskin is decaying and turning to ashes." The thief will then be in pain until he returns the stolen object. (Some extremely talented diviners, however, are able to simply sit in an empty room and stare at a corner until they know where the lost item is.)

The healing of illness is the most common form of practice among village sorcerers. In fact, magical healing of all kinds is a subject of great fascination among Russians generally—one of the best ways to start a wild and lively debate among Russians is to mention the name of the well-known healer Anatoly Kashpirovsky, and then listen to the fireworks while everyone argues about whether or not he was a genius or a fraud. Even Leonid Brezhnev, in his declining years, sought to prolong his failing vitality through the arts of a koldunya named Duna Davitashvili. Healers come into fashion, then drift back into obscurity. At the time of my visit, Polyakov himself was one of the best-known magical healers operating in Russia.

The many methods of healing are varied; although the kolduny hold various cultural assumptions and mystical beliefs in common, theirs is a world where dogma is subordinate to individual inspiration, and where a healer may well develop his or her own "special" methods.

Polyakov's most basic method was to draw forth illness from the body by using beeswax in "charged" water; the illness is "charmed" into the wax and water. In this nineteenth century spell,[2] an egg is used as the vehicle in which the illness may be captured.

A Spell to Capture Illness

Get an egg. Make the sign of the cross over an icon three times, then say: "At an auspicious time does a good business begin." Move the egg from left to right across the head, face, arms and body of the patient while whispering:

"At this auspicious time, I do not come to give, but to remove, an ailment, from her hands, her feet, her head, her brain, her brows, her eyes, every vein, every joint. I do not remove the ailment myself. Most holy Mother of God and all the saints come to my assistance."

Then speak to the illness directly, as if it were a spirit in its own right: "Did you appear at noon? Did you appear at dinnertime, did you appear at night? Were you sent? Did you appear at a joyful time? I expel you, I send you to the waters, where the water swirls, where people don't walk and birds don't fly and beasts don't run. That's where you should walk, that's where you should roam. Don't break the yellow bone!

"Lord, purify me! Mother of God, purify me! Mother Earth, purify me! All ye saints, come to my assistance!"

Run the egg over the person's body three times, uttering the spell three times. Have the patient stand, then carve a circle in the earth around him or her with a knife. Fill a glass half full of water. Break the egg into the glass. The illness is in the egg and goes into the water.

This spell, though recorded in Russia, contains elements that are quite universal. I have seen Mexican *curanderas* "sweep" a patient's body with an egg while calling upon a garden variety assortment of Catholic saints and pre-Columbian spirits, thus conjuring the illness into the egg. The Santeria tradition makes use of similar methods.

In Slavic countries, the use of beeswax to "capture" the spirit of an illness is also very old (the Pagan Slavs were known as superb beekeepers; they sold honey to the Byzantines). Here is yet another nineteenth-century spell:[3]

Using Beeswax to Capture Illness

Place a cross in a bowl of water over which a charm has been uttered. Place three candles in a dish. Then say loudly "God has risen"; recite a psalm, the Lord's Prayer, a prayer to the Mother of God, and so on. Then whisper, "Coffin and grave, be thrice censed." Take the candles out of the dish and lower three drops from each candle into the water. If the drops of wax coalesce into a single mass, all will be well. Get the sick person to drink the water.

OVER THE COURSE of the next two weeks, I witnessed several more healing sessions with Dr. Polyakov, and had the chance to discuss his methods at greater length.

Polyakov's philosophy of healing was based on balancing the universal polarities, which exist within all human beings just as they exist within the structure of the cosmos and the seasons of the year. In Polyakov's world view, Chaos was as necessary as Order, Water as valuable as Fire; hence true healing, whether physical or psychological, lay in achieving a state of equilibrium between the two. In order to accomplish this, he made use of three basic techniques:

- Conjuring the illness into wax and water
- Imprinting positive mental imagery
- Energy massage

In detailing some of these techniques, I make no claim that they will be effective in healing anyone's physical problems. As we shall see, Polyakov's methods are essentially shamanic, and in all shamanic healing a great deal depends upon the personality of the healer, the quantum of energy and "fire" that he or she is able to muster and put into action. An individual with a true shamanic gift can accomplish cures with almost any method (or sometimes without any perceptible method at all); in fact, Slavic sorcerers are extremely individualistic, and each healer seems to have his or her own "favorite" method.

If you are physically ill, by all means see a physician. The exercises given here are intended for those who wish to experiment with the quality and nature of energetic fields within the human body, and not as a substitute for professional medical care. I also believe that these methods may be psychologically useful—magical healing is as much a matter of psychology as it is of medicine, and just as effective in harmonizing the soul as it is in curing the body.

Let us begin with a simple technique used by Polyakov to ascertain whether the various centers of energy within the body are equilibrated or whether they are out of balance.

Like yoga, shamanic magic has always recognized distinct foci of spiritual energy within the body. In India, these centers of spiritual energy are, of course, called chakras or "wheels," though Igor and Olga believe that in Pagan Slavic terms it might be more proper to imagine them as "zones" or "regions" of the body rather than as wheels.[4] This notion of inner centers of power may be found in almost all cultures with a shamanic world-view; the Aztecs, for example, recognized three centers of power, one in the crown of the head, one in the heart, and one in the liver.[5]

Slavic sorcerers have highly individual notions about the nature and significance of these zones of power; all agree concerning the existence of a center of power in the belly or *dzivot*, and we shall consider this notion in more detail later on. Aside from that, a sorcerer or sorceress may well find his or her own special center of power almost anywhere. But as we have noted, the spiritual nomenclature of India has become a kind of universal metaphysical language, and consequently the better-educated and more urbanized students of traditional Slavic magic, including Dr. Polyakov, now attach the same locations and meanings to these zones as those which pertain to the more familiar chakras:

- the crown of the head governs consciousness and our connection with the higher self
- the space between the eyes (the so-called "third eye") governs psychic perception and the higher mind
- the throat governs intelligence and communication
- the heart governs love and compassion
- the navel or solar plexus governs anger, ego, and the power of positive assertion
- the generative organs govern sexuality

- the coccyx or base of the spine governs the survival
  instinct and the physical plane at its most basic level

What follows here, then, is the basic method for ascertaining whether these psychic centers are in harmony:

Dowsing the Psychic Centers

Charge a bowl of water, whether by magically changing it to the Water of Life (as described in the last chapter), or, more simply, by adding a few drops of holy water. This is equivalent to the nineteenth century practice of placing a cross in the water and then praying over it, as described above.

Have the "patient" sit upright in a chair, without crossing his or her arms or legs. Standing behind the patient, bring the bowl of water close to the person's body, holding it close to the back of each chakra in turn.

Place yourself in a deep state of relaxation; if possible, "turn off" your mind and think of nothing at all. The bowl of water will probably want to "drift" or "float" away from the chakra. Allow it to do so, continuing to hold it in your hands and, if necessary, walking backwards to accommodate its "drift." If it floats quite far away from the chakra in question (let's say around three feet) then the chakra is out of alignment. If it remains relatively close to the patient's body, the chakra is balanced and in harmony.

If a chakra proves to be seriously out of alignment, you may balance it as follows: Using all your powers of imagination, fill yourself with positive energy, breathing in light and healing with each deep, rhythmic breath that you take. Meanwhile, approach the patient again, bringing the water closer and closer until it is again in contact with the patient's chakra.

Dr. Polyakov teaches that charged water should be moved slowly away from the body in order to draw forth undesirable intrusions; this is healing with the yin polarity, useful for drawing forth toxins, ulcers, or "watery" psychological disturbances like depression, anxiety, and so

Doctor Vadim Polyakov uses positively charged water and natural beeswax to draw forth illness. He asserts that the key to this method lies in holding the water at exactly the right distance from the body.

forth. To heal with the yang polarity, the charged water should be brought closer and closer to the patient's body; this is good for "attacking" things like tumors or anything (again including psychological states) that needs to be "burned out" of the body, as well as for creating warmth to aid the muscles, the circulation of the blood, and so on. When the healer approaches a patient's chakra while "charged" with positive energy, he brings the fiery yang force into play, using the inner fire to push the drifting, dissociated Water of the unaligned chakra back into balance.

The beeswax method—which, as we have seen, is very old and can be found in nineteenth-century charms—works on the same principle. Polyakov places a great deal of emphasis on "finding the right distance" at which to begin. This "distance" corresponds to the patient's auric or energetic field—in other words, the wax and water must initially be positioned at the edge of the patient's natural vibratory field; moving away from that field draws forth illnesses through the yin method, while moving the wax and water closer towards the patient's body attacks illness through the yang method. Either way, the illness or (to use a shamanic term) "intrusion" is charmed out of the body and into the wax.

Here, then, are some basic techniques for healing with beeswax and water:

Healing with Beeswax and Water

Charge a bowl of water with positive energy; if you wish, you may also add a few drops of holy water (the village healer in a hurry may well use the holy water alone, without taking the time to formally "charge" the water with energy).

Melt a wafer of pure, natural beeswax and pour it into the charged water (equivalent to allowing the wax of three candles to drip into the water, as in the nineteenth-century spell). Before it congeals, bring the bowl close to the patient's body. If the problem is digestive, hold the bowl at stomach level; if circulatory, hold it near the heart and so on.

Get your mind out of the way and allow the bowl to "float," as in the exercise regarding the chakras. It will soon come to rest at a particular distance, one that will be constant throughout the body, whether high or low. This distance represents the edge of the patient's bio-energetic field.

Next, you may either draw the problem out of the body by moving the bowl away from the body, or attack it vigorously by moving the bowl closer. Continue to do this, back and forth, for some time, allowing your intuition and the charged water itself to set the pace, the flow, and the distances. If you like, you may also use the kind of verbal suggestions or positive imagery which will be discussed a few pages farther on.

Continue for a few minutes, until the treatment "feels" like it's over. The illness will have been transferred into the wax, which should now be removed from the water. Talented psychics may be able to discern details about the problem by studying the contours of the wax.

Now throw out the water, fill the bowl again, and charge the water with positive energy once more. Take the congealed wax and melt it down in order to burn away the essence of the disease which is now vested therein. Pour the hot wax into the new water until it hardens again. Remove it, place it in a carefully sealed plastic bag, and store it in the refrigerator.

Repeat this process (using the same wax) again and again, perhaps once or twice a day until the problem is gone. Then bury the bag of wax deep in the earth.

This technique is equally effective if you do it for yourself. Sit down, hold the bowl of water close to your own body; let it establish the distances, and proceed as indicated above.

WAX AND WATER were not the only tools Polyakov used; he also worked with herbs and gemstones (malachite, he said, was good for the kidneys). The use of positive mental imagery was another foundation stone of his practice—one that may remind some readers (whether favorably or otherwise) of New Age methods of "positive thinking." Such words and images, however, are part of the traditional arcanum of all sorcery.

These cakes of wax were used to determine the nature of the illness of one of Dr. Polyakov's clients. The contours of the wax can tell an experienced healer much about the infirmity.

The power of the spoken word is the very essence of magic, and examples of the "magic word" are virtually countless. In ancient Egyptian myth, Isis chants an incantation over the dismembered corpse of Osiris in order to resurrect him, just as the sorceress mother of the Finnish hero Lemminkainen chants over the pieces of her son's body which she has retrieved from the river of the Underworld. The "barbarous words of evocation" found in medieval grimoires have their origins in Gnostic incantations intended to transport the speaker through the myriad palaces of heaven, and in India the incantation is formalized into mantras—Sanskrit words, syllables, or phrases held to have the power to manifest particular states of consciousness or mundane events.

In Slavic sorcery, those kolduny who healed or accomplished their magic primarily through the spoken word or incantation were called "whisperers." The best-known example of a traditional Russian "whisperer" is Rasputin, "the mad monk," whose remarkable ability to control the Czarevitch Alexi's hemophilia was based on his words alone. The Slavic incantation may be long or short, spoken, chanted, or sung. It can even be turned into literature, like the chant of the witch Kubarikha in Boris Pasternak's *Dr. Zhivago*, performed to heal a sick cow named Beauty. [6]

> Aunt Margesta, come and be our guest. Come on Wednesday, take away the pest, take away the spell, take away the scab. Ringworm, leave the heifer's udder. Stand still, Beauty, do your duty, don't upset the pail. Stand still as a hill, let milk run and rill. Terror, terror, show your mettle, take the scab, throw them in the nettle. Strong as a lord is the sorcerer's word.

The power of an incantation is vested in its verbal rhythms as well as in the imagery it evokes. Polyakov's voice rose and fell, grew louder and softer, faster or slower, at various times while he talked or "whispered" to his patients. In his view, however, the image was ultimately more important than the word, for it was the imprintation of a positive image upon the mind of the patient which, in fact, assisted the "healing."

Sometimes words and actions were combined to create a complete ritual; in such instances Polyakov dropped his academic posture altogether and became a shaman pure and simple, for his rituals had nothing to do with science, whether parapsychological or otherwise.

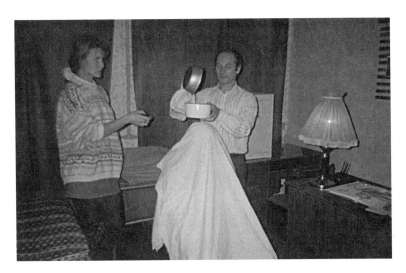

Vadim Polyakov and his assistant Arina Kol'tsova perform an exorcism, combining actions and words into a complete ritual in which the healer acts as shaman.

In Russian villages, people still fear black magic; any mysterious ailment or misfortune, whether it befalls people or their livestock, is likely to be attributed to the spells of sorcerers. In such cases, the sorcery or *koldovstvo* must be overcome by exorcism, banished from the individual's body and soul.

The following ritual is precisely that—an exorcism to remove the spells of evil sorcerers. Those who prefer their magic in the form of psychology may regard this as a method for removing an unwanted "complex" or other psychological "intrusion."

A Ritual Exorcism

Seat the patient in a chair, sitting upright, then cover him or her completely with a white sheet. The color white represents purity, the angelic realm or Heaven; it also acts as a protective shield.

Stand behind the patient, elevating a bowl of charged water over his head. Pour the hot wax into the bowl (or, better still, have someone else do it for you).

Slowly, begin to circle the patient, holding the bowl at the standard "auric field" distance from the body, as described above. Say:

"I summon this sickness, this sorcery, this witchcraft, into this water, into this wax, away from this man and into this water, this wax."

Repeating these or similar words, continue all around the patient's body, beginning at the head and ending at the feet. Then place the bowl of wax and water at the patient's feet and say:

"This sickness, this sorcery, disappears in the earth. Under the earth is a river, and in the river a fish. This fish is eating the sickness, eating the sorcery. He has eaten it up, eaten it all. And now he's burning in the fire!"

At this point, breathe the power of fire into your hands, as described in chapter two. Fill your hands with fire until you can literally feel them burning. Then exhale the fire from your hands into the ground beneath you, all the while repeating:

"Burn it in the fire! Burn it in the fire! Burn it in the fire!"

After the wax has completely hardened, reheat it to burn away the indwelling negativity, as before. Charge another bowl of water and pour in the melted wax. After it has hardened once again, place the wax in a small plastic bag and bury it deep beneath the ground.

In traditional societies, no single act, whether magical or mundane, can be separated from the fundamental cosmovision of that society in which the act takes place. The very definition of human action in traditional societies demands that such action take place in harmony with the entire cosmos. Though much of the ritual described above may seem as incoherent as it is bizarre, I believe that it nevertheless contains within it a portrait of the pre-Christian European cosmos.

As we have seen, the ancient European universe was imagined as a central World Tree, which served as the axis for three discrete levels of reality: the Upper World or Heaven, the Middle World or Earth, and the Underworld where the spirits of departed ancestors dwell. Because

"Burn it in the fire!" Vadim Polyakov draws the sickness out of the afflicted client's body and into the water and beeswax during a ritual exorcism, filling his hands with the power of fire to destroy the illness.

the World Tree is everywhere, it is also within us. Each human body is a World Tree: our minds, like the topmost leafage, reach for Heaven; our bodies themselves are the trunk (and so they are actually called), with arms like great spreading branches; and our feet are planted in the ground like roots reaching deep into the Underworld. Hence, the three worlds are contained within us—the three chakras or psychic centers above the level of the heart hold all the attributes of Heaven, while the three that lie below are symbolic of the Underworld; the heart chakra itself is the center of our inner tree, the Middle Earth of each human individual. Mircea Eliade has argued[7] that all yoga derives from this shamanic model of the universe, for the yogi, like the shaman, is a master of the "inner fire," the vital energy or power which flows through the human spinal column or trunk of the World Tree and animates our lives even as the sap animates the tree.

In this Exorcism Ritual, the operator begins by holding the Water of Life above the patient's head, thus drawing down the energy of Heaven at the top of the tree. He circles the patient even as the sun, the symbol of Fire and Spirit, circles the World Tree, meanwhile employing the fiery, "charged" energy of Heaven to draw the impurities out of the human tree even as the sun itself heals and "grows" the World Tree.

Finally, the operator places the bowl at the foot of the patient. He has reached the very roots of the World Tree. In most shamanic systems of thought, there is a dark reptilian or amphibious creature at the roots of the great tree, which in European myth systems is generally a serpent or dragon (the Maya specify a crocodile and North American Indians a turtle). In this folk magic version, the creature at the base of the World Tree is a "big fish." Just as the primeval serpents of Slavic and Teutonic myth gnaw away at the very roots of the World Tree—chewing up our ancestral and collective karma—so does the "big fish" eat the garbage and detritus represented by the spell or witchcraft.

The primal dragon is in eternal opposition to the God of Thunder, master of celestial fire: Marduk slays Tiamat, Apollo the Python, Thor the Midgard Serpent; in Slavic hero tales, Ilya Muromets, a Christianized version of Perun the Thunder God, is a dragon-slayer as well. Thus the King of Heaven uses the power of Fire to overcome the Dragon— another mythic metaphor for the triumph of Order over Chaos. Thus the operator in this ritual plays the role of the Thunder God, using his own inner fire to "burn up" the fish or primal dragon. This combat is, of course, repeated eternally; the dragon, though slain for a day, cannot really die, for the dynamic conflict between Light and Darkness, Order and Chaos, is the very rhythm of the cosmos.

As we began with the Water of Life, holding it above the patient's head, so we end with it as well; for, as the myth of Indra and the dragon Vritra teaches us, to slay the primordial dragon is to release the power of the Water of Life, the poison and elixir that lies sleeping in the coils of the Underworld serpent.

THE THIRD COMPONENT of Polyakov's practice was what I have called "energy massage," the rudiments of which may be described rather easily. The operator massages the patient's body as if he were scrubbing a load of dirty dishes, thereby cleaning the auric field. Typically, he uses an imaginary instrument for the purpose, such as a brush. Meanwhile, he clairvoyantly examines the patient's aura, hunting for "dark spots" or other evidence of imbalance. These troublesome areas receive special attention, whether in the form of more energetic scrubbing or, as with Polyakov, by attacking the problem with the inner fire, burning it away, perhaps extracting it from the patient's body with an imaginary knife or axe.

In regard to magical healing in general, the "energy massage" may well be a universal phenomenon. Certainly it is not limited to the Slavic tradition; I have seen Mexican curanderas perform similar operations, which are usually called "sweepings." The traditional Mexican healer "sweeps" the patient's aura clean with an imaginary broom (sometimes they use actual whisk brooms, the same ones people use to clean the insides of their cars), just as the Slavic healer "scrubs" the aura.

Polyakov never worked on me personally; Galina Vaver, however, "scrubbed" my aura on a regular basis for several days in a row. Her ex-husband, Vladimir Antonov, had insisted that she get me "cleaned out" before he worked with me. While I practiced self-denial in the form of fasting on meat and alcohol, I was also receiving Galina's energy massages.

Galina spoke no English, and I spoke no Russian. The situation struck her as rather humorous, and she was generally chuckling at our futile attempts to understand one another. Fortunately, neither scrubbing nor being scrubbed requires much discussion. At various times during each session, Galina had me lie down on a couch, sit in a chair, or stand up so that she could reach me better. She moved softly and quietly around my body, scrubbing all the while, pausing to shake the auric gunk off her hands at frequent intervals. Though the actual motions she made were the same as Polyakov's, her style of approach was entirely different. Where Polyakov was always vigorous and fiercely energetic, Galina was tranquil and deliberate. She shook her hands clean in a thorough and business-like manner. Unlike Polyakov, she did not shout "burn it in the fire" or anything of the sort; she rarely spoke at all.

Her gentleness was deceptive. I am accustomed to being worked on by energy healers of every description; I may even be a bit jaded about it all. Usually, the enthusiastic healer keeps asking me something like: "Can you feel the warmth coming from my hands? Do you feel your crown chakra opening?" And, just to be polite, I say "Oh yes, it's very warm up there," or something of the sort.

However, I usually feel nothing at all. I sometimes try to convince myself that I feel something, if only due to my own desire to have

Energy healer Galina Vaver works on Dr. Ina Kirtchik. Her method employs a swift, gentle touch to cleanse the auric "gunk" from her patients.

"something" happen. But the effect, if any, is seldom perceptible (the next day, the healer will call and ask me if I can feel the change in my energy system, and I say "Yes, oh yes" even though I still feel nothing).

When Galina began to work on me, I figured I would soon be exuding all kinds of sweet blandishments, founded upon nothing. Her touch was so gentle, so soft, that I could not imagine it would have the slightest effect on me. Yet I found myself drifting away under her hands. Even when I was fully awake, even if I were downright nervous when she began, I would soon start to fall asleep. Whether in the evening or in the middle of the afternoon, I found it hard to stay focused, to pay attention to what she was doing—my mind kept wanting to float off somewhere else. And not just my mind—my whole body and soul were drifting as well.

At one point, I actually lost consciousness while sitting upright in a straight-backed chair. If Galina hadn't caught me, I would have fallen face down onto the floor.

Endnotes

1. For my own survery of this "traditional lore," I have relied upon Linda J. Ivanits, *Russian Folk Belief* (London: M.E. Sharpe, 1988).

2. Ibid.

3. Ibid.

4. Igor Kungurtsev and Olga Luchakova, "Earth and Spirit," in *Gnosis*, Fall 1994, 16–17.

5. I personally believe that the Aztec material preserves an archaic world view in which there were only three chakras: the crown represented Heaven or the Upper World, the "liver" represented the Underworld, and the heart was symbolic of this world, the point of equilibrium between the two opposites. In a sense, the Hindu system merely doubles this concept, placing three chakras in the Upper World, three in the Lower World, and one in the center, thus making seven, which is the number of "heavens" recognized in many shamanic systems.

6. Boris Pasternak, *Dr. Zhivago*.

7. In *Yoga: Immortality and Freedom* (Princeton: Princeton-Bollingen, 1970).

FOUR

ICONS AND ARCHETYPES

THE WALLS OF POLYAKOV'S OFFICES WERE decorated liberally with reproductions of old Russian icons. He frequently enjoined his patients to meditate on such figures—a discipline he himself practiced regularly. In the calm faces and frozen Byzantine postures of the iconic saints, claimed Polyakov, there was a perfect regularity and balance that promoted healing.

Russian icons are a great deal more than a style of art or an adjunct to Christian piety; the folk tradition surrounding them is a species of archetypal therapy, a form of magic; and in the legends, images, and folklore of some of these "saints" we may glimpse the lineaments of the ancient goddesses and gods who reigned in the collective mind of the Slavic (and indeed of most European) peoples. The saints who inhabit the world of the icons are archetypes, which, according to Plato, means that they are primal ideas in the mind of the infinite; hence their lore may have little or nothing to do with the long-dead human beings who were canonized by the Byzantines so many centuries ago. St. Paraskeva spins the web of human destiny while St. Elijah brings the rain; St. John the Baptist and St. George attend the fertility of the earth while St. Nicholas wanders through a magical landscape working his wild miracles. All of this has little to do with Christian doctrine and a great deal to do with the archetypal world.

The use of icons entered Slavic folklife through Byzantium; in fact, we could say that one of the principal differences between "western" and "eastern" Europe lies in the influence of the Byzantine or Greek Orthodox Church over the cultural development of Eastern or Slavic Europe. Even in Byzantine times, however, icons were looked upon with suspicion by ecclesiastical reformers; the iconic saints were branded as Pagan gods in Christian disguise, and the worship of holy images denounced as a form of subversive Paganism rather than authentic Christian worship. The reformers who cried out against the veneration of images were the first "iconoclasts"—the "image breakers" who, under a succession of Byzantine emperors, sought to eradicate the cult of icons by the simple expedient of smashing the sacred relics.

The iconoclasts failed—and all those who appreciate a symbolic, archetypal richness of myth and image in religion will be glad that they did. Icons are still venerated throughout the Orthodox world, though seldom with as much fervor as in Russia, where they are regarded as a species of Western mandala, a meditative tool to open doorways into the infinite.

During our tour of the Hermitage, Polyakov had pointed out that many icons are in fact cosmograms, mandalic maps of Heaven, Earth, and Hell. Such icons, he insisted, constituted diagrams of human consciousness, with Heaven representing the positive or "spiritual" polarity, the solar force, and Hell representing the negative or "soul-centered" polarity, the lunar world. Earth, in the middle, was the point of harmony between the two, the reconciling point of balance. "When you meditate upon these icons," Polyakov said, "let your eyes be guided naturally to the center, to the earth as a place of equilibrium. That is where true healing lies."

One wonders if the early Christian icon painters, intent upon Heaven and in fear of Hell, would have agreed with Polyakov, whose interpretation is overtly magical. Yet this focus upon the center, upon the still point in the middle of the icon, is a theme Polyakov believed to be inherent in the entire icon tradition. Some icons feature a border made up of little "scenes from the life of the saint," a series of miniature paintings, roughly square, which extend all the way around the icon as a kind of border or frame (these are known as "biographical" icons). Polyakov says that one should meditate upon each scene separately, working around the entire icon in a circle, treating it as a meditation wheel ultimately resolving into the center of the circle, the face of the saint.

Icons such as this one depicting St. George and scenes of his life are frequently used by healers and sorcerers as tools for meditation. Often mounted on simple boards, they hang in countless Slavic homes.

The faces themselves are painted with what Olga calls "a precision that illustrates the refinement of human features through ascetic practice." They also partake of a circular or mandalic symbolism, for many, if not most, of the portraits that occupy the center of icons are laid out according to a precise geometry. A vertical line runs down the center of each face, usually defined by the part in the hair, the nose, and perhaps the cleft of the chin. This vertical axis is intersected by a horizontal one, typically the line of the eyes. Thus the saint's face itself forms a cross of the four directions.

As we have seen, a directional or seasonal cross of this nature should (symbolically speaking) be contained within a circle, the circle of life or of the year. Again, in many if not most cases, the cross of the directions is encircled by the saint's halo, which is typically a perfect circle. This quartered circle, if focused upon in meditation, will lead your consciousness to its center, which is the ajna chakra or "third eye center" of the saint. The center is where the magic happens, for each saint bestows a particular gift or quality upon us, be it health, success, or love—gifts or qualities appropriate to those archetypes we call the gods.

IN THE 980S, Vladimir of Kiev tried to shape the unruly natural forces of pre-Christian Slavic worship into an organized system (though as we have seen, he soon discarded his own handiwork in favor of Orthodox Christianity). He "set up idols on the hills outside the castle: one of Perun, made of wood with a head of silver and a moustache of gold, and others of Khors, Dazh'bog, Stribog, Simar'gl, and Mokosh."[1]

Vladimir's pantheon is of interest to us both for what it includes and what it omits. There is only one goddess, Mokosh; and the important god Volos, Lord of the Underworld, does not appear in this "official" list of deities. Perun the Thunderer was clearly the chief god of medieval Kiev. The solar god Dazhbog also merits mention—perhaps twice, for Khors may have been identical to Dazhbog; nothing is known of him beyond his name, which seems to come from the Persian *khorsid*, meaning "sun." Early chroniclers compare Khors to Apollo, and the khorovod or sacred round dance—which we have already encountered in reference to the seasonal festivals and Stravinsky's *Rites of Spring*—is a dance performed in honor of the sun. Stribog, probably a god of wind, storm, and dissension,[2] may have been the god of cold and frost as well, and thus an ancestor of the "Grandfather Frost" who is known in Russian fairytales and folktales to this very day. The winds are said to be the "grandchildren of Stribog, god of the winds"—they had a warlike character and were imagined as sharp arrows flying from the sea. The Simargl was a winged dog, guardian of the seed and new shoots, related to the magical Persian bird called the *simurgh* and hence the probable ancestor of the Firebird so popular in Russian folklore.

The gods of Vladimir's Kiev are a somewhat arbitrary bunch; they were assembled on the hill outside of Kiev only in the last few years of Slavic Paganism and there were older goddesses and gods, too humble to be noticed by Vladimir's warrior society, who have survived much longer, and it is these who most commonly appear in the icon tradition.

In finding our way through this vast landscape of archetypes, we shall focus only on those that have survived—whether by way of icons or folklore—into the present day, or at least until comparatively recent times. In so doing, we shall journey, like shamans, down the World Tree and through each of the three worlds.

The stars, planets, and constellations circle around the uppermost branches of the World Tree; here, in Heaven, live the gods of the sky and of the celestial order. Though we begin our journey in the Upper World, it will concern us less than Earth and the Underworld, for little remains of the old sky gods save for some fragments of folklore.

The rulers of the ancient Heaven were the sky god Svarog and his sons Dazhbog and Svarovitch, as well as Perun the Thunderer. Yet Svarog and Svarovitch do not even appear in Vladimir's pantheon, and only Perun has left clear traces in the icons of later times. Svarog (from the root *svar*, meaning clear or bright) was the god of the daytime sky and creator of the world. He seems to have fashioned the earth as a smith would hammer out a sword, for he was often equated with the Greek Hephaestus or Roman Vulcan, god of smithcraft. As a personification of the sky, he was sometimes lighted by the sun's rays, sometimes covered with clouds, and sometimes brilliant with lightning. In the shadows of the clouds, he kindled the lightning's flame. Splitting the clouds with flashing arrows, he lit "the torch of the sun which had been exterminated by demons of the shadows." Svarog ruled the universe, and, after becoming father of all the other gods, he transmitted his sovereign creative power to his children. To invoke him, sorcerers called out: "Sky, you see me! Sky, you hear me!"

Some scholars have seen a survival of Svarog in the figures of Sts. Cosmas and Damian, whose legend involves the magic of smithcraft (Svarog was the divine smith). There is, however, some evidence that the ancient Slavs worshipped the Divine Twins who appear in India as the Asvins and in Greece as Castor and Pollux, the Gemini twins. If Cosmas and Damian have any Pagan antecedents, I suspect that these are more likely to be found in the myth of the Divine Twins rather than a "doubling" of old Svarog. There are two other folkloric saints, Flor and Lavr, who probably represent the Divine Twins, for the Twins were known as horsemen, and these saints are the patrons of horses. Rather, we should perhaps seek the iconic equivalent of Svarog in the cult that centers around St. Michael the Archangel; according to Mircea Eliade,[3] sky gods are serene and detached, meditative and contemplative rather than active, and the cult of St. Michael is one centered in intense forms of meditation and in the search for prophetic vision.

Svarog was said to be the father of Dazhbog the Sun God and Svarovitch (i.e., "son of Svarog") the God of Fire. All three of these deities seem to have been widely worshipped among the Slavic peoples, though it is Dazhbog who appears prominently in the Kiev pantheon, as well as in the old Russian epic entitled *The Lay of Igor's Campaign*, where he is said to be "the grandfather of the Russian people." His name probably means "the Giving God"[4]; the Sun God is a god of blessings. Until quite recently, the Hutsuls of the Carpathians still spoke of "Our Lord Sun" or "the Sacred Sun."

According to folktales, the Sun lives in the East, in a land of eternal summer and abundance. He emerges from his golden palace every morning in a shining chariot drawn by white horses who breathe fire. In this, he rides across the vault of heaven. He possesses twelve kingdoms—the signs of the zodiac or months of the year. He lives in the solar disc, and his children live on the stars. They are all served by the solar daughters or Dawn Maidens who bathe them, look after them, and sing to them. Sometimes the daily movement of the Sun is perceived as a change in the deity's age: he is born in the morning, appears as a handsome child, reaches maturity towards noon, and dies in the evening as an old man. In Poland, he was said to ride in a two-wheeled diamond chariot harnessed to twelve white horses with golden manes, and in other tales to live in a golden palace in the East whence he makes his journey in a car drawn by three horses, one silver, one golden, and one of diamonds. The Serbs imaged the Sun as a young, handsome king who lives in a kingdom of light and sits on a throne of gold and purple. At his side stand two beautiful virgins, the Morning and Evening Stars, seven judges (the planets), and seven "messengers" who fly across the universe as comets ("stars with tails").

The Moon was called Myesyats, which is a masculine name. He is sometimes described as the Sun's "old bald uncle," but in other legends, Myesyats is a beautiful young girl whom the Sun marries at the beginning of summer, abandons in winter, and returns to in the spring. One may invoke this feminine Moon as "pretty little moon" and call upon her to heal illnesses.

The Sun's daughters are the Dawn Maidens who stand at the side of their father. Zorya Utrennyaya, the Dawn of the Morning, opens the gates of the celestial palace when the Sun comes forth on his daily journey, while Zorya Vechernyaya, the Dawn of the Evening or Twilight, closes them again when the Sun comes home. It is sometimes said that the Dawn Maidens guard a dog who is tied by an iron chain to the constellation of the Little Bear. When the chain breaks, the world will end.

In some myths, the Dawn Maidens are accompanied by two sisters, the Morning Star and Evening Star; they help the Zoryas tie up the Sun's white horses. In another sense, however, the Dawn Maidens and the Morning and Evening Stars are not separate entities, but identical. Zohra, the probable origin of the name Zorya, is the Persian word for the planet Venus, which frequently appears doubled in myth as the Morning Star and Evening Star. Sometimes the name Zorya was also used to refer to a single deity; in Kiev, Zorya was known as a virgin goddess and companion of Perun who protected warriors with her long veil. The following verse is an invocation to Zorya,[5] which was still used as a protective charm into the nineteenth century.

O Virgin, unsheath your father's sacred sword.
Take up the breastplate of your ancestors.
Take up your powerful helmet.
Bring forth your steed of black.
Fly to the open field,
There where the great army with countless weapons is found.
O Virgin, cover me with your veil.
Protect me against the power of the enemy,
Against guns and arrows, warriors and weapons,
Weapons of wood, of bone, of copper and iron and steel.

THE CHIEF DEITY of the Kiev pantheon, and the most important of the sky gods, was Perun. The Byzantine historian Procopius says that "he is the god who wields the thunderbolt, and the Slavs regard him as sole lord of the universe." He rode through the sky in a chariot drawn by wild horses, shooting his thunderbolt arrows and bringing both the nurturing rains and the fierce storms.

His name testifies to his great ancestry. The Vedic Thunder God Indra was sometimes called Parjanya, which has the same linguistic root as Perun. The god was known as Peron in Slovakia and Perkunas in Lithuania, while the Polish word *piorun* actually means "thunder." His pre-eminence throughout the Pagan Slavic world is attested in numerous place names as well: in Slovenia there is a Perunja Ves and a Perunji Ort; in Istria and Bosnia many hills and mountains are called Perun; in Croatia there is a Peruna Dubrava, and in Dalmatia a Mt. Perun. Additionally, there is a Perin Planina in Bulgaria, a Peruny and Piorunow in Poland, a Perunov Dub in Little Russia, and a Perun among the Elbe Slavs.

The Mater Verborum of 1202 equates Perun with Jupiter, almost certainly because both gods were kings and wielders of the thunderbolt. However, his closest equivalent is the Norse god Thor, whose mother, Fjorgynn, bears a name that is an almost exact linguistic cognate for Perun. Thor bears a hammer, while Perun casts his thunderbolts with a bow and arrow; aside from this, the two deities are virtually identical.

Like most Indo-European thunder gods, Perun was also a god of the warrior class. An old chronicle tells how Olga, an early ruler of Kiev, led her warriors into battle, and how they swore by their weapons and by Perun. Igor, Prince of Kiev, placed his arms, his shield, and his "personal god" by the image of Perun on top of the hill to celebrate a victory in battle.

The idol of Perun with its "head of silver and moustache of gold" was thrown down by Vladimir when Kiev was Christianized in 988; a church to St. Basil was built upon the spot. But Perun was long remembered; his worship continued into the next century. He was sometimes conceived as a divine and mighty laborer who traced furrows in a copper sky with his miraculous plow. In the folklore of Belarus he still carried his bow and arrow but roamed the sky on a millstone rather than in his chariot of war.

He can be met with in other guises as well. For instance, Ilya Muromets, the principal hero of the old Russian epics, bears a strong resemblance to Perun. Ilya Muromets, "son of the peasant," was sickly when he was born. For thirty-three years he only sat, and could not walk. Then two wandering minstrels gave him a "honey draft" to drink, and the miraculous liquid restored his strength, making him a hero. He had a horse that flew through the air, and the arrows shot from his miraculous bow could bring down church cupolas and split mighty oaks (the Thunder God's sacred tree). When it came time for him to die, he built a cathedral in Kiev and then, upon death, turned to stone.

In Carpathian folklore, Perun lives on as a nature spirit called the Thunder Emperor, a stormy figure who is greatly feared. A lord of hail and lightning, he dwells in the rocky fastnesses of the mountains. He rides forth from his castle when the beech forests are green and the meadows are flowering. His horses, their saddles, bridles, and saddle cloths are all made of iron, and the thunder is his drumming. His horse is black and foreboding, and his retinue is comprised of the princes of thunder, the nobles of the clouds, his sons and grandsons and kinsmen. They, too, are clothed in iron. In front of him travel the pipers and trumpeters, violinists and cymbal players of the thunder realm.[6] The Thunder Emperor points his scepter at houses, fields, and livestock, and his legions blast them all with thunder and hail, stripping the leaves from the forests, trampling the fields, and overturning the houses. Farmers sometimes hired exorcists to chant against the Thunder

Emperor, and on Christmas Eve they often attempted to propitiate him by inviting him into their houses for the feast.[7]

Perun survives in the icon tradition as the prophet Elijah. Like Perun, Elijah is a master of the "fire from heaven." In the Biblical Book of Kings, he ends a drought by calling the priests of Baal to a contest, challenging them to make Baal's altar take fire by magic. They fail, of course, while Elijah, with a single word, causes fire to descend from the sky and consume the altar of Yahweh. Afterwards, a great rainstorm blows in from the sea and renews the land. When hostile armies are sent against him, he again draws fire from the sky to burn them up. And finally, when his time on Earth is done, a fiery chariot drawn by horses of fire descends in a whirlwind to carry him away.

And so he is typically depicted, especially in the icons of Novgorod —riding through the sky in a chariot of flames, the sky itself painted a brilliant red. In Slavic folklore it is said that the sound of thunder is Elijah driving through the sky in his chariot of fire, and the Serbians in fact call this saint the Thunderer. When sudden thunderstorms strike, Russians often call out "Prophet Elijah, protect me," and they typically pray to St. Elijah for rain, for the growth of the crops, and for protection from natural disasters in general. The Feast of St. Elijah is celebrated on July 20 with great feasts of bulls, lambs, and calves, which are consecrated in the church beforehand. Among the southern Slavs, this feast day is a time of rest, with no man or woman doing any work.

Perun, Ilya Muromets, and Elijah are all figures representing the psychological quality of positive action, as befits wielders of the Fire, the active, dynamic polarity. Svarog may have created the universe, but he has retired to a life of contemplation. The dynamic world of action is relegated to the Thunder God, the "right hand" of the Sky God, his nephew or son who makes things happen in the world. Whenever we undertake a quest, fix our attention upon a goal, and strive to accomplish something, we partake of his archetype. To struggle and to achieve are magical acts rather than mere worldly pastimes, for Perun and Elijah release the waters of magical as well as creative power, even as did the god Indra in the *Rig Veda*.

FROM THE UPPER World, we descend to Earth, the blossoming Middle World, symbolized in the Zbruch idol by a ring of people dancing to the sun. Though the old Neolithic deities of forest and field make only a very faint echo in Vladimir's warlike pantheon, they have survived powerfully in the hearts and souls of the Slavic people.

The only goddess present on the hill outside Kiev was Mokosh, the Earth Mother. She was more commonly known by her title, Mati-Syra-Zemlya, "Mother Moist Earth." An old charm says:

> The first mother is the Holy Mother of God,
> The second, Moist Mother Earth,
> The third, the mother who gives birth in pain.

The word Mokosh itself probably means "moist," while Zemlya, the ordinary Russian word for "earth," is semantically equivalent to the name of the Greek figure Semele, mother of Dionysus. There are other linguistic links with Avestan goddesses like Harahvaiti and Aredvi, all of whom are but reflexes of the great river-and-land goddess Anahita, who in turn is yet another "goddess of all" like the Vedic Saraswati, herself a river. (In Russia the waters, and especially the rivers, were known as "mothers.") Her archetype is difficult to define simply because it is so all-encompassing; yet every woman who has grown to maidenhood, become a mother, and lived to be old is a participant in Mother Earth's symbolic round of flowering, giving, nurturing, and growing wise.

Mother Earth's body is made up of the stones beneath us; her bones are the roots of trees and her hair the trees themselves, as well as the grasses which cover the earth. Not only is she a mother, she is also a beautiful young girl. The Earth Mother in her springtime glory was personified by the goddess Lada, and the animal and plant life which arrived in the world at that time was said to have come from Vyri, a mythical, lush, evergreen land which lay far in the southeast.

Mokosh spins the web of life and death, and in earliest times she may have spun the world itself into being, as is suggested by the following old Russian folksong[8] in which a young girl, awaiting her future husband, sits in a white tent in the middle of a green meadow and embroiders the world.

The first thing she embroidered, that was the Moon,
First the shining Moon and then the stars.
The next thing she embroidered was the beautiful Sun,
Beautiful Sun and the warm clouds too.
The next things she embroidered were the damp forest pines,
Moist in the woods with wild animals all round.
And then she embroidered the shining sea, the waves....

Mokosh survives in folklore as an old woman with long gray hair who visits the homes of peasant women at night and helps them with their spinning. Like a troop of shoemaker elves, she works while the world sleeps. The "Mothers" or Rodzhenitsye who spin the web of human destiny appear to be the same goddess in triple form—but since they are usually ranked among the more humble Otherworld spirits who hover all around us, we shall deal with them in another chapter.

Yet another spinner is Paraskeva, an obscure Byzantine saint whose cult was reminiscent of Pagan worship of the Earth Mother. Though many of the Earth Mother's attributes were subsumed in the figure of the Virgin Mary—who appears in some icons as the Tree of Life itself —it was Paraskeva who bore the closest resemblance to the ancient goddess (and not only to the Earth Mother, but to the crone Baba Yaga as well).

In many icons, St. Paraskeva carries a spindle to symbolize her spinning, though she was a solitary woman like Baba Yaga rather than a spinner of domestic harmony. Pictured as a long-haired crone, she was called "dirty," for like Mokosh she symbolized the fruitfulness of the black earth as opposed to the white purity of the sky, the feminine polarity as opposed to the masculine. Like the Mothers, she spins the world from her wild hair; and when she combs her locks, she brings the rain.[9] Her rites were celebrated on Fridays, the day which, in the old astrological alphabet that stretched from India to Scandinavia, was always the day of the Goddess.

Those rites were not accepted with good grace by the Orthodox Church. In the time of Ivan the Terrible, Christian patriarchs thundered against the "orgiastic" cult of Paraskeva. Women young and old loosened their hair and stripped naked and danced in her name— sometimes the men danced along with them. Icons of Paraskeva were frequently placed in trees, especially birches, for she was symbolically linked with the sacred birch. Her image was found by sacred springs as well, and in fact was frequently dipped into springwater in order to invest the statue or icon with healing power. Paraskeva was also found at crossroads where the spirits of the dead were said to dwell.

On Fridays, her sacred day, the world rested. Men were not to hunt or fish, for Paraskeva was a protector of animals; nor were women to spin, for upon that day the saint grew weary and felt each prick of the needle as a kind of torment. Only those things which promoted the greening of the world were permitted—especially the overtly sexual dances which, as we have seen, were dedicated to Paraskeva's name.

The worship of Moist Mother Earth survived longer than that of all other Pagan deities; Mokosh lives on in Russian embroidery as a woman with uplifted hands flanked by two horsemen. She protects women's work and the fate of maidens, along with her usual function as a goddess of fertility, bounty, and moisture. She also survives in the veneration of Mary Theotokos, the Mother of God, who in the icon tradition may appear as Tree Goddess, Horse Goddess, or as the Goddess of Heaven, again with arms uplifted in blessing.

Even today, adults discourage their children from striking the ground with sticks, because "It is a sin to beat the earth, for she is our mother." In Belarus, plowing was formerly forbidden until March 25, because until then the earth was pregnant and should not be disturbed. Legal quarrels related to property could be settled by calling on the Earth as a witness: peasant judges in land disputes were obliged to eat a bit of soil before delivering their verdict, while the opposing parties had to place a clod of earth upon their heads and walk around the disputed piece of property. In fact, if one were to swear any oath with a clod of earth on his head, the oath was considered binding. The Orthodox Church tried to persuade peasants to make their circuit of the disputed land with an icon rather than a hunk of soil; but the Church failed.

Peasant women were the priestesses of Mother Mokosh: in some parts of Russia the women slept upon the ground clad only in their shifts in order to hear from Moist Mother Earth herself when rain might come; the dreams and voices they experienced were regarded as significant weather predictions.

Until the time of World War One, Slavic women performed the following ritual, which was meant to preserve a village from plague or cholera.

At midnight the old women would circle the village and summon other women in secret, so that the men knew nothing about it. Nine virgins and three widows would be led out of the village. There they would all undress down to their shifts, as in the rain ritual. The virgins would let down their hair and the widows would cover their heads with white shawls.

One of the widows would be hitched to a plow which would then be driven by another widow. The nine virgins would seize scythes and the other women would grasp animal bones and skulls. The procession would march around the village, howling and shrieking, plowing a furrow to permit the powerful spirits of the earth to emerge and annihilate the germs of evil. Any man who had the bad luck to meet this procession would be "felled without mercy."

There were quieter, gentler rituals[10] dedicated to the Earth Mother as well, including the following.

Prayer to the Earth Mother

In August, go to the fields at dawn with jars filled with hemp oil. Turn east and say: "Moist Mother Earth, subdue every evil and unclean being so that he may not cast a spell on us nor do us any harm."

Then turn west and say: "Moist Mother Earth, engulf the unclean power in your boiling pits, in your burning fires."

Then turn south and say: "Moist Mother Earth, calm the winds coming from the south and all bad weather. Calm the moving sands and whirlwinds."

Then turn north and say: "Moist Mother Earth, calm the north winds and the clouds, subdue the snowstorms and the cold."

Oil is poured out after each invocation and, finally, the jar is thrown to the ground.

According to Slavic tradition, the earth can help you predict the future, as we have seen in the example of the rain ritual. In some parts of Russia, a peasant might dig in the earth with a stick or his fingers, apply his ear to a hole and listen to what the earth said. If he heard a sound resembling a well-filled sleigh gliding over the snow, his crop would be good. If the sleigh sounded empty his crop would be bad.

Russian peasants used to ask forgiveness of the earth prior to their deaths (even in the twentieth century). One could always confess one's sins to Moist Mother Earth. In the absence of a priest, country people sometimes underwent their final baptism with earth rather than with holy water—a last rite which was administered by the friends or family of the dying person.

MOST ENGLISH-SPEAKING people are familiar with St. George. As a more-or-less medieval knight in armor, he slays a dragon. And it is as a dragon-slayer rather than as a religious figure that most of us know him. In Eastern Europe, however, St. George takes on an altogether different role. He is the protector of the land itself, and thus in a sense the protector of the nation as a whole. When the czar or a member of his family was seriously ill, special church ceremonies were held in honor of St. George to pray for his recovery. As a dragon-slayer, George was also a figure of chivalry, a protector of women and of the feminine principle—and the land itself was Mother Russia, or Moist Mother Earth, and hence feminine.

St. George was not simply a dragon-slayer, as he is in Western

.f the land and the earth was rooted in a far

: he was the master of the forest and patron

lay falls on April 23, when the forest is just

gain after the long winter. Throughout the

h was chosen to dress in branches and early

orge's Day, and to ensure the health and

eeding them ritual food; he was called Green

s, it is said that on the day of St. George the

s' horn, and that the echoes fly through the

into song.

Man of Spring who leads a host of wild ani-

of an ancient Neolithic deity whom we may

male spirit who served as protector of the

any incarnations are the Greek god Pan, the

nnos, and even Robin Hood. In Slavic myth,

The Leshy: Lord of the Forest. This is the mischievous male nature spirit who served to protect the wildwood.

this primordial deity is called by his rightful name, the "Lord of the Forest," though he is regarded as a mischievous nature spirit rather than a god.

The creature called the Leshy is quite literally the Forest Lord, for that is the meaning of his name. In the Christianized folk tradition he is said to be the offspring of a demon and a mortal woman. It is said that he looks "almost" human, and that his cheeks are blue because that's the color of his blood. His flashing green eyes pop out of their sockets, his eyebrows are tufted, and he has a long green beard. His hair is "like a priest's." Sometimes he wears a red sash, and his left shoe is on his right foot. He buttons his kaftan the wrong way around. He doesn't cast a shadow. Sometimes he is said to sport hair, horns, and a tail. He carries a cudgel and a whip and can assume other forms—often the forms of animals, but sometimes a mushroom. He may appear to the forest traveler in various disguises: as a bear, wolf, hare, or even as an ordinary person or an individual well-known to the traveler.

The Leshy's job is to guard the forest. When thieves or "bad people" enter the woods, the Leshy scares them away by crying out and playing tricks on them. The Leshy protects the deer, the birds, and all other forest creatures and is sometimes seen leading herds of wild animals—however, he is especially fond of the bear, with whom he feasts and revels, and of the wolf, who is his totem.

The wolf, in ancient Europe, was associated with outlaws who lived in the woods. The Leshy has several characteristics relating to outlaws; he and the wolf are both social rebels who have abandoned the habitations of ordinary folk to live in the wild.

When he walks through the forest his head protrudes above the trees, but when he reaches the forest's edge he becomes a tiny dwarf, capable of hiding under a leaf. Some say that he is a family man, with a wife called Leshachika (or Lesovikha) and children called Leshonki. They all make mischief together. The Leshy's wife may appear as an ugly woman with huge breasts, as a naked girl walking in the woods, or as a woman as tall as the trees and clad in peasant clothing. Most stands of forest have only one Leshy; but sometimes the Leshys may gather together in an especially large forest and under the hegemony of a king.

The Leshy won't trespass on anyone else's land, but he jealously guards his own kingdom. He leads wanderers astray in the forest, removing or re-arranging signposts and markers. After leading you back to your starting point over and over again, he will finally release you. The Leshy especially hates loggers, and weeps over the death of every single tree in his domain. He seldom hurts anyone, for he is basically good-natured; though some Leshys have been known to become extremely vindictive, tickling their victims to death. If he takes a human child into the forest, that child is likely to emerge as a dishonest tramp (if male) or slut (if female) forever afterwards. Leshys may sometimes substitute one of their own children for one of yours; such a child will grow up strong, but stupid and of voracious appetite. On occasion, Leshys make pacts with hunters or herdsmen whom they have especially befriended. They protect these individuals from predatory beasts and grant them occult powers. Sometimes such people would disappear into the forest, supposedly as captives of the Leshy. They might return mute, wild-looking, and covered with moss. Many simply remained peculiar for the rest of their lives, though some made use of the Leshy's occult power to become sorcerers.

At the beginning of October (October 4), the Leshys all begin to die, though they will return again in the spring. At such a time they roam the forest angrily, whistling and shouting, sounding like "over-excited women," sobbing in a human voice, crying out like birds of prey or savage beasts. They will return again in the spring, disguised as St. George, garbed in greenery and leading the village animals in a kind of animal dance which extends back to the dawn of time.

You can hear the Leshy in the rustling of trees, as well as in odd bits of laughter, whistling, or the sound of clapping hands. His voice is the echoing of the forest, and there is always a wind around him, so that no one ever sees his footsteps, whether he walks in sand or in snow. He is the archetypal Wild Man, the male spirit as a solitary inhabitant of the forest, at one with nature, communicant of animals and trees. Whenever a man camps alone in the woods and wanders far from any trail, he is in communion with the Forest Lord.

As WE HAVE seen, the rites of the summer solstice were dedicated to a deity named Kupalo. As the dying vegetation god familiar to Western mythologists ever since Frazer's *Golden Bough*, Kupalo is the Slavic variant of a most ancient deity indeed, for the vegetation god, like the Master of the Forest, extends all the way back to the European Neolithic.

The name Kupalo has the same root as the verb *kupati*, which means "to bathe." The veneration of healing water was closely connected with the cult of this god. In addition to his role as the spirit of water, Kupalo was also a god of plants and herbs, for he personified the active vegetative life-force. During Kupalo's Night, trees had the power to leave the ground, move about, and speak among themselves in their own secret language. Only one who possessed the magical "fire-flower" of Kupalo could understand their speech, but on this night it was believed that those who sought it might find it.

Kupalo was not the only name of the vegetation god in Eastern Europe, for he also appears as Yarilo and Kostroma. Yarilo was a particularly important figure, for the Slavic peoples were very devoted to him, and even in the 1700s the Orthodox bishop of Voronezh had to take strict measures against country people who still worshipped him. According to legends from Belarus, Yarilo is young and fair. He wears a white cloak and a crown of wildflowers, and he rides a white horse. He goes barefoot and carries a bunch of wheat ears in his left hand. His principal rites were celebrated in the early spring, though his "funeral" was celebrated at the summer solstice. Like other rites in honor of Yarilo, this festival persisted for centuries, despite all efforts on the part of Christians to eradicate it.

St. John the Baptist, called St. Ivan in Russian, has become the seemingly unlikely substitute for these vegetation gods—unlikely because John was an ascetic, dedicated to rigorous control of the life-force rather than celebration of its abundance. For the most part, the syncretism between the two figures (the summer solstice was actually called the Feast of Ivan-Kupalo) is due to the fact that St. John's feast day falls upon June 24, close to the old Pagan solstice. There are archetypal similarities and points of convergence as well: John, like Kupalo, is associated with the healing waters, for John baptized with water; and just as Kupalo is slain and dismembered every year, so was John dismembered, for he suffered decapitation at the hands of Herod (his passing was even attended by a woman wildly dancing, just as the annual funeral of Kupalo featured ecstatic dancing by all the women of the village).

The dying vegetation god is both the child and the consort of the Great Mother; whenever a man plays the role of lover, champion, and worshipper of the Goddess, he takes on the archetype of the lover-son, the man enraptured by woman. He is the soft man who has realized his "inner feminine," in contrast to the overtly masculine Perun and the wild Leshy. Possessed by Kupalo or Yarilo (or, to use the more familiar Greek cognate, by Dionysus), a man can do nothing but surrender to the inevitable power of Mother Earth, whether embodied in the seasons, in a particular woman, or in the spirit of all womankind. Surrendering, he dies. Dying, he is reborn.

LET US PASS now from the greening Middle World of Earth and enter the Underworld. Its god, Volos, was not an "official" part of Vladimir's pantheon; rather, he was worshipped in the "lower" part of Kiev, the district dominated by merchants and common people. The fact that his idol was here, rather than in the upper town, may have signified that he was, in a sense, Perun's mythic antagonist. Sometimes, however, he seems to have been linked with Perun as a friend rather than an enemy. An old Russian chronicle relates how Princess Olga's warriors invoked "Volos, god of beasts" along with Perun when they swore on their weapons. When Prince Svyatoslav concluded a treaty with the Greeks, he bound himself by oath to both Perun and Volos—the Upper World and the Lower.

Volos' survival in later folklore has been just as powerful as that of Perun himself—perhaps more so. In addition to his role as Lord of the Underworld, he was the god of cattle, wealth, divination, and probably the arts. After the downfall of Kievan Paganism, he survived in folklore as a simple shepherd watching over his flocks. Until the nineteenth century, Russians would leave one sheaf of corn in the fields at harvest and "curl" or plait the ears into a knot, which was spoken of as "curling Volos' hair" or "plaiting the beard of Volos." In some areas, a piece of bread was placed among these corn ears.

Though any genuine myths concerning Volos have been lost, we may glean a fair portrait of this deity's role as Underworld Lord by comparing him with the god Velinas, the God of the Dead among the Pagan Balts and a figure who still survives in Lithuanian folklore. Velinas is the one-eyed, prophetic, treacherous god of those ancestral spirits who comprise the Wild Hunt—a troop of ghosts who march through the sky on certain nights, causing terror to ordinary people but inviting witches and sorcerers to join them on an ecstatic Otherworld journey. Like one-eyed Odin of Norse myth, Velinas is associated with hanging and the hanged; and in fact the name Velinas is related to the Old Norse word *valr*, meaning "the host of the slain" (from whence Valhalla, Odin's shining palace in Asgard).

This link between Volos and Odin mirrors, once again, the ancient structure of the universe. Scholars have theorized that the three gods worshipped at Uppsala in Pagan Sweden were the lords of the three worlds—Thor ruled Heaven, Freyr Earth, and Odin the Underworld.[11]

Similarly, a medieval chronicler informs us that the Pagan Balts reverenced a great oak tree at a place called Romuva, and that three gods were worshipped there—Perkunas in the topmost branches, with a perpetual fire of oak wood as his symbol; Potrympus in the middle, a smiling young earth god whose symbol was a snake; and Patollus at the bottom, an old man with a turban who ruled the Underworld (the turban may echo Odin's floppy, wide-brimmed hat and even the turban of Rudra, a Vedic god who was ancestral to Shiva "of the matted hair").[12]

In the icon tradition, Volos is sometimes known as Saint Vlas or Saint Blaise, from St. Blasius, a shepherd and martyr of Caesarea in Cappadocia whom the Byzantines regarded as the patron saint of the flocks. His day is March 11. This is Volos the agricultural deity rather than Volos the Lord of the Dead. One may pray to him thus: "Saint Vlas, give us good luck, so that our heifers shall be sleek and our oxen fat."

When cattle epidemics broke out in the Russian countryside, the peasants would carry an icon of Saint Vlas (without telling the priest) to the sick animal. An ewe, sheep, horse, and cow would be tied together by the tails and pushed into a ravine,[13] then stoned to death while an exorcism was chanted: "We kill you with stones, we bury you in the ground, O death of cows, we push you into the depths. You shall not come again to our village." Then the people would cover the bodies with straw and wood and burn them completely. Churches dedicated to Saint Vlas are always situated at the edge of former pastures.

Perhaps the most interesting incarnation of Volos—and one who more nearly approximates the Underworld god of magic and mystery —is St. Nicholas. A bishop in the Anatolian city of Myra during the late Roman period, the historical St. Nicholas has, throughout northern and eastern Europe, vanished in a sea of Pagan attributes modeled on the Underworld Lord. As every child knows, St. Nicholas is, of course, our Santa Claus—and yet Santa Claus, like Odin and Velinas, leads a Wild Hunt (in the form of some rather tame reindeer) around the North Pole of the sky, the top of the World Tree where those ancestral spirits who constitute the Wild Hunt may generally be found.

In Russian folklore Nicholas is a wanderer, like Odin and Velinas. He roams the countryside and is called Nicholas the Miracle Worker, for his primary function is to make magic—again like wandering Odin, who in the Norse sagas often appears unexpectedly, carrying his staff and garbed in his hat and gray cloak, to touch the lives of mortals with a sudden stroke of his wild magic. In fact, the prayers of the Slavic people to St. Nicholas constitute convincing evidence that Volos must have greatly resembled Odin and Velinas. They pray to this saint for protection in general, but especially for protection while traveling, and Odin, as we have seen, was a wanderer.[14] They pray to him for help in study and in passing their exams, and Odin was a god of wisdom and knowledge, master of the runes. They also pray to him for healing, and for success in any risky adventure—whenever miraculous intervention is needed. Whenever we wander, whenever we seek out the mysteries of life, living by intuition and sheer magic, our outward lives in shadow and our inner vision turned toward the ancestral world, we embody the archetype of Volos, or St. Nick the master of magic, the Underworld Lord.

Even today, Volos may still be found in his rightful place—beneath the World Tree. In 1383 an icon of St. Nicholas was miraculously discovered beneath a tree near Velikoretskaya in the Vyatka region. A pilgrimage to the sacred tree has taken place every year since then (except in 1551, when snow fell on the village in midsummer). The pilgrims crawl beneath a hollow under the tree to pray and to perform their devotions.

WE HAVE TRAVELED down the World Tree to its roots, where the dead dwell beneath the earth. We have met the Lord of the Underworld, leader of the Wild Hunt. Still we are not finished, for somewhere in the deepest caverns of Hell lives a most ancient goddess, the most ancient of all. In the villages of Neolithic Europe her image is found again and again, stiff and white and carved of bone. Even today, those of us of European descent have not quite forgotten that death is a spectral white lady, a banshee; for this is the goddess who, long before Volos, Odin, and their male kin, ruled the Underworld alone. This is the Death Crone, the Goddess of Old Bones.

Bone Mother destroys us, then resurrects us, even as the earth from which we have our being is born and resurrected each year. She collects our whitened bones, pours the Water of Life and Death upon them, and sings her magic songs. Thus, having died, we return.

Her psychological function mirrors our deepest nature: whenever we experience a darkness, a depression, a spiritual emptiness so profound that we feel ourselves dead and in the depths of Hell, we have paid the Bone Mother a visit. The terrors we see there in the Underworld depths may be enough to crush us—especially if we should chance to behold our own shadow, our darker nature.

But if we are wise, we may be transformed in the Bone Mother's realm, and rise reborn.

Let us, now, spend some time in Baba Yaga's hut....

One encounters her, most often, when one is on a quest. In the deepest, darkest part of the forest, the hero or heroine suddenly comes upon her dwelling, which is said to be an *izba* or peasant's hut, for Baba Yaga is an archetype who speaks to the common people, not to kings or bards.

This is no ordinary peasant's hut. Surrounding it is a fence made of human bones, and upon the top of each bony stake there is a human skull. The hut itself is sometimes said to be made of human body parts, and sometimes of food, like the witch's hut in the story of Hansel and Gretel. Most peculiar of all, the Yaga's hut stands upon two chicken legs, and is prone to spinning round according to the rise and fall of the daily or seasonal tides.

The day itself revolves around Baba Yaga's hut. In the best-known Baba Yaga story, the tale of Vassilisa the Wise, it is said that three horsemen ride out from and return to the dwelling of the Yaga: one of them is white and rides a white horse and signifies the dawn; another is red on a red horse and signifies the day-bright sun; while the third is black upon a black horse and signifies the night. As we know, the day, like the seasonal round, is a microcosmic image of the universe at large; the white horseman rides from the world of Heaven, the black from the Underworld, and the red from Middle Earth.[15] Yet they all begin from, and end in, Baba Yaga's house. She is the World Tree itself, the ancient goddess who is both a Rusalka or tree nymph and the Mother Goddess as Tree of Life; she is the shakti or kundalini power at the base of the human and cosmic tree, and her roots are deep in the ancestral well of souls.

To enter Baba Yaga's hut is a dangerous thing; in many stories she is the archetypal *vedma* or witch, and she may try to pop the hero or heroine—especially if such a hero or heroine is but a child—into her

Baba Yaga: The Old Bone Goddess. This archetypal character signifies the ongoing recreation of our universe.

oven. The fairytale protagonist almost always prevails, escaping the cannibalistic urges of the Yaga and shoving her into her own oven—again like the witch in Hansel and Gretel, who, like Baba Yaga herself, is but another folkloric memory of the Old Bone Goddess.

Baba Yaga's hut is the place where transmutation occurs; it is the dark heart of the Underworld, the dwelling place of the dead ancestors who are symbolized by the grinning skulls around her house—and also by her oven or stove, for in Slavic folklore the spirits of the ancestors are said to dwell in the flames of the household oven or else in the fireplace. From this ancestral well the Yaga rides out upon her witchy errands, typically traveling in a mortar and steering herself with a pestle.

If the Underworld is a place where we may easily be eaten alive, it is also a place where we may be forever transformed. Let us remember that Baba Yaga keeps the Water of Life and Death. In one of her many incarnations, she is a great serpent or dragon who sleeps coiled around the fabulous water, like the alchemical dragon who guards the elixir; hence she is the primal energy of chaos which sleeps at the root of the World Tree, the ground of being (Sanskrit: *mulaprakriti*) from which all things are created. In order to achieve positive transformation, in order to make Baba Yaga our helper instead of our devourer, we must learn humility. Vassilisa the Wise, who was sent into the forest by an evil stepmother in order to fetch some light, did all the chores that Baba Yaga asked of her, working in a gentle silence—just as the "good girl" worked for Mother Hulda in the fairytale from the Brothers Grimm, for Mother Hulda with her long nose and fierce teeth is yet another Bone Goddess. So Baba Yaga gave to Vassilisa a torch that burned in a skull, and which in time was to burn up the evil stepmother herself. A torch in a skull—enlightenment from the dark heart of the ancestral Underworld.

Baba Yaga may destroy us or enlighten us. In this sense, she resembles yet another Bone Goddess, the Hindu Kali who dances with a necklace and girdle of human skulls, who slays and destroys, whose worshippers meditate among corpses in graveyards, but who, to those same faithful devotees, may in time appear as an ineffably beautiful woman who bestows the most precious of spiritual gifts. For this is the function of the Bone Mother: to break down the boundaries of our personality, to "slay our ignorance" like Kali by forcing us to examine ourselves in the dark mirror of the Underworld, and then to resurrect us, pour forth the Water of Life upon us, and grant us the deep wisdom that only a close acquaintance with the Underworld may bring.

THE GODS AND goddesses, far from being completely separate entities, are also interdependent participants in the eternal dance of duality, of Water and Fire, Darkness and Light. Their relationships create patterns, mandalas, cosmograms.

Let us, for example, return to one of our most basic symbols, the Cross of the Four Directions, which is also the cross of the seasons, a mandala of the waxing and waning of Darkness and Light. The celebration of returning spring was dedicated to the goddess Lada, returning from Vyri with her flock of birds, while the summer solstice was dedicated to Kupalo, the spirit of growing things. It is likely that the Pagan festivals of the harvest season were dedicated to Mother Mokosh (the same time of year is now marked by the important Orthodox festival of Pokrov, dedicated to the Mother of God), while the Koliada, replete with rites of divination and remembrance of the ancestors, was the season of Volos, Lord of the Underworld. Thus the seasonal cross of the year is a cross of goddesses and gods as well, as seen in the diagram below.

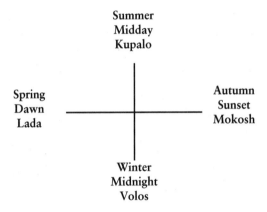

Summer
Midday
Kupalo

Spring
Dawn
Lada

Autumn
Sunset
Mokosh

Winter
Midnight
Volos

Like the seasons of the year and the times of the day, the goddesses and gods have their stations on the Cross of the Four Directions.

We can also pattern the ancient deities in threes as well as fours. Most students of mythology and folklore are familiar with the concept of the Triple Goddess—the Goddess as Maiden, Mother, and Crone. In Slavic myth, these archetypes may easily be matched with Lada, Mokosh, and Baba Yaga respectively. We may place the three of them on a triangle; in most Western magical and Hermetic systems the element of Water, which is of course a primary symbol of the feminine principle itself, is represented by a triangle pointing downwards, as shown in the following diagram.

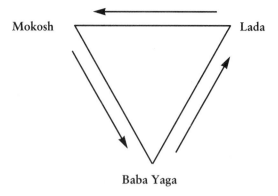

The Feminine Triad.

There is another, masculine triad which has often escaped the notice of contemporary mythologists. As we have seen, the Pagan Norse worshipped three gods at Uppsala: Thor as Lord of the Upper World, Freyr as Lord of Middle Earth, and Odin as Lord of the Underworld. This same triad may be identified in the Baltic as the three gods of the Romuva World Tree: Perkunas in the Upper World, Potrympus in the Middle World, and Patollus in the Underworld. In Slavic myth, we may easily identify this masculine triad as follows: Perun in the Upper World, Kupalo in the Middle World, and Volos in the Lower World. Fire, like Water, is symbolized in European magic and Hermeticism by a triangle, in this case pointing upwards, because Fire is the masculine element.

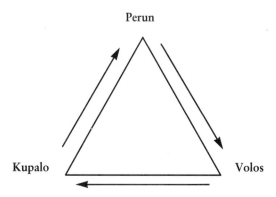

The Masculine Triad.

Finally, we may resolve the polarities of Darkness and Light into two sets of three deities, masculine and feminine, like this:

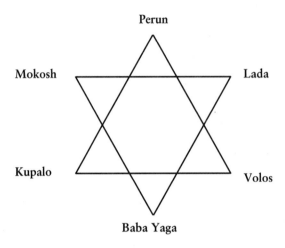

The Hexagram: The masculine and feminine triads combined.

There are, of course, an infinite number of variations. Goddesses and gods, witches and saints, icons and archetypes all unite in the sacred dance of Darkness and Light.

Endnotes

1. Quoted in Geroge Vernadsky, ed., *A Source Book for Russian History from Early Times to 1917, Vol. I: Early Times to the Late Seventeenth Century* (New Haven and London: Yale University Press, 1972), 25.

2. His name may possibly mean "scatter goods" or "spread wealth," but it may also derive from *Patri-bhagos or "Father God."

3. Mircea Eliade, *Patterns in Comparative Religion* (Lincoln: University of Nebraska Press, 1996).

4. From *Dadhi-bhagos, cognate with the Vedic term *data vasu*, meaning "giver of goods," and hence related to Bhaga, the Vedic god of good fortune.

5. Quoted in Alexinsky, "Slavonic Mythology," 294.

6. The Thunder Emperor's noisy retinue of storm spirits recalls the Maruts, thunder beings who, in the *Rig Veda*, accompany Indra on his wild chariot rides through the sky.

7. Vincenz, *On the High Uplands*, 62–5.

8. Quoted in Hubbs, *Mother Russia*, 24, and adapted by the author.

9. The same rain-making activites were attributed to the Rusalki, the tree and water spirits who were almost certainly identical to the "nymphs" mentioned by Procopius. For more on the Rusalki, see chapter seven.

10. From Alexinsky, "Slavonic Mythology," 287.

11. Actually, the term used by academics is "the three estates" rather than "the three worlds," in accordance with Georges Dumezil's theory that ancient Indo-European society was based upon three classes: kings and priests, warriors, and agriculturalists. Yet these three estates are most probably mere analogues of the three worlds of shamanism.

12. Jaan Puhvel. *Comparative Mythology*. (Baltimore: Johns Hopkins University Press, 1989) 227–8.

13. In this animal sacrifice, we may once again see the mythologem of the three worlds; animal sacrifices with three different kinds of victims are known from the literature of India, Persia, and Rome. Though the animals vary from culture to culture, the Slavic version is identical to the Persian, where the sheep or ram is equivalent to the priestly caste or Heaven, the horse to the warriors and Perun who perform the actions of Heaven in this world, and the cow to the Earth and Underworld. See Mallory, *In Search of the Indo-Europeans*, pp. 134–5.

14. St. Nicholas is sometimes regarded as the special patron of those who journey by sea, although this aspect of the tradition appears to come from Byzantine Greece, where St. Nick doubles for the sea god Poseidon.

15. Black, red, and white are frequently found in folk and fairytales from all over Europe. In the Grail Legend, Perceval is reminded of his lover when he sees black ravens pecking at spots of red blood in the white snow, and Deirdre of the Sorrows in Irish myth is likewise reminded of a lover when she sees the exact same sight. Black, red, and white are also the three colors most commonly associated with the alchemical process, though in a different sequence: black for the dissolution of the personality, white for its purification after darkness, and red for the solar power and vivifying life-force that results.

FIVE.

Earth Magic: The Green Hills

The Slavic landscape is comprised of immense spaces covered by forests and cut up by marshes, lakes, and rivers. In ancient times, particular places on the land were regarded as powerful or sacred, especially the rounded tops of hills (the "bald mountains" of Mussorgsky's musical composition "Night on Bald Mountain"). However, the old gods were worshipped primarily in groves of trees. There was a sacred grove on the Baltic isle of Rugen, while between Stargard and Lubeck was a great oak grove guarded by a wooden fence with two gates. This sacred place was regarded as a sanctuary for escaped criminals and wrongdoers who, once inside the grove, were considered to be under the protection of the gods. In Bohemia, it was not until 1092 that the sacred groves were cut down and the trees burned.

In addition to groves of trees and bald mountains, rivers, fountains, and especially the banks of streams were also regarded as sacred places where worship was frequently conducted. Here the old women performed rites dedicated to the Bereginy or river nymphs.

Because Slavic Paganism was primarily rustic in character, a great deal of the surviving Pagan sorcery may best be described as Earth Magic. At that time I lived in a rural area and spent a great deal of time camping and hiking in the wilderness, so I was especially eager to learn everything I could about this aspect of traditional Slavic sorcery. Before traveling to Russia, I had even asked Olga about finding a park or woods near St. Petersburg, someplace where I could experience nature (as opposed to civilization).

"Don't worry about it," she told me. "Vladimir is the master of the forest. He will take you there."

My actual "training" with Vladimir began with a phone call.

"Ken," he said, "Galina tells me you are clear now. I think we will go to the forest tomorrow. Meet me at the Udelnaya metro station at nine tomorrow morning."

I hung up the phone and told Ina I would be in the forest tomorrow.

"Udelnaya isn't a forest," she said. "It's just a park."

Forest or park, Udelnaya was a rather distant metro station, and I found myself up before dawn on a cold, gray day, trudging to Chernyshevskaya station bundled up in sweaters and a jacket, with a backpack on my shoulders. When I got to Udelnaya, Vladimir was sitting there dressed like an old tramp—stocking cap, ragged jacket and workman's gloves, and heavy rubber boots. There was a big, shapeless, disorderly pack on his back. We walked out of the metro station and there before me, in the gray mist, was the Udelnaya park. I started towards it, but Vladimir steered me in a different direction.

"We're taking the train," he said.

"Where are we going?"

"As I said. To the forest."

We took a seat near the door of the railway car. For companions we had old women in scarves, hunched over large bags, and young men wearing caps, drinking beer and vodka at nine in the morning and looking generally disgruntled with life. As the train moved sluggishly through the suburbs of St. Petersburg and out into the woods, Vladimir explained his ideas about power spots.

"The earth is a multi-dimensional organism, so of course it contains various manifestations of multi-dimensional space, from the densest physical plane up to the plane of the Creator. Therefore it is filled with specific geographic zones, whether large or small, that possess powerful energy fields. Such a zone of energy is a *svyato mesto*, a place of power. Some power spots may feel like dark holes in a dense dimension, filled with a very thin layer of energy. Others may vibrate with great spiritual and creative power. Such places of power can be found almost everywhere—on the earth's surface, near water, or under the ground. I have even identified various places of power in the metro.

"Different power spots resonate with different centers in our body. There are some that activate the throat or the heart center and allow us to enter a state of bliss. Also, they produce different feelings, different states of consciousness. Some places produce a groundless joy, filling us with laughter, while some make it possible for us to heal ourselves and others. Then there is the opposite effect: some places can devastate our bio-energetic systems with such intensity that they may even cause disease to those who live near them. Others increase our egotism; in such places we feel bloated with arrogance. Still others fill us with an aggressive feeling of drunken animosity. Some places of power generate fear and alarm. This is why we must learn to recognize them. If we understand what is happening, we may simply take a few steps backwards and feel better. But if we don't understand, we fall prey to mystical dread, which is an irrational, uncanny fear that occurs seemingly without reason."

"How do we learn to recognize these places of power? Many people work with pendulums. Can you find positive or negative places of power with a pendulum?"

"Yes, of course, but this is a primitive method, and not very precise. When we learn to sense the power places with our own body, using our entire organism, then we really know them.

"Also, the way that most people use the terms 'positive' and 'negative' is mistaken, because most people say that yin energy is 'negative,' while yang energy is 'positive.' And this may be true in the magnetic sense, but just because a place has yin energy doesn't mean it is negative in the emotional sense. And a yang spot is not always positive emotionally.

"A 'negative' power spot can suck out disease or other harmful things, can purge the human organism and heal it. Or a place which causes loneliness and anguish may help us to learn what true aloneness—as opposed to simple loneliness—is all about."

"And what is 'true aloneness'?"

"Being alone with the entire universe, which is to say, detachment from worldly things and entering into the great aloneness of the void. By the same token, some 'positive' power spots possess too much energy, and can fill us with alarm, depression, and so on."

"And that," said Vladimir, "is why we should never call a place 'positive' just because it has yang or masculine energy. That is why we should not call a place 'negative' just because it has a female energy. The categories are all wrong. I evaluate by only one criterion: how a place really makes me feel. And perhaps even that is the wrong way to think about it. Because even the grossest, most dense sort of place may be of value to someone.

"When we really learn to know the places of power, we can see that there are seven kinds. I would call five of them positive in the emotional sense, and two of them negative. So when I speak of negative places of power, I mean those which take away our vital life energies, but also those which may be used to treat problems, like I just said. Positive places of power are more complex."

Vladimir proceeded to elaborate upon the five kinds of positive power places, holding up a finger for each variety—which earned us a grim, disapproving look from the old woman sitting across from us.

"First, there are those which contain an excess of favorable energy which they give to us freely, as an act of love. These favorable energies may be either subtle or dense, yang or yin, but if they are too dense we may transmute them into something higher. We can do this if we learn to transfer our consciousness into different centers of power within the body and therefore become able to perform inner work at the place itself. Secondly, there are the places which activate a particular chakra or inner center of power, and which therefore create specific emotional states. Third, there are places which give a specific form to our consciousness, which allow us more easily to shift our consciousness from one inner center to another, and which help us develop mobility, activity and strength. Fourth, there are the places which naturally shift our consciousness into an entirely different dimension. And fifth, there are those spots which bear the imprint of some very high or enlightened soul, such as the meditation places or graves of the masters."

"How, then, do we learn to find these places of power? And how do we learn to shift our consciousness from one center to another?"

"That is what we will be doing today. The next stop is ours."

We got off the train at a place called Zelinogorsk, which means Green Hills. There were no hills in sight, just small groups of people on the train platform, milling around with blank stares in the cloudy gray morning. Vladimir began walking swiftly towards a collection of ramshackle wooden houses at the edge of town. Soon we were on a well-established dirt road leading into the woods.

"Before 1940, this was all part of Finland," he told me, "and in those days these were real roads. Now it's part of Russia and the roads have fallen into disuse; there are only hikers, bicycles, and cross-country ski trails here now."

We passed the final house, where two burly men sat on the front porch gazing curiously at us. We continued on, and the curtain of pines and birches, already naked and winter-barren, rose between the town and us.

"Now we enter the forest," Vladimir announced. "Let's make water."

"I don't have to."

"You must. It's obligatory."

We pissed vigorously around a stand of birches, then started back down the trail. After about ten minutes, we struck a smaller path bending off to our left. Here, Vladimir paused.

"Down this trail there are several places of power. But right here, where the path forks off, this too is a rather powerful spot. There is a cone of energy above us, in the sky, focused upon this spot. Can you feel it?"

I stood there, attempting to quiet my thoughts and activate my senses. Vladimir waved dismissively at my efforts.

"Walk!" he commanded. "You can't feel anything if you're standing still. In places of power, it is always best to keep moving."

I began to walk, while Vladimir kept shouting at me. "There, now you are at the boundary! Keep walking! See how it feels different?"

The difference was, in fact, perceptible. Walking beyond the invisible line Vladimir called the "boundary," I felt a distinct lifting, less a feeling than an absence of feeling, as if a certain quality of intensity had left my life. Turning around and walking back through the "place of power," I felt not so much a weight, but a force pressing against me. It was like swimming through a pool of electrically charged energy.

Thinking of Vladimir's dissertation about the different kinds of power spots, I called out, "And this particular spot, what is it good for?"

"Yes, that's what I'm showing you now. Drop your backpack."

I dropped it.

"Now, stand straight and tall, and raise both arms."

He raised his arms as if in an open embrace to the sky.

"And now like this," he said, bringing his arms down gently to his sides. "This place is perfect for drawing spiritual power down into your body. Just like this." He raised his arms and brought them down again.

I tried it. Nothing much happened. Vladimir didn't seem satisfied.

"You're not imagining your body as a tube. You must do that. You must see your whole body as a tube through which energy may flow, a vessel into which spiritual power may be poured."

I closed my eyes and raised my arms, palms upward and extended to the heavens. I tried to feel the cone of energy Vladimir insisted was hovering above me. Soon, my hands and feet and throat and the crown of my head all began to tingle. I envisioned my body as a funnel for power, a vessel into which energy might flow. Breathing deeply, I brought my hands slowly to my sides, and felt the tingling increase, encompassing my whole body as something flowed into me from above, filling me, enlivening me.

I opened my eyes. The trees were still barren and the sky still a muddy gray, but I could see waves of energy trembling before my eyes, much like the patterns of motion one sees on a mild psychedelic trip.

Vladimir was watching me, as if studying. He nodded.

"Very good. Let's continue."

We turned left, deeper into the woods. "This path leads to the cemetery," he said.

"Is that where we're going?"

He shook his head vehemently. Later I was to learn that most Russian kolduny and magi have very negative feelings about cemeteries. But for the moment, Vladimir was already on to another topic.

"I have said that one may discover places of power with a pendulum, but this is a primitive method, not very effective or precise. Better to use one's entire organism. And the same is true of divination, seeking answers to questions. In the villages, the kolduny use pendulums for answering such questions, but not the fancy pendulums with crystals and so on. A rag tied around a rock, that's enough. But again, it is better to use one's entire organism. Like this."

Vladimir abruptly turned off the trail and to our right. He stepped into a mossy depression where a stand of fir trees grew in a circle perhaps six feet in diameter.

"Here, inside this circle, I have built a fire and meditated. I received much information. You may do the same. Please."

I stepped into the circle.

"Yes, just stand there. Think of a yes-or-no question. Now, concentrate. Make your mind perfectly still. And in that stillness, ask your question. Then listen to your body. Soon you will feel something. If it feels good, the answer to your question is yes. If it's uncomfortable, the answer is no."

With that, he stalked off deeper into the woods, leaving me to my own devices. And there I stood, not even knowing what to ask.

I have always found it remarkable that, as soon as you attempt to still your mind, you begin to worry. Even if you weren't worrying about anything beforehand, you'll probably start worrying as soon as you make a concerted effort to relax your mind.

The first thing I started to worry about was whether or not I was wasting my time. True, I was enjoying my ramble through the woods, and I liked Vladimir personally, but despite Olga's reassurances I couldn't shake my gnawing suspicion that this was all some pseudo-yogic spin-off on Asian traditions rather than a surviving chunk of Pagan European Earth Magic.

So my first question was: Should I put an end to my so-called "training" with Vladimir?

I breathed myself into silence, waiting patiently for the thoughts to quit chattering in my head. It was only through an effort that I was able to float free, and through yet another effort that I was able to feel my whole body—the "entire organism," as Vladimir put it—as a unit. Finally, I became aware of each limb, each finger and toe, the hair on the back of my neck and the teeth in my mouth. I struggled to hold onto the awareness of all of it, a oneness, undivided. There in the stillness I felt my mind moving around, scurrying from one portion of my body to the next, hunting for sensation. At last I became aware of a dim ache in the back of my leg, just above the ankle and below the knee. It felt something like a pulled muscle.

So I assumed that the answer must be a "no"—that I should set aside my reservations and experience this session in the forest with a whole heart. I decided to try another question.

I had not seen my nine-year-old son Nicholas for several weeks now, and he had been on my mind. He lived with his mother, my ex-wife, and I saw him only every other weekend at most. There had always been a distance between us, though I never really knew whether the distance had arisen because he harbored some resentment towards me, or whether it was just a product of his own nature (and mine). In any event, I had often experienced the distance as an actual gulf between us, and wondered if healing were possible.

So that was my next question: Is it possible to heal the distance between my son and me?

This time it was easier to wait and listen and watch. This time the sensation came more swiftly, once again as a kind of tingling, in the center of my chest. I examined that sensation for several minutes—trying to ascertain, I guess, whether or not the tingling was pleasurable or otherwise. I decided that it felt good; it was a warm sort of tingling. Therefore, healing must be possible.

I turned around to see Vladimir watching me.

"Take a picture," he said.

I extracted my camera from my pack and pointed it at him.

"No, no! A picture of this place of power!"

I stepped back a few feet from the circle of firs and snapped a picture.

"Photographs," he explained, "carry a psychic imprint of the person or place whose image they have captured. If you wish to ask questions and receive good answers, just look at a photograph of this place. Formulate an image of this place in your mind. This will help you enter into its vibration—in case you cannot find such a spot for yourself where you live."

"And how would I find such a spot, if there were one to be found?"

"I will teach you." He began striding down the trail again. In a few moments, we had reached another fork, a very faint one this time, bearing off to the right. We turned off the path to the cemetery and moved deeper into the woods.

IN THE FOREST, I didn't have time to think much about the meaning of my experiences. Afterwards, I thought about it a great deal. For example, there was Vladimir's practice of drawing energy or spiritual power into the body as if it were an empty tube. Let me repeat the technique here. It is a disarmingly simple exercise, but one which has resonance with the whole spectrum of Slavic magic.

Accessing Spiritual Power

Standing straight, take a few deep breaths in order to enter a state of relaxation. Raise and extend your arms. Imagine your body as a hollow tube, waiting to be filled. Imagine that an endless source of energy and spiritual power hovers just above you. Now, bring your arms slowly to your sides, and, as you do so, feel that energy flowing down into the hollow tube that is your body.

I have used the term "spiritual power" to describe the type of energy that was drawn into the body. At various and sundry times, Vladimir also described it as "the Holy Spirit."

As we have seen, the Holy Spirit refers primarily to the positive polarity of cosmic energy, the yang or masculine force. Vladimir called this energy the "creative" aspect of the infinite, which is yet another "positive" or yang attribute, equivalent to the Firebird of Russian folklore and to all the other magical birds or tongues of flame which, during visionary episodes, descend upon saints and holy men everywhere. Just as one may charge a bowl of water with the power of the inner Fire, so this exercise charges the entire organism with that same power,

Vladimir Antonov drawing spiritual power into his body at Zelinogorsk. This exercise, which has a resonance with the whole spectrum of Slavic magic, is detailed on page 109.

thus enhancing the Upper World polarity or "spiritual" aspect of the human entity. Seen in that sense, Vladimir's exercise might well be called "The Descent of the Firebird."

Similarly, the exercise that Vladimir described as "divination with the entire organism" may well have extremely ancient roots. Here, for example, is another nineteenth century charm[1] from rural Russia:

A Nineteenth Century Divination Charm

During Yuletide, let a woman lift her skirts above her head while backing up to the bathhouse. Let her put her naked bottom through the half-open door of the bathhouse and wait patiently. If the spirit of the bathhouse (known as the Bannik) scratches her with his claws, it's a bad omen. However, if he caresses her backside tenderly with the soft palm of his hand, then her future will be bright.

This ritual is not quite as silly as it sounds. In the first place, an old Russian bathhouse was not a simple bathroom with a tub; it was a type of sauna, closely related to the Native American sweat lodge, the Finnish ritual sauna, and to other ceremonial sweat houses of the "circumpolar tradition." The bathhouse was a log shack set at some distance from the main house, with an outer area for dressing and an inner chamber for steaming oneself. Not only did it have its own tutelary spirit, the Bannik, it was also regarded as a habitation of witches and the ghosts of the dead. Christian icons were never hung there; no laughing, singing, or boisterous conduct was ever allowed. Despite its rather spooky associations, children were often born in the bathhouse.

In short, the bathhouse was a Pagan temple; and in fact it was called "the temple of the Mothers," the Three Fates who represented the female ancestors of the clan and whom we shall meet later on. Its association with "witchcraft" reminds us that the bathhouse was often the setting for esoteric rites of sorcery. A sorcerer might heat himself up in the bathhouse, then dive into ice-cold water and, through his own shamanic inner heat, warm the water and change its polarity.

The bathhouse—like the circle of trees in which I pondered at Zelinogorsk—was a sacred enclosure, a place well suited for divination. Though images of the bare backsides of peasant girls may produce their own set of associations, it is important to remember that this village mode of divination may essentially be defined as follows: Pose a question, enter the sacred enclosure, and wait patiently for a physical sensation, whether pleasant or unpleasant. This, of course, was precisely how Vladimir described "divination with the whole organism."

Divination with the Physical Body

Enter a "sacred enclosure," whether it be a sweat lodge, a tight circle of trees, or simply a darkened room. Take a few deep breaths in order to relax. Let your mental chatter fade away of its own until the mind is relatively free of thoughts, adrift, without direction. Then pose a simple yes-or-no question.

Now wait. Try to keep your question foremost in your mind, but don't expend any mental effort by thinking about it; just let it rest there in your consciousness. Be patient. In time, you will begin to feel a particular sensation somewhere in your body, whether it be an itch, an ache, or a soft gentle glow.

If the sensation is pleasant, the answer to your question is "yes." If it is unpleasant, the answer is "no."

After a great deal of practice with this exercise, the location of the feeling—in your neck, your foot, stomach, or whatever—may yield meaningful insights which add depth and detail to the initial yes or no.

RANGING THROUGH THE woods, we identified several more power spots, though Vladimir simply told me where to stand rather than actually teaching me to find them for myself. Between these foci of energy, we moved briskly and energetically through the deepening woods, and at last we were hungry.

We hunted for a fallen pine—the birch, according to Vladimir, is a marvelous tree but doesn't burn well. The pine tree we found was covered with edible mushrooms. First we stripped the mushrooms, then the branches from the tree.

Vladimir tumbled the branches together, needles and all, in a heap, then set it on fire with scraps of paper that he kept in his pack. We unrolled his folding rubber mat across yet another fallen log, and sat with our feet to the fire, dining on cans of mushrooms and rice (Vladimir was mad about mushrooms, as I was soon to discover), bread, and hard-boiled eggs. We sat for a while in the deepening gloom of the forest as the afternoon settled in and the fire burned down.

Afterwards, we hiked over a hill and into a completely different landscape. Here were the green hills for which the town was named, rolling on and on, northward to Finland. A watery sun was trying to break through the clouds, and the hills were clothed in mist. The birches and the other deciduous trees gave way to a coniferous forest of firs and pines, what Vladimir called a "dry forest," or, more affectionately, a "real Finnish landscape."

Here, he insisted, the best mushrooms could be found. "In this region, there are fifteen edible varieties. I know all of them."

It was rather late in the year, he explained, and the gathering season was more or less over, but our harvest from the fallen pine tree had convinced him that a few stragglers might yet be found. Complaining

Vladimir Antonov preparing a meal of mushrooms and rice in the woods at Zelinogorsk.

that he had no money, he went on to boast proudly of how he subsisted largely on wild food—of which mushrooms were the crowning glory.

We hunted up and down the green hills in the gathering mist, but found only a few mushrooms. The sun began to hover below the cloud cover, dark and orange, and we knew that in a short while it would sink below the horizon. We turned back toward the train station.

Moving to lower ground, back into the realm of the birches, we picked our way across a bog, stepping gingerly. I followed Vladimir along a ridge of relatively firm ground, with moist marshy earth to either side of us.

Suddenly my right foot slipped and landed in the bog. I was sinking, the marsh sucking me down like quicksand and swallowing my right leg all the way to the thigh.

I clawed for a hold among the trees. For a moment I was suspended there, between the bog and the sky, till Vladimir turned back, extended a hand, and pulled me out of the swamp.

I slogged on behind him, the water and the muck squeaking and squishing in my shoe until we reached a paved road. Sitting on a fallen log, I tried to wring out my sock and trouser leg. I poured water out of my shoe. It was hopeless. I was cold and wet and the sun was vanishing. A bitter wind began to blow.

We hurried down another forest trail to reach the train station before dark. The woods were beautiful in the graying twilight; the birches and pines took on new height and grandeur, closing us in as if the ancient darkness of a fairytale night were about to overtake us. However, I was impervious to the charms of the evening, for my foot and leg were bitterly cold.

Suddenly, Vladimir stopped in the middle of the trail.

"This is a very great svyato mesto," he said. "The power is above us, a circle of energy, focused here on the trail. This place holds the power of the heart center."

He set down his pack.

"Now you must learn to shift your consciousness and enter your heart center," he said.

Something in my look must have told him that I was reluctant, that I was willing to learn the techniques of finding my own power spots some other day, and that all I wanted right now was to get to the train station. He paid no attention to me.

"Imagine that your head is sinking into your chest. Imagine your face as if it were right there in your heart. Here are your eyes"—he pointed to the center of his sternum—"and here is your mouth" —he pointed to his upper diaphragm. Then he smiled: "And here are your ears." Holding his hands to the sides of his ribs, he wiggled his fingers as if two ears were flapping.

"Do this," he commanded.

I stood there in the cold, breathing deeply and slowly until I was able to imagine—and even to feel—my head in my chest.

"Now walk," said Vladimir. Slowly I walked, and he walked behind me, still talking.

"You must no longer look at the world from the eyes in your head, but only from the eyes in your heart center. From this vantage point within yourself, you may learn to perceive all places of power. Keep moving, keep walking! Now we are at the edge of the svyato mesto. We are crossing the boundary into normal time and space. So turn around and walk back through the place of the heart center's power."

It was true that I was seeing the world from an entirely different angle. The last remnants of autumn color seemed more vibrant now, despite the gloom. Or was I just imagining things?

Vladimir Antonov explores a place of power with his heart center. A similar technique appears on page 118.

"There is a whole world, all around you but invisible. It is the Otherworld. When you look at the world from your heart center you can see behind yourself, and when you can see behind yourself you can see into the Otherworld. Can you do this?"

I didn't know. I didn't know if I was actually seeing what was in back of me, but I could feel, perceive, perhaps actually see a cord of energy connecting Vladimir and me, and I could feel—or maybe see—him stalking along behind me.

"So how do you feel now, Ken?"

"Lighter. As if my feet were barely touching the ground. As if my feet were about to start dancing."

"That's a very good idea!" roared Vladimir. "Let us dance!"

Vladimir started to lumber across the trail like a big dancing bear, waving his arms slowly.

"The arms are very important," he said. "Your arms are connected to your chest, to your heart center. You have energy arms as well as physical arms. When you dance from your heart center, move your arms. Not just your physical arms, but your energy arms too. Dance with your energy arms!"

As I learned to access my heart center, Vladimir and I danced with our "energy arms" in a clearing in the forest.

I danced. My arms moved in slow meanders, circles, patterns. I could almost see my "energy arms" moving too, like the fiery after-image from a Fourth of July sparkler.

"So many arms! Now you dance like Shiva!"

And so we danced.

Soon we were finished. We picked up our packs again and continued down the trail. I could hear the train whistle now; soon we would be out of the forest. I no longer even felt the swamp water slogging in my shoe. Instead, I felt a deep inner contentment as I moved, swiftly but lightly, along the trail.

MY OWN TRAINING was highly individualized, and not entirely typical, for throughout my various journeys with Vladimir I was taught to locate the places of power by using my heart center rather than my dzivot.

Slavic sorcerers work with the life-force that animates and vitalizes all of us; the Russian word for it, *dziz'n*, is related to the Sanskrit word *jiva*, which, in yogic tradition, signifies the soul.

The Slavic dziz'n, however, has its own set of associations. The word dziz'n, to begin with, refers to the life-force as an aggregate—a universal vital principle that ensouls us all. But each of us has his or her own individual life-force, and this is called dzivot. Whoever you are, you make magic by the use of your dzivot, for it is the life-force which is the active agent in all magical operations.

This life-force should not be imagined as something soft, nebulous, and "spiritual"—rather, it is a fierce energy that carries within it both passion and courage. Olga Luchakova told me: "If one engages in a spiritual struggle, in the sense of struggling for some great cause or vision—something which requires great effort, something wherein victory is even more precious than life—we say that such a person is 'sacrificing his dzivot.'"

Yet the word dzivot is also the common Russian word for "belly" or "stomach." The life-force, then, with all its power and passion, has its physical locus somewhere between the solar plexus and the genitals—a region which, despite its passionate associations, Polyakov describes as yin or feminine. As Igor Kungurtsev points out: "The Russian magi are very individualistic; their power may be vested anywhere. More often than not, however, they work from an area somewhere in the belly. If we were talking in Hindu terms, we could say that the magi find their greatest power zone to be somewhere in the region of the solar plexus, sexual, or root chakras."

Those who are familiar with the Hindu teaching on the chakras or wheels of energy in the body will remember that passion, courage, and fear are attributed to the solar plexus, while the sexual vitality which accounts for life in general is attributed to the so-called sexual chakra, in the genital region. Thus the teachings of the sorcerers are in basic accordance with Hindu doctrine, save for one important difference— Hindu yogis often speak with disdain of the "lower chakras," preferring to seek the powers and experiences characteristic of the "higher," more "spiritual" centers. Forces such as courage, vitality, passion, and sex are regarded as "low," and somehow unworthy. The sorcerer, however, finds his source of power and magical ability precisely in those chakras or centers which carry the spirit of commitment, energy, passion, and sex. In this, he closely resembles the shamans of those cultures, such as the Siberian or Native American, wherein the source of shamanic power is also said to emanate from the solar plexus, or the alchemists of ancient China, who likewise placed the source of ch'i or life energy in a metaphorical "cauldron" located in the belly.

In order to access those states of consciousness in which the sorcerer does his work, he begins by allowing his awareness to spread throughout his entire body or bio-energetic system—that complete spectrum of physicality and awareness that is animated by his dzivot or life-force.

At this point, his heightened awareness can begin to travel around the body. He can drop his entire perceptual field into one area of the body. He can become an infinitely small point in a specific spot—which is typically in the stomach, the seat of the life-force. From this vantage point, he can look out at the world around him as if his eyes were, in fact, centered in the life-force of his belly. From this vantage point, he can diagnose disease, gaze into the spirit world, and locate zones of energy and power.

As I have said, Vladimir insisted that I work from the heart rather than the belly—for reasons I will explain a little later. But those readers who want to make use of this particular variety of Earth Magic may have better luck working with the dzivot. The technique given here is, in part, drawn directly from Vladimir, and in part from Igor and Olga, both of whom studied extensively with sorcerers (including Vladimir) in Russia. This technique is broken into three parts over the following pages, each marked by an indention of the text.

Accessing Your Center of Power

First, select a location that is as natural and unspoiled as possible. Ideally, this should be someplace where you can hike far away from other people or any kind of disturbing influence. You need a place where you can feel completely relaxed and not worry about whether anyone is going to see you and think you're crazy.

Close your eyes and take a few deep breaths. Then empty your mind of all thoughts, and shift the focus of your attention to your physical self. Let your awareness flow like light throughout your body, vitalizing it so that your unclouded mental state becomes an equally clear state of physical awareness.

For most of us members of Western civilization, this is the most difficult part of the entire practice. The stilling of the mind is something to which meditators may aspire—perhaps unsuccessfully—for years.

This emptying of the mind is a prelude to the main event—the shifting of one's consciousness to the locus of personal power or dzivot. In ancient times, it may have been possible for sorcerers and magicians to accomplish this shift more easily. Igor Kungurtsev speculates that "primitive Europeans living in nature probably had a different distribution of awareness. It was centered in the whole body rather than in the mind alone. In modern times, however, the magi begin with certain techniques for stilling the mind which do, in fact, closely resemble yogic practices. This is perhaps the only way that modern man can approach the total awareness our ancestors accessed so easily."

To help calm the mind and eradicate mental chatter, you can begin by releasing all negativity from your mental and physical sphere—it is surprising how much "thinking" falls into the category of "negativity." Natasha had a very simple way of releasing negative emotions—one which, far from being specific to Slavic sorcery, is common to many metaphysical traditions:[2]

> Take a deep breath and relax. Let your hands hang freely at your side. As you breathe, imagine that all the negativity within you is flowing out through your fingers. With each breath, try to feel the negative energy actually flowing out through your hands.

To still the mind further, you can either take a very aggressive approach—such as literally forcing the thoughts out of your mind—or you can just let thoughts come and go until (hopefully) they stop by themselves. This is a gentler path, but takes a lot longer. Personally, I imagine my thoughts as clouds on an endless, infinite horizon. When a thought arises within me, I mentally envision it as a cloud in my sky of mind. Then I watch as a brisk wind begins to blow and either scatters the cloud altogether or else blows it away, beyond my field of inner vision. When at last my sky remains clear and no more thoughts arise, I let go of the image of the sky as well.

When you feel that your mind is calm and empty, you can begin to let your awareness flow throughout your body. Vladimir images this total awareness as a "bell-shaped skirt" of energy, beginning at the neck and flowing down all around your body, even into the earth. Igor and Olga speak of mentally opening "an umbrella of awareness underneath you"—one which reaches down into the earth itself and connects with the energies that dwell therein.

Then imagine your head sinking down into your body and entering that cocoon of energy, coming to rest somewhere beneath your rib cage but above your groin. Don't worry too much about exactly where to place your "head"— everyone's dzivot is slightly different and individualized. The main thing is to know, with firmness and clarity, that your "head"—or, rather, your consciousness—is now centered in your dzivot. Vladimir recommends that you build up a mental image of your own head and face right there in your belly. See and feel your nose pressing against the wall of your stomach, see and feel your ears about to press out from your sides. Feel your eyes peering out from your diaphragm and know that everything you see is being seen from that vantage point.

When at last you are certain that your consciousness now dwells in your dzivot, you can begin walking. Don't look at or concentrate attentively on anything in particular. Keep your perceptions free and unfocused. Vladimir compares this to "letting your bell-shaped skirts of energy roll you along the surface of the ground like a big ball."

In time, you will find yourself attracted to a particular spot. Explore it. Don't just sit there and try to "meditate" in a passive fashion, but keep walking, keep moving. Feel the boundaries and differing levels of intensity associated with your spot. Feel its energy wash over you.

No matter how many visits it takes you to achieve this, or how many times you visit your power spot, always begin with the meditation detailed above, so that you can maintain your sense of heightened awareness whenever you are in contact with your power spot. Use that awareness to answer the question: What kind of a place is this? Is it masculine or feminine, yang or yin? Does it exude positive, loving energy, or does it drain sickness and negativity out of your sphere? Does it activate a particular center within your body? If so, which one?

Different power spots activate different psychic centers. The type of power spot you choose will give you a clue as to the nature of your own shamanic or magical gifts, because it will activate a particular psychic center. The center thus activated will tell you where your own personal power comes from.

Having said all this, it is only fair to state that Vladimir—who speaks in terms of the chakras himself—warns students about falling victim to rigid formulations concerning the inner centers of power:

"There are many points of view. Some teachers and gurus say there are seven chakras, while others say there are five or twelve or...whatever they say. In the same way, teachers and gurus tell us that each chakra must have its own color. Of course, they all disagree about which colors should be linked with which chakras, and yet they are all too willing to try and force their own color systems on everybody else.

"I say that worrying about these things—the number of chakras in the body or the colors associated with them—is simply an obstacle on your path towards the infinite. These systems do nothing but place limitations on that which is, ultimately, limitless. If you must envision the centers of power, envision them as white light, nothing more. But don't worry about it. That will only impede your progress."

Endnotes

1. from Alexinsky, "Slavonic Mythology," 290.
2. Natasha did, however, enhance the exercise with a typically Russian addition: she mentally recited the Orthodox "Prayer for Every Need" while imagining negativity draining away from her.

SIX

EARTH MAGIC: THE MAGIC OF TREES

VLADIMIR HAD GIVEN ME A TASK—TO keep my consciousness in my heart center as much as possible. Over the next few days, I tried to do so. Upon arising in the morning, I meditated, expanded my field of energy, and dropped my head down into my heart. I tried to keep it there while I ate, talked on the phone, walked across town to change money, and so on. In the beginning I was able to stay focused in my heart for only a few brief moments at a time. Afterwards it became easier, and I was able to sustain it for perhaps half an hour.

It didn't make me feel any better, though. In fact, I became highly emotional and subject to moods. When someone on the street glared at me with that disdainful look reserved for foreign "outsiders," I became fiery and angry. If

I saw homeless people begging on the Nevsky Prospect, I became sad. Everything in life was felt more intensely. One gray day a light snow began to fall; it made me think of home, and how far away from that home I was. I became seized with a nameless anxiety that lasted all afternoon.

Vladimir claimed that human souls, upon first coming into incarnation, develop from the level of pure instinct to that of great intellectual attainment. Having done so, they begin to work (after a lifetime or two of basking in their intellect, apparently) towards developing the higher, more "refined" set of emotions associated with the heart center. This, apparently, was why Vladimir had insisted that I work with the heart center rather than the dzivot—he believed that I had gone about as far with the intellect as I was likely to get, and that it was time I began to work on those "higher emotions."

For the moment, however, I was merely fried from emotional excess. So when it came time for our next journey into the forest, I may well have been more open, less resistant, and a great deal more sensitive.

This time we took the train to a place called Moreskaya, which means "by the sea" and lies upon the shores of the Baltic just north of St. Petersburg. After leaving the train, we crossed a paved road and struck off into the forest again, pissing amidst the trees to mark our entry into sacred space.

The day was sunny but cold, and the greenery—or what was left of it, for it was the beginning of November—stood out sharply in the brightness. The trail upon which we were walking was one of Vladimir's favorite locations for gathering wild food, an activity that (in warmer weather, at least) occupied a great deal of his time.

"The only season I love without reservation is the spring," he said. "In spring the world wakes up after winter. The forest turns green and everything is full of life. But in the summer there are clouds of mosquitoes, while in the autumn I am very busy gathering mushrooms to be stored for the winter, while the winter, of course..." he shrugged.

"In the summer there are nettles here, a rich source of vitamins which can be made into a very tasty soup. And the needles of the fir trees are also strong with Vitamin C, though bitter even after boiling. And rose hips—I gather these as well—also provide Vitamin C."

Vladimir knelt and pointed out a vibrant little fern, nestled beneath a tree and illuminated by a shaft of sunlight that broke through the forest cover. It was bright green, and very springy to the touch. Its tiny stalk curled gracefully at the tip.

"The dreopteris fern," he said. "It is small, but it is a plant of great power. Can you feel its energy?"

I could feel it. The shining little fern was genuinely glowing with an internal brightness.

Next Vladimir pointed to a mushroom, white with red spots, which, like the dreopteris fern, was growing alone at the base of a tree.

"Do you know what this is?"

I figured I did. "That looks like *amanita muscaria*, the fly agaric mushroom."

I knelt down to examine that most celebrated of plants. "This mushroom induces a state of ecstasy," I said. "Some people believe that *soma*, the divine nectar of the gods in ancient India, was made of the juice of this plant. The special drink which was given to initiates at Eleusis may have come from this mushroom as well, and the original intoxicating mead that was sacred to Dionysus. And in Siberia, the fly agaric is—or was—the drug of choice among shamans."

"So I have heard," shrugged Vladimir. "I myself have no interest in drugs. But I will tell you something even more interesting. If you boil this mushroom down to a juice, and mix the juice with sugared water, the flies will be attracted to it. They will drink of the mixture and die. People do this in the villages to rid themselves of flies, which can be quite a problem in the summer."

Now I knew how the fly agaric had acquired its name.

Our landscape had changed, and we had reached the shores of the Baltic. This was not the open sea but the Bay of Finland, and today, in this gentle weather, its waters were as quiet as those of a lake. The previous night had been so cold that there was a thin film of ice in the shallows, sculptured in crystal out of the foam and binding the reeds which grew by the shore. The forest came down almost to the sea, and we followed its edge, walking north with the beach on our left and the trees on our right. A sharp crackling accompanied us—the sound of the ice breaking up as the cold morning sun beat down upon it.

That was when we saw our first bird sign. A mating pair of rather fat birds, brown-speckled with long thin beaks, hopped along with us, just to our right. Though they were not particularly frightened by our presence, they were still prepared to disappear into the forest at the slightest provocation. Vladimir tossed a few scraps of bread at them, but they showed no interest. They were in search of some different food, pecking on the ground as they waddled about.

"A very rare bird," he said. "We call it the *kedrovkia*." He pulled a small, battered Russian-English dictionary out of his coat pocket and studied it for a moment or two. "Ah yes, that means cedar bird, because the cedar is its tree. This bird is native to Siberia—I don't know how it got here. Even in Siberia it isn't common; I only saw two of them during all the time I spent there."

He paused and watched the birds.

"At a place called Orechovo there is a special tree, very useful for awakening the power in the dzivot. I think we shall go there."

It was only later that I discovered there was another name for the kedrovkia, which was *orechovkia* or hazel-tree bird. Orechovo was the place of the hazel trees.

The path we followed veered away slightly from the shore now, and into the woods. Vladimir walked ahead, shouting back at me.

"Let us learn another exercise! You remember how to place your consciousness in your heart center. You will do it, please."

I took a few deep breaths until I had awakened the umbrella of light all around me. Then I "dropped my head" down inside of it, and reformulated my face—eyes, nose, mouth, and all—inside my heart.

"Now we shall walk. And as you walk, you will allow your consciousness to expand, moving out from your heart center to encompass all these trees, the whole environment. When you have done this, you will do one thing further. Just as you relinquished the seat of consciousness in your mind, you will relinquish the seat of consciousness in your heart. There will be no more you. There will be only the environment."

And with that, we turned away from the shore and into the forest.

IN ANCIENT TIMES, plants and herbs were associated with the worship of Kupalo, the vegetation god to whom the Slavic summer solstice festivals of yore were dedicated. Plants that were to be used for magical purposes were typically gathered on the summer solstice, or, after the coming of Christianity, on June 24, St. John's Day. On the morning of the solstice, for example, one might rise at dawn and hunt for the "tear weed," also known as purple loose-strife. The Pagan Slavs believed that the root of this plant had the power to control troublesome spirits. The sorcerer who possessed this magical root could control demons by chanting these words,[1] which, according to tradition, should be spoken in a church in front of icons:

Tear-weed, tear-weed,
you have wept much and long but gained little.
May your tears not drown the open field
nor your cries sound over the deep blue sea.
Frighten off the demons and the witches!
If they do not submit to you, then drown them in your tears!
If they run from your glance, throw them over cliffs or
into pits!
May my words be firm and strong for hundreds of years!

Another herb associated with Kupalo was the saxifrage, called the "herb which breaks" because it was said to be able to break metal into tiny bits simply by its touch. It should be gathered in the daytime where a harvest or a great deal of gardening and landscaping has been going on. To find it, one must take the mown grass and crops, and throw them in the water. The saxifrage will float to the top.

Kupalo's principal herb was the mystical fire-fern. It was said that the flower of the fire-fern bloomed only on Kupalo's Night, St. John's Eve. This flower was extremely powerful and could control demons, as well as discover buried treasure, provide riches and attract lovers. It was said that even kings had to bow to the possessor of the fern-flower.

Finding the Fire-Flower

The fire-flower of the fern must be gathered at midnight. Go to the forest and find the right fern. The fire-flower will climb up the length of the plant like a living being, then explode into a bloom of fire exactly at midnight, causing such a luminous glow that no one can look directly upon it.

To gain the flower, trace a magic circle around it. Stay inside and try not to gaze at the guardian demons who will take monstrous shapes in an attempt to frighten you off. Pay no heed to their voices. If you do, you will be lost.

Though the tale of the fire-fern may seem entirely legendary, it may well have a basis in fact. Some sorcerers believe that the tiny dreopteris fern that I spotted in the woods, and which Vladimir described as "a plant of great power," is in fact a "warrior plant" capable of producing a protective energy so powerful that it is sometimes visible to those who know how to see. Just as water naturally changes its polarity on certain powerful holy days, so the dreopteris grows in power towards Midsummer, so that by Kupalo's Night the energetic cocoon of the plant is intensely vivid and glowing. A sorcerer knows how to perceive the energy inherent in plants and trees, and may recognize the mythic fire-fern in a dreopteris of sufficient power and energy. The dreopteris is also regarded as a species of wild food, peaceful enough in small amounts, but, according to some, capable of producing psychedelic effects when eaten in large amounts.

Vladimir, however, was concerned primarily with the practicalities of herbs rather than with their mystical properties; my foray into herblore was only a prelude to our real work of the day, which was tree magic.

All Earth Magic emerges from a specific environment, a landscape. It is the land itself which gives birth to all land-based or earth-centered traditions. The magic of Castaneda's Don Juan cannot be separated from the landscape (and plants) of the Sonora Desert, just as the traditions of Amazonian tribes cannot be separated from the jungle which surrounds them. Even T'ai Ch'i and Hatha Yoga have origins in the poses and actions of animals indigenous to China and India, respectively.

Tribal European peoples north of the Alps lived in a woodland environment. In ancient times, a vast hardwood forest stretched from the British Isles across Germany and deep into Eastern Europe; today almost nothing survives of this primordial woodland save for a rather large remnant in eastern Poland and western Belarus. To the north, the hardwoods gradually become mixed with evergreens and other conifers, and around the latitude of St. Petersburg the mixed forest itself begins to give way to an evergreen forest, so that pines and firs predominate somewhat over the elms, oaks, walnuts, and so on. Farther north still, as in Scandinavia and northern Russia, the European forest becomes purely coniferous; and this evergreen forest, at least, still survives, especially in Sweden and Finland.

Because ancient Europeans lived in a forest environment, the old Pagan mythologies—whether Celtic, Teutonic, or Slavic—are rich with the magic and the lore of trees. Ancient Slavic villages and towns were simply places where the forest had been cleared away for human habitation; beyond the village limits, the trees still reigned supreme. Whole groves and individual trees alike were venerated. Many trees were believed to be the homes of the ancestors or departed spirits like the Rusalki, while large old oaks in high or isolated places were sacred to Perun the Thunder God. The European white birch (which is very similar to the canoe birch that grows in the northern forests of our own continent) was often used in village festivals as an image or model of the World Tree that served as the central axis of the universe and the mystical highway of the cosmos. Because each clan holding or village community was a cosmos unto itself, the World Tree was everywhere; whoever and wherever we may be, we are always at the center of the universe. Hence specific trees were venerated locally as "world trees," and folk magic practices involving sacred trees may be found in European folklore from Ireland to Russia. The most famous example in Eastern Europe was the tree of Romuva, the location of which is still a mystery but which, if the old sources are accurate, was served with a perpetual fire and held three idols to represent the divine guardians of the three worlds— Heaven, Earth, and the Underworld. The Ogham alphabet, in which the Celtic Druids wrote monumental inscriptions and (presumably) ritual formulae, was in fact a tree alphabet. It was an elaborate magical system in which each letter was equivalent to a particular tree and in which each tree had a host of symbolic and divinatory attributes.

I never uncovered a "tree alphabet" of such depth and detail in Russia, but I did learn that Vladimir and other Russian sorcerers had very definite mystical ideas concerning trees.

In the first place, trees, like all other plants and animals, possess an aura or energy field. This concept in itself is familiar to many people, and has been very nicely chronicled in Peter Tompkins' well-known book *The Secret Life of Plants*.[2] In the tradition of Slavic sorcery, trees are something quite special, highly evolved beings whose energy field, more than all other animals and plants, comes closest to the human

"Trees are highly evolved beings..." In the tradition of Slavic sorcery, trees have energy fields to similar to those of human beings—only more highly evolved.

condition. There are some smaller plants, such as the dreopteris fern, which are highly charged with healing energy, but in general it is the trees who hold pride of place among Slavic sorcerers as potential friends and allies from the plant kingdom.

AS WE WALKED through the woods, I tried to keep my consciousness focused in my heart center and my heart center more or less absent, merged with the environment, though I confess that I kept swinging in and out of phase—primarily because my mind was trying to take in everything Vladimir was saying. During the moments of occasional silence I had to keep starting at the beginning again, dropping the old noggin into the heart and reaching out from that vantage point to everything around me. Meanwhile, Vladimir was teaching me to perceive the auric field of trees.

"Here is a grand old oak," he said, leaving the path to head towards the shore again, where a great spreading oak stood upon the margins of the woodland. "It is very powerful, and you can feel it all the way from here"—we were perhaps twenty feet away from it—"but the oak is not like other trees. It has the densest energy field of any tree in the forest.

Communicating with an oak is almost like communicating with a rock, a member of the mineral kingdom."

"Do certain trees have negative energy, then?"

"No. All trees have positive energy. The oak may have a relatively dense field, but it is a positive field none the less. All trees seek to give us their love; if we reach out to them with love, they will return their love to us."

"But it is said that not all trees have positive energy. Some, like the oak and the pine, are givers of energy, and if we are weary or depressed we can be restored by taking part in their energy. But other trees, like the aspen, suck energy out of us, just like negative power spots. But this isn't necessarily bad—these trees can suck out disease or distress, as with the negative power spots."

"Yes, some people say that."

"So?"

"So, I think they're wrong. That's all."

After spending some time with the oak, we approached an alder tree. This one seemed energetically fainter, less well defined than the oak. Indeed, according to Vladimir, the alder is a very "nice" tree but has a very soft, faint aura.

"In general," he said, "old trees are more powerful than young ones. But with the alder, it doesn't matter much. Its aura is very tenuous, almost not there at all."

Finally, we came upon a birch tree standing alone—a bit of an unusual sight, since birches usually grow together rather thickly. Vladimir approached it with great joy.

"You see, the most powerful trees are those which stand alone, like this birch here. Birches are especially light and airy and joyful. One may caress a birch tree as if it were a pet, a small furry animal." He did so. "But the birch is not at its greatest time of power right now.

"You see, all trees are positive. Their energy is highly evolved, and they are truly much closer to us humans than any of the animals can ever be. They are like us. But if we are to derive the greatest benefit and knowledge from working with trees, we must be aware of their seasons. The birch, for example, is the earliest tree in the forest to leaf out in the spring, and that is its power time. Work with a birch in the spring. Pines, on the other hand, love the sunlight and hold the warmth very nicely; working with pines is best in the summer. The fir trees are calm and quiet and give us tranquility, so one should work with them later in the year, starting in the autumn."

DURING THE COURSE of the day, Vladimir led me from tree to tree, explaining their energies, attributes, and powers. He did not concern himself with finding a "special" tree for me personally—before too long I would return to the United States anyway, and would be unable to make use of Moreskaya on a regular basis.

Because trees are highly evolved beings—in the Slavic tradition, they have a special affinity with human beings—they may serve as our teachers and allies, and it is sometimes possible to identify a particular tree with which you have a very close personal link on the spiritual level. According to Igor and Olga, the technique for discovering your own personal "tree of power" is very similar to the one used for discovering power spots.

Finding Your Tree of Power

Begin by finding a likely place for communication with the trees—a national forest or extensive park—then enter into meditation and empty your mind of all thoughts. As before, become aware of your entire organism or bio-energetic field. Then drop your consciousness into your dzivot.

When you have entered that state of awareness—which might almost be called the characteristic or defining state of consciousness operative in all Slavic sorcery—you are ready to begin walking. However, you must walk in an undirected fashion, allowing yourself to be drawn through the forest rather than leading yourself or moving with conscious intent. You must be able to see the trees without really looking at them. Don't choose a tree and then stare at it, thinking. Rather, allow yourself to be led—by your energy field rather than by any conscious or intellectual intent—to a specific tree.

Igor Kungurtsev (standing second from left) and Olga Luchakova (standing first from left) leading a workshop on Slavic Earth Magic in California.

A tree discovered in such a fashion may become your teacher, friend, or ally. Examine it with your senses. What kind of tree is it? If it is an aspen, and if you agree with those who, contrary to Vladimir, regard aspens as "sucking trees," then it is possible that you need an ally who can help you release psychological or physical negativity, or that you yourself have a healing talent which may help other people release such negativity. If it is a pine or an oak, you may be in need of receiving power, energy, and strength.

In what season does your tree express its power? If it is a summer tree, such as a pine, then perhaps summer is your own "power season" as well—or spring if it's a birch, or autumn if it's a fir. If you happen to find yourself in relationship with a tree I haven't mentioned here, perhaps one which simply doesn't grow in an Old World forest environment, then you will have to explore its seasons for yourself, studying it over a long period of time from the vantage point of your dzivot.

One may even try to merge one's own consciousness with that of a special tree teacher or tree friend. According to Vladimir, the best way to do this is as follows.

Merging with Your Tree Teacher

With your consciousness centered firmly in your dzivot, approach your tree. Lean your back up against it. Rub yourself against its bark in a friendly way; trees appreciate physical affection. Then, feel your consciousness expanding from your dzivot, surging out as if to unite itself with the environment, but imagine that it is leaving you from behind (which, as I mentioned in the last chapter, is the direction of the Otherworld), flowing out by way of your back and hence into your tree. After a few deep breaths, you should feel as if your consciousness has in fact traveled out of your dzivot and into the tree.

From that point, you are on your own. You can ask questions and wait for a resonance or certainty within yourself to acknowledge the answer that your tree is giving you. Or you can simply wait for your tree to tell you whatever it wants you to know—for that still small voice (or big, resounding feeling) that makes you know you are receiving communication from another life form.

If you wish, you may call on a tree to help you enhance your own visionary abilities, for it is with the help of our "tree teachers" that we may learn to perceive the auras and energetic cocoons surrounding all living things. When you merge your own energy with that of a tree, as above, you can try this technique, as taught to me by Olga Luchakova:

Perceiving the Aura of the World

You have been standing with your back to your tree, eyes closed, your own energy merging with that of the tree. When you feel that you have thoroughly become one with your tree, open your eyes. Now, however, look at the world through the tree's eyes rather than your own. When you have managed this shift of consciousness, you will eventually be able to see the world as your tree sees it—glowing with the vital energies and fields of power that are usually hidden from us.

Vladimir also taught me an exercise which seems to derive from extremely archaic shamanic rituals. As we have seen, a great tree stood

Olga Luchakova (right) with a group of Earth Magic students on Mount Tamalpais in northern California.

at the central point of the old shamanic cosmos. This World Tree was not only the central pivot around which the world revolved in its cycle of days and nights and seasons, it was a highway. The shaman could climb up the World Tree to visit the land of the gods and communicate with them, or he could climb down to the roots of the tree, to the Well of Souls where the spirits of the ancestors lived. Here he could speak with the dead, retrieve lost souls, and delve into the past, whether individual or collective. More often than not, the shaman's journey was accomplished by leaving the body and "traveling in the spirit," though some Siberian shamans, as recently as the end of the last century, actually cut down a birch tree, raised it up again inside their tents, and proceeded to climb it while in an altered or ecstatic state of consciousness.

Vladimir calls this exercise "climbing a tree with energy arms."

Climbing a Tree with Energy Arms

Find a tree that feels right. Sit, stand, or lie down nearby—preferably in such a way that you can follow the tree's trunk upwards with your eyes, up into the highest branches.

As always, begin by emptying your mind of all thoughts. Focus your awareness on your energy body, then drop your consciousness into your heart center (for this practice, it is important to work from the heart rather than from the dzivot).

Just as your physical arms are connected to your chest, your spirit arms or energy arms are connected to your heart center. So, just as you would use your imagination to grow a new "head" in your heart or belly, imagine an extra pair of arms attached to your physical arms. These energy arms are just as tangible and real as your ordinary arms, but they take their motive power from your heart rather than merely from your shoulders.

Now become accustomed to moving your energy arms. Allowing consciousness to rest firmly in the heart, begin moving them slowly, freely, without purpose or plan. When you have imaged them so fully that you can actually feel them—when you know, for example, that your left spirit arm is making circles in the air just above your physical left arm while your right spirit arm is waving back and forth below your physical right arm—then you are ready to begin "climbing."

Close your eyes and reach upwards with your energy arms. Unlike your physical arms, these energy arms have no limitations in terms of space—they can extend forever, from your heart all the way to the boundaries of the universe. With your energy arms, grasp the trunk of the tree you've chosen. Start climbing.

You may climb from branch to branch, or go straight up the trunk; it doesn't matter. As you climb, you will begin to feel an extraordinary lightness, a sense of open space and vastness. Climb for as long as you like, then come back.

In time, and after many repetitions of the exercise, you may find that your experiences go beyond a simple feeling of exhilaration. You may find that you have entered strikingly real landscapes in your imagination; you may see visions and omens of significance, or hear voices that reveal powerful truths.

For you have, in fact, entered the Otherworld.

I will soon have more to say about the nature of the old Slavic Other-world and its inhabitants. But at first, it is enough simply to learn to climb.

"THIS CACAO WILL take a while to boil," remarked Vladimir, hanging the can of tepid liquid over a pine branch just above our fire. We had stopped for lunch and, like last time, built ourselves a fire with branches from a downed pine tree.

"While we are waiting, I may be able to find some mushrooms," he said.

Vladimir extracted a sharp knife from his pack, then, slowly and deliberately, took a few steps in the direction of the sea. He opened his palm, balancing the knife upon it. Then he closed his eyes.

"You know," he said, "there is a Forest Guardian in these woods. It is the spirit of the man who, before the Revolution, owned the property. When he died, he remained as a protector of the forest he loved. He is a good friend of mine. He shows me where to find the best mushrooms. All I have to do is allow my knife to lead the way."

Slowly, he extended his arm, as if the knife were in fact pulling him along. He began to walk, following the knife until, quite suddenly, he leaned over and stabbed at the ground. Triumphantly, he held up a mushroom.

"The Forest Guardian has rewarded me again," he smiled. "He is friendly with me because I too watch over these woods, in my own way. I remember, last summer I was walking here when I came upon a smoldering peat fire. Certain industrial companies start fires in these woods, and they are very careless—the workers just walk away without taking care of their mess. When I saw the fire I ran back to the road, to where the traffic police had a guard booth. I told the policeman what I had seen and he called the fire department; they came and put out the fire. I continued on my way. I was walking along, quite unconcerned, when I saw the biggest, grandest mushroom I had ever beheld! And in the summer! Mushroom season, of course, occurs in the autumn. So I knew it was an Otherworld mushroom, sent to me by the Forest Guardian. I took it home and cooked it up. And do you know what? It was utterly tasteless!"

Vladimir roared with laughter. "It was like eating air! Otherworld mushrooms have no substance!"

I remembered that the Leshy or Forest Lord of Slavic folklore often took the form of a mushroom himself.

"This Forest Guardian, would you call him a Leshy?"

Vladimir shook his head. "No, Leshys are tricky characters. They aren't to be trusted. The Forest Guardian is completely benevolent. He's a good fellow."

The cacao was boiling now. Vladimir took a long swig and handed the flask to me.

"You know, Ken, the Otherworld is all around us. I know a place, somewhat to the north and east of here, where the Rusalki live in a pond in the forest. They are sad; when I visit that spot, I can hear them weeping. The Rusalki, of course, are souls who, because of special karmic conditions, must take the form of tree and water nymphs for a period of time, in between incarnations. There are many such spirits, living in between the worlds—the Forest Guardian, for example. And not half a mile from the place where the Rusalki weep, there is a spot where the good people, the happy dead, are feasting. They, of course, are on the other side, in a different dimension. But whenever I walk by that particular part of the forest, I can hear them laughing at their feast.

"Nor are all the inhabitants of the Otherworld members of the human kingdom. The souls of plants and animals may spend time between the worlds, for they too must sometimes wait in the Other-world before they are reincarnated into new plant bodies, new animal bodies. Some of these plants and animals are responsible for diseases in humans—the spirit plants, though quite small, are especially dangerous.

"Let me tell you another story," he said, leaning back against the fallen pine where we had made our camp. "Once Galina and I were working on a patient who was quite ill; he had a bad back, and no one could cure him. We suddenly realized what the problem was: a croco-dile from the spirit world had attached itself astrally to the man's back, and he was carrying it around with him! You see, not all spirit plants and animals are indigenous to the particular region in which you find them—they may very well be wanderers, in search of bodies to inhabit.

"In any event, we were able to rid the patient of his crocodile. But the next morning, I woke up with terrible pains in my back! I knew that I had acquired the crocodile. So I came here, to these woods, and I had a long talk with him. I told him about Egypt, where there are many croco-diles. I described it to him in great detail, so that he would know it when he encountered it in his astral travels. I encouraged him to go there, because he could easily find a nice crocodile body to live in. Then I went home and took a nap. When I woke up, my back was no longer sore.

"You see, Ken, this is how one must deal with creatures from the Otherworld, whether of plant, animal, or human origin. Don't try to banish them, exorcise them, or do battle with them. To do so is to give in to mystical dread, just like when we encounter a negative power spot and don't understand what is going on. With annoying spirits, the best thing is to simply talk to them and send them on their way to an appropriate place. They listen surprisingly well and always go gratefully."

"But how do you contact them in the first place? How do you learn to perceive the spirits of the Otherworld?"

"As I have told you, the best way is to enter your heart center and then look behind yourself. Looking behind yourself from the eyes in your heart, you will be able to see into the Otherworld. But here, let me show you another way. Stand up."

We walked a few steps into the forest, until we came to a birch sapling about ten feet tall, and almost empty of branches.

"Now, lean your back against this birch," he told me. I leaned into the birch tree, slowly, to make sure it held my weight.

"Now, bounce gently against the tree."

I began to bounce against the sapling, which was just light and springy enough to sustain my motion.

"Relax. Let everything around you disappear. Bouncing gently back and forth, you relax and let the whole planet disappear. Now you are part of the world of consciousness. Bouncing, bouncing, gently back and forth, bounce your way into the Otherworld. You are one with all other conscious entities—with all the spirits, all the gods. You can reach out and touch them with your energy arms, for they are the arms of love."

And, bouncing softly in the forest, I bounced into the Otherworld....

VLADIMIR AND I emerged from the forest at the village of Lisy Nos, "the fox's nose." We found a stand of birches and pissed there to mark our re-entry into the ordinary world. Then we made our way to the train station. Two trains were waiting, one on each side of the platform. One of them was headed north and the other was bound for St. Petersburg. People stood on the railway platform in the cold sunlight, talking as they waited. A lone bird flew frantically about, bumping into one train window and then another, seemingly confused at being trapped between the trains.

Vladimir and I climbed aboard. The car was empty, save for an old grandmother with a shopping bag. We took a seat.

The car door opened again as a man in a business suit came aboard. Still soaring frantically, the bird came in with him. The man eyed the bird disapprovingly, shook out his folded newspaper, and sat down. Meanwhile the poor bird plunged around the train car, banging its head against the windows.

Vladimir leaped up and opened a window, motioning me towards one end of the car while he went to the other. Slowly, we began to move towards the middle, holding out our arms to prevent the bird from passing us, doing our best to charm it towards the window. We looked as if we were engaged in a kind of dance, and must have appeared quite silly to the man in the business suit, who studiously ignored the whole thing.

In time, however, the old woman leaped up and joined us. All three of us danced about the train car, moving our hands this way and that in a wild attempt to guide the bird toward the open window. Yet the poor creature kept getting past us. The man in the business suit continued to shake his newspaper.

Again the car door opened and a middle-aged woman with a fur hat entered. The bird sailed past her, out the door, and into the freedom of the sky.

Vladimir, the grandmother, and I were left standing in the aisles, the air around us suddenly empty, the train whistle blowing. We stared at each other blankly; then the grandmother went back to her seat. Vladimir and I did the same.

Endnotes

1. quoted in Alexinsky, "Slavonic Mythology," 296.
2. Peter Tompkins. *The Secret Life of Plants* (New York: HarperCollins, 1989).

SEVEN

OTHERWORLD SPIRITS

LIKE SO MANY OF THE OTHER EXERCISES Vladimir taught me, the technique for "entering the Otherworld" is deceptively simple.

Entering the Otherworld

Find a sapling that can support your weight and (for the sake of your comfort) has very few branches. Lean your back against the sapling and begin to bounce gently, back and forth.

Close your eyes. Relax, and let all thoughts leave your mind. Let awareness of the physical world disappear.

When you are completely relaxed, clear of all thoughts and still bouncing gently back and forth, allow your clarified consciousness to drop into your heart center. Rest there for a moment, still bouncing.

141

As in the tree-climbing exercise, imagine an extra pair of arms attached to your heart center. These are your energy arms or spirit arms. Move them gently, gracefully back and forth as you bounce.

Now reach out with your energy arms. Feel them growing, expanding, reaching out forever to embrace the Otherworld and all its inhabitants.

It is difficult to say what will happen next. You may have to practice this exercise many times before you experience anything except a mildly euphoric feeling. In time, however, you may see, hear, or somehow enter into communication with the spirits of the Otherworld.

Every culture, of course, has its own Otherworld geography—the *bardos* of Tibetan Buddhism, the *lokas* of classical Hinduism, the Faerie Realm of Celtic legend and lore. The Slavic peoples had a particularly rich Otherworld tradition—so rich, in fact, that it is often difficult to say where the realm of the nature spirits ends and the realm of the gods begins. The early chroniclers attest to the fact that the Pagan Slavs worshipped nymphs and ancestral spirits, and that they propitiated the wrathful dead who walked the earth as vampires. Much of this vivid Otherworld has survived into recent times; though Vladimir was the only person I met who claimed to be on a conversational basis with the Rusalki, he was certainly not the only person who believed in them.

A Christianized legend tells us that when God created Heaven and Earth, one group of spirits revolted. They were driven from the sky and cast to earth. Some fell onto the roofs of people's houses or into their yards. These became benevolent from living close to humankind. Others fell into the waters or the forests. These remained wicked.

The fundamental dualism of Pagan Slavic philosophy pertains to the Otherworld as well: the Otherworld spirits are subject to the duality of Order and Chaos as manifested in the polarities of the village and the wilderness. Spirits were either *beregyni*, which means protective spirits, or *upyri*, the Russian word for "vampires," signifying threatening spirits, evil spirits like werewolves, or personifications of illnesses. Sometimes the distinctions were blurred: the Rusalki, who lured men to their deaths, were nevertheless sometimes regarded as beregyni because of their association with rain, water, and fertility. Though Vladimir believed that all of these Otherworld spirits were, in some sense, related to the spirits of the dead, most practitioners of Slavic sorcery regard them as separate entities or life-forms in their own right.

The Otherworld was present in our own world as well; the traditional Slavic peasant's hut or izba was a microcosmic universe in itself. In the center of the house was the pech or stove, an image of the alchemical, Otherworldly cauldron flaming at the center of all things as well as in one's own belly or dzivot. The fires that burned in stove or hearth held the spirits of the ancestors; on cold winter nights, the household grandmother might make her bed on top of the stove for warmth.

Up until the nineteenth century, a six-petaled rose inside a circle was still carved on rooftops in northern Russia, while above it there was often a wooden horse's head, perhaps symbolic of the horse goddess, an aspect of Mother Mokosh. The six-petaled rose itself has been regarded by some as a solar symbol, sacred to Dazhbog or Khors, and by others as a sign of thunder, thus linked with Perun. The rose may also be the symthe Rod, and hence of the family's ancestral stream.

The word *rod* literally means "kinfolk," though it may also be used in a broader sense to signify collectivity in general. Natasha Sviridova sometimes referred to the Tree of Life as the Tree of Rod. A related word, *rozhenitsa*, means "one who gives birth," hence "mother," and spirits called the Rozhenitsye or Mothers were honored well into the nineteenth century. Hence the Rod may represent the general power of birth or reproduction, while the Rozhenitsye are the special mistresses of individual birth and destiny.

The worship of the Rod and Rozhenitsye was constantly condemned by churchmen, and therefore must have been very widespread. Long after the gods of Kiev had faded, the father and mother spirits of clan and tribe were venerated. Their cult was private and domestic; old women were their priestesses and the bathhouse was their temple. They were worshipped with offerings of bread, porridge, cottage cheese, and mead.

The Rod, the collective psychic imprint of the fathers of the family or clan, has survived in Russian folklore as the Domovoi or house spirit; his name is derived from the word *dom* meaning "house." He is always referred to as "Grandfather" or "Master of the House" or "himself." Of all the Slavic domestic spirits, he is the most important, a genuine "household god," like the *lares* of ancient Rome. He is often said to be vaguely human in shape, though hairy. He is covered in silky fur—even to the palms of his hands, which are otherwise quite human. He wears a long cloak tied around the waist with a light red belt or, occasionally, just a red shirt. In many ways he resembles an old man with a grizzled, bushy head of hair and flashing eyes. Sometimes he has horns or a tail (though this is not typical), or appears in the shape of a domestic animal (your dog or cat) or even a bundle of hay. Most often, however, he appears in the shape of a well-known resident of the house, perhaps the master of the house or an elder, whether dead or alive. There are folktales that tell of times that the master of the house would be sleeping or away, yet seen in the yard or stable.

Sometimes the house spirit was a snake, especially in Bohemia, Lithuania, and East Prussia.[1] Such a snake was said to live behind the oven or below the threshold; to kill it would be to destroy the happiness and prosperity and health of the family. When the family was absent, the snake watched over the house and the animals, and it was very fond of the children. When the snake died, it was said, so did the master of the house. Frequently there were two snakes, a male and a female. The "house snake" may well represent the survival of an extremely archaic practice; Marija Gimbutas believed that in Neolithic times a Snake Goddess was the protective deity of hearth and home.[2] When Lithuania was forcibly Christianized beginning in 1387, the harmless house snakes were rounded up and tossed into bonfires.

It is both difficult and unwise to attempt to see a Domovoi (if he appears to you, it will usually be during the Easter season), though his voice can sometimes be heard. Ordinarily he speaks softly and caressingly, though he can also be abrupt, gloomy, or groaning and sobbing—though any poltergeist type of activity means he feels neglected and is displeased with you. The Domovoi loves to live near the stove, under the threshold of the front door. He may also dwell in a branch of pine or fir in the yard (such a branch should be abundant with pine needles and very green). If you have a pine tree on your property, that is the best thing. Otherwise, bring in a pine bough. In any event, the bough must be hung with offerings. Sometimes a house may acquire a Domovoi which doesn't belong to it. These aggressive creatures will make noise, harm your pets, or push you out of bed.

The Domovoi may be a bachelor, though he may also have a wife called the Domania, Domovikha, or the Kikimora. She prefers to live in

The Domovoi.

the cellar or behind the oven, and comes out at night to spin. Sometimes she looks after the chickens; at other times she takes part in all household tasks, though only if the mistress of the house is herself diligent and hardworking. If a woman is lazy, the Kikimora will give her a lot of trouble and tickle her children at night, or simply keep people awake by whining and whistling. She is invisible and never grows old. However, when seen, she is usually spinning and resembles an ordinary peasant woman, though without any headdress. Hopefully, you will not see her spinning—it is a bad omen.

The Domovoi is a useful spirit to know. He will promote your general prosperity, keep everything in order and do housework at night while you sleep. He will forewarn you, usually by howling and moaning, if trouble is approaching, and weep before the death of anyone in the family. He will pull on a woman's hair to warn her if a man is about to abuse her.

A Domovoi is so closely connected to a house that he never willingly leaves it, unless you are really living a dreadful life or neglecting your Domovoi. There are many folk rituals from all over the Slavic world that are intended to help you make friends with the Domovoi. Here are a few:

Making Friends with the Domovoi

When moving into a newly built house, cut a slice of bread from your first dinner there and put it under the stove (or in the right-hand corner of the loft) in order to attract your Domovoi to the new house, meanwhile saying: "Our supporter, come into the new house to eat bread and obey your new master."

If you move from one house to another, you can take your Domovoi with you. Have the oldest female member of the household heat up the stove in the old house. Scrape out the cinders. At noon, put them in a clean pan and cover it with a napkin. Open the window and turn toward the corner of the room in which the oven stands. Invite the Domovoi to come with you to the new house. Take the pan to the new house. Have the master and mistress wait there with bread and salt in their hands. Have them bow and again invite the Domovoi into the new house. Let the old woman and the master of the house then enter the room, carrying bread and salt in their hands. Let the old woman put the pan by the fireside, remove the cloth, shake it towards all the corners to frighten away any rival or earlier Domovois, then empty the coals into the oven. Break the pan and bury the pieces below the front corner of the room.

Sometimes, a house without a Domovoi may acquire one if you put on your best clothes, go outside, and kindly say: "Grandfather House Lord, come and live with us and tend our flocks."

If you attract a rival and unwelcome Domovoi, go outside with a stick. Pound on the walls, the fence, or whatever. Shout out: "Go home! You're not our Master of the House!"

If your own Domovoi becomes angry with you (which is usually your own fault), put salt on a slice of bread and wrap it in a white cloth. Put the bread in the hall or the courtyard and bow to the four directions, meanwhile whispering phrases of honor and apology to your Domovoi. Or put clean white linen in front of the Domovoi's favorite room, which is an invitation to join the meals of the family.

To make friends with a troublesome Kikimora, go into the forest, gather ferns, make fern tea, and wash all the pots and pans with it.

Hang your old shoes up in the yard. The Domovoi likes this.

Second in importance only to the Domovoi are the Rozhenitsye, or Mothers, as they are called in Russia, Slovenia, and Croatia. These female spirits—or, more properly, goddesses—are also sometimes called by their ancient Greek name, the Fates, notably in Bulgaria and Bohemia. They may appear as pretty girls, or sometimes as cheerful old crones. Usually, there are three of them, as befits the folkloric descendants of the Fates, the Teutonic Norns, Celtic Parcae, and even the three fairies of the Sleeping Beauty story; however, seven or nine Rozhenitsye have also been reported. They are said to be beautiful, like fairies, tall with bright cheeks and white clothing. Their heads are covered with a white cloth, and sometimes their entire faces are shrouded with white veils. They wear gold and silver jewelry around their necks, and sometimes flowers or precious stones in their hair. In their hands they carry candles, so that their misty, almost transparent figures may easily be seen on moonlit nights. Their eyes sparkle with such a glow that they may easily bewitch people. Beware if you should see them, for you will be so struck with awe and terror as to be virtually paralyzed. This experience seldom occurs at home, however, and is more likely to befall you if you are traveling in the wilds at night.

When a woman gives birth, the Fates come to her as she lies sleeping with her newborn. They place an enchantment on the mother, then lift the child onto the kitchen table in order to decide his or her fate. The first Fate spins the child's destiny, the second one measures out the thread, and the third one cuts it, thus establishing the limit of the child's life. They determine whether the child will be rich or poor, as well as how and when it will die. Sometimes they disagree with each other and argue.

There are many methods of propitiating the Fates and inducing them to favor a newborn. The following are two of the most common, which come from Slovenia:

Propitiating the Fates

Set a table in the room where the mother and newborn child lie. Cover it with a white tablecloth and place chairs all around. Furnish the table with candles, wine, bread, butter, and salt—and, if you wish, with cheese and beer as well. Speak a prayer to the Fates, inviting them to take part in the feast. If the child is christened, perform the same ritual for the christening, or leave the leftovers of the meal for them.

It is said that the Fates live in caves. If there is a cave near your home, bake some bread and take it to the cave. Place the bread underneath a stone near the cave's entrance.

THERE ARE ALSO a number of familiar spirits that hover around the household, though somewhat outside of it. These are regarded as somewhat more mischievous and unreliable than the Domovoi and the Fates, for they live in closer proximity to the wild places, outside the warm circle of hearth and home.

The Dvorovoi or Yard Spirit, for example, can be downright malicious. It is said that he hates all white animals, whether cats, dogs, or horses. Only chickens are immune, because these are protected by a special divinity of chickens, who is represented by a round stone with a hole in it that is sometimes found in fields. A Dvorovoi can even be fatally dangerous. An old tale tells of how a Dvorovoi fell in love with a mortal woman and lived with her for several years, plaiting her hair. When she decided to marry another mortal and combed out her hair on her wedding night, the Dvorovoi strangled her in her bed. Like the Domovoi, the Yard Spirit often resembles the head of the household or

some other male ancestor. The following charms are among the folkloric methods for keeping him under control.

Dealing with the Dvorovoi

> To appease a Dvorovoi, place a bit of sheep's wool, a slice
> of bread, and something small and shiny in the stable. Then
> say "Master Yard Lord, friendly little neighbor, I offer you
> this gift as a sign of gratitude. Be kind to the cattle, look
> after them and feed them well."
>
> If a Dvorovoi becomes too mischievous, you can punish him
> by sticking a pitchfork into the wooden fence around the
> yard, or by beating him with a whip into which must be
> woven a thread drawn from a winding sheet. He also dreads
> the dead body of a magpie hung up in the yard, as does the
> Domovoi.

The Ovinnik or Barn Spirit is a related creature, neutral or even
malicious like the Dvorovoi. He lives in a corner of the barn and looks
like a large, disheveled black cat. He can bark like a dog or laugh his
head off. His eyes shine like burning coals. He is a bit nasty and might
even set your barn on fire. At his best, he can function as a spirit of divination, much like the Bannik. He likes pancakes.

It is the Bannik, however, who is the most important of these medial
spirits, those who dwell in the gray areas between the warm pech and
the wild woods. As we have seen, he lives in the bathhouse and can be
consulted for divinatory purposes. The Bannik, like most other spirits,
may appear as a familiar person—if you walk into your bathroom and
see a friend or relative bathing in your shower (someone who isn't actually there), you've seen the Bannik.

There is something primal about the Bannik—if disturbed while he
is taking a bath, he might very well pour hot water over the intruder, or
even kill him. His domain, the bathhouse, was always regarded as a
kind of Pagan temple and was never decorated with icons. It is said that
the Bannik sometimes invites devils and forest spirits to visit him, and
the story, quoted in Chapter 3, of the woman who became a witch by
entering a bathhouse and passing through the mouth of a spirit frog,
gives one a feeling for the kind of spirits that dwelt in an old Slavic

The Bannik.

sauna. Even though children were often born in the bathhouse (which was also sacred to the Rozhenitsye), mother and child were never left alone there for any length of time, for fear that the mother might be possessed by evil spirits.

Beyond the bathhouse lie the fields, which have their own spirit, the Polevik. He has the appearance of a deformed dwarf, and can speak in human language. Green grass grows on his head and he has eyes of two different colors. Sometimes he appears dressed in white, while at other times he is as black as the earth. He generally appears at noon or just before sunset. Like the Leshy, he misleads travelers who wander through the fields. He might even strangle a drunk who falls asleep while he's supposed to be doing his farmwork. For this reason, one must never nap in the fields, or the Polevik may ride over you on his

The Polevik.

horse or afflict you with disease. His children run through the fields, catching birds for their parents to eat. To appease a mischievous or annoying Polevik, place two eggs and a cock too old to crow in a ditch, but without letting anyone see you.

Until harvest time, the Polevik is as tall as a cornstalk, but then shrinks to the size of a stubble. He runs away from the farmers with their scythes, hiding among the stalks, but he is always caught and brought to the barn with the final sheaf.

The Polevik is not the only spirit who wanders the fields at noon. The Poludnitsa is quite literally the Midday Spirit, for her name comes from *poluden* or *polden*, meaning "noon." She is usually perceived as a beautiful young woman, tall and dressed in white, though her age may vary greatly—sometimes she is said to be only twelve years old, while in Siberia she is an old woman dressed in rags. The Midday Spirit walks through the fields during the summer harvest, and if she finds men or women working at noon, she pulls their hair. She mischievously leads children to get lost in the fields. When not in the fields, she drifts about on the air currents. In Poland, it is said that she carries a scythe and accosts people in the fields, asking them difficult questions; if they are unable to answer, she strikes them with illness. The Lusatian Serbs also say that she may force you to talk with her about one single subject for a whole hour, with illness as punishment if you change the topic. She may make herself manifest in your house during a storm, and the phenomenon called *fata morgana* or "will-o'-the-wisp" is sometimes attributed to her presence. She is occasionally accompanied by seven black dogs.

Sometimes the Poludnitsa may be truly malicious. She can cause death with her touch, and may ambush women who have recently borne children if they go out in the streets at noon. If a mother leaves her child alone in the fields at harvest time, it may be stolen by this spirit. In the old days, Russian children were quieted by being told that the Poludnitsa would get them if they weren't good.

BEYOND THE FIELDS lies the true wilderness, a place of beauty, magic, and danger. And here live the Fairies.

There are many different types of Fairy folk, ranging from benevolent to malicious. All of them, to some degree, are to be regarded as spirits of the dead, for the common Slavic term for "fairy" is *vily*, related to the Lithuanian *veles*, which also signifies the spirits of the dead and in turn is related to the name Velinas, the Baltic Underworld God, and of course to the Russian Volos as well. Vladimir Antonov looked upon all the Otherworld inhabitants as disincarnate human beings, living out elemental spirit lives in accordance with their karma while they waited to reincarnate again in human form.

The Fairies, in general, are female. They are the "nymphs" to whom, according to Procopius, the ancient Slavs were especially devoted. Nor were the Slavs altogether alone in their veneration of these female nature spirits—the gods of ancient Greece are, for the most part, long gone, but until recently Greek peasants still worshipped the tree nymphs. In the most ancient days, it seems to have been the female ancestral spirits who were the most deeply revered and who had become one with rivers, lakes, and trees. Some of this deep regard for the ancestral feminine survived in the cult of the Rozhenitsye. The Fairies, however, are rather different than the Mothers. They are wilder, more treacherous, and more overtly sensual—they bring the rain, and watch over the fertility of the earth.

Though the Russians and Ukrainians ordinarily associated nymphs and Fairies with rivers and trees, the southern Slavs of Serbia, Croatia and Slovenia regarded them as spirits of the air.

It was said that Fairies were the souls of young women who had been frivolous in their lifetimes, and hence, after death, floated midway between heaven and earth. They may often be seen dancing by moonlight near the graves of those who have died a violent death. They are beautiful women and forever young, with pale cheeks and dressed in white. Their long hair is usually blonde, and their power is vested in it. Should a Fairy lose a single hair, she will die, or, according to the Slovenians, she must reveal her true shape to anyone who succeeds in cutting her hair. The bodies of the Fairies are as slender as pine trees and as light as birds; they often have wings. If a man steals a few of a Fairy's feathers she must serve him, but she will disappear as soon as she gets her wingfeathers back. The eyes of Fairies flash like lightning, and their voices are so beautiful that anyone who hears them sing will remember the experience forever. In fact, a man who hears them is capable of listening for days without eating or drinking. No one, however, knows what language they speak, save only their best friends. They are strong and brave, and the forest resounds and the ground shakes when they battle each other, which they often do. They can cure illness and foretell the future. Fairies ride horses and deer, and can transform themselves into horses, wolves, snakes, hawks, and swans.

Some of these southern Slavic Fairies live in clouds.They sit among the whiteness, sleeping, singing, dancing, or causing winds and storms. They have eagles for their helpers, and sometimes take the shape of birds, descending to earth to prophesy the future or help people. They also live in the stars. Still others live on mountains thick with trees, or in caves and ravines; these have magnificent castles for houses. They ride horses or stags and chase the deer with bow and arrow. They kill

men who defy them and perch on trees, with which they are insepara-
bly united.

Fairies of all kinds love to sing and dance, and entice shepherds,
singers, and other young lads to dance with them. They may give a lad
either happiness or misfortune, depending on their mood. Their dancing grounds may be recognized by fairy rings of thick, deep green grass.
One must never step inside—it's bad luck.

In Slovenia, it is said that in ancient times, when people lived in
peace and goodwill and the fields produced all by themselves, the
Fairies were closer to humankind, helping us to harvest our crops, feed
our cattle, build our houses, plow, sow, and perform proper funeral
rites. All they asked in return was a bit of food, which they ate during
the night. When humans became evil and war began, the Fairies
became more scarce. Now only a few lucky mortals see them dancing
in the fields or sitting on a barren rock or deserted cliff; sometimes they
can be heard singing mournfully.

It is also said, in Slovenia, that a Fairy may become a mortal man's
sister. Every young lad or honest man has a Fairy for a sister who helps
him in time of need—and in fact certain animals, such as deer and
mountain goats, may also be favored with Fairy siblings. Fairies help
their brothers in times of danger, bless their property, and give them
gifts. Sometimes a man will marry one: she will make an excellent wife,
but the man must never remind her of her descent, or else she will disappear, returning only to watch over the children left behind. Fairy
children are frequently given to mortal women to raise, and are said to
be amazingly clever, with wonderful memories.

Here are a few traditional Slovenian ways of honoring the Fairies:

Honoring the Fairies

The Fairies, like the Mothers, are said to inhabit caves. Take
fresh fruit or vegetables straight from the fields—or flowers,
or silk ribbons—and place these offerings on a stone in a
Fairy cave.

Sometimes the Fairies are associated with sacred trees and
wells or springs: Hang the silk ribbons on a tree, or bake a
small round cake and place it near a well.

The best-known Fairy women are the Rusalki, the nymphs of river and tree who, in Slavic folklore, have a stature all their own. Their bewitching image has provided material for Russian writers such as Pushkin, Lermontov, Gogol, and Turgenev. Without question, the Rusalki were once worshipped as goddesses in their own right, and a major folk festival was celebrated in their honor well into the present century.

It was said that when a woman drowns, whether by accident or on purpose (or when a female child dies unbaptized), she becomes a Rusalka. Along the Danube and Dnieper, the Rusalki are thought of as gracious maidens. Their faces are pale like the moon, and they wear robes of mist or green leaves, or perhaps a white robe without a belt. Their hair is green, or perhaps a soft brown, decorated with flowers.

The Rusalki are both silvan and aquatic. Until Rusalki Week at the beginning of summer they live in the water, in crystal palaces that may be approached by paths strewn with gold and silver gravel. At Whitsuntide they emerge from the rivers and go into the woods, meadows and fields. (As spirits of the dead, it was natural for them to live in the green trees, which ancient Slavic belief regarded as the homes of the departed.) When the sun has not yet entered "the abode of summer," the Rusalki can remain under water, but when the waters are warmed by the rays of life-giving light, they have to return to the trees, the houses of the dead. A forest where the Rusalki live is usually said to have a magic well whose waters cure all diseases.

The autumnal waters rise and foam when the Rusalki leave their abodes on moonlit nights. They dance on the shore and drown young men who happen to be bathing there. If they see a man on the opposite side of the stream, they can even grow so big as to step across the stream. They like to dance by moonlight with wandering shepherds and other village lads, and, as with Fairy women generally, it is believed that the grass is always thicker and the wheat more abundant where the Rusalki have been dancing. Some village lads become their lovers; in fact, the Rusalki are jealous of mortal women. A man may even capture one in a magic circle, take her home, and marry her—but she will disappear again during Whitsuntide, going back to the trees.

In northern Russia, however, the Rusalki were sometimes perceived as wicked girls, unattractive and with disheveled hair. They were naked, wan, and cadaverous, like drowned corpses, and their eyes

A Rusalka.

shone with evil green fire. They brutally seized anyone who was fool-
ish enough to walk by the water's edge late at night, torturing their
victims and pulling them to a watery death. These dark Rusalki ruined
mill-wheels, dikes, and fishermen's nets. They sometimes sent down
storms and torrential rains. On summer nights they swam to the surface, bathed, and splashed water at each other. They liked to sit on the
mill wheel, splashing each other then diving deep and away. Groups of
them lived in lonely places by the rivers, or in the deep waters or under
the rapids. They stole linen and thread from sleeping women and were
said to be fond of spinning and hanging their yarn on trees. After
weaving their linen, they washed it and left it on the river banks to
dry. If a man were to tread on such linen, he became weak and lame.

In general, however, the more positive, joyous, and magical aspect of
the Rusalki prevailed in Slavic lands. Their festival, called Rusalye or

Rusalki Week, was celebrated at Whitsuntide, when the summer began and the Rusalki left their winter homes in the lakes and rivers and went into the fields for the summer. Though the word *rusalye* (and hence the modern name for these nature spirits) comes from the Greek Rusalia or "feast of roses," the Rusalki are surely the *bereginy* or female creative spirits of the river banks mentioned by medieval chroniclers, and their festival shows the remnants of the ancient worship of the tree and water nymphs mentioned by Procopius.

Their processional "leading-off" included dramatic rituals and games, songs and music. In some places, there were processions through the fields accompanied by magic spells and invocations. Though there were many local variations, the festivities usually included three distinct common features:

- rituals connected with birch trees

- offices for the dead, normally held on Semik (the Thursday of Rusalki Week), and

- a precessional farewell or burial of the Rusalka.

On Whitsun Monday a small shed, adorned with garlands, flowers, and fragrant grasses, was erected in the middle of an oak grove. A straw or wooden doll, dressed in holiday garb, was placed inside. The people came from all over, bringing food and drink, dancing around the shed and making merry.

In some parts of Russia, people went into the woods on the Thursday preceding Whitsunday, singing ancient songs and picking flowers, which were then bound into wreaths. The young men cut down a birch tree, which the girls dressed in women's robes decorated with bright ribbons and pieces of cloth. The tree was carried along while festive songs were sung. (Sometimes, however, the tree was left standing in the forest.)

A ritual meal of flour, milk, and eggs, with plenty of beer and wine was enjoyed and then, after dinner, the tree was carried into the village to be placed in a house specially chosen for the purpose, where it was left until Sunday. During this time, it served as a focal point for girls' songs, ring dances, and vows of eternal friendship. In the end the tree, dressed like a woman, was thrown into a river or pond. Girls wove garlands of birch branches during this week, and on Trinity Sunday threw them into a river for divination. If a garland floated, its maker would find a fiancé in the direction it was flowing; if it sank, the girl would die during the year. Men who happened on these divination rites were ceremonially dunked in the river. On the Thursday of Rusalki Week, Semik was celebrated and a funeral office for victims of unnatural or premature death was sung.

The doll that lived in the shed was, of course, called the Rusalka. She was finally torn apart in the grain fields, tossed into the water, or burned, though there were many variations on this theme. The Rusalka was not always a doll or effigy, but sometimes a girl or a horse who underwent a mock funeral. The procession that accompanied the Rusalka beyond the village to her death in the fields sometimes treated her with respect, sometimes with jeers. The effigy might be burned, drowned, or torn to pieces. A doll might be placed in a coffin and carried to the river with girls who pretended to be priests or deacons, making a censer from an egg shell and singing "Lord have mercy." At the river the girls combed the Rusalka's hair and bade her farewell, both laughing and crying. Then the coffin was fastened with a stone, thrown into the river, and the khorovod was danced.

The Rusalki are, of course, said to be especially powerful at their own time of year. Leaving the waters, they choose willows or birches hanging long and slender over the river and climb into the branches. When the corn begins to ripen, they hide in the fields, ready to punish anyone who might pluck at the tender ears of corn. At night they swing on the branches in the moonlight, calling out to each other, singing, laughing, clapping their hands, and then climbing down to dance in the clearings. They dance the khorovod adorned with many-colored blossoms of poppies, their hair flying free, and run through the meadows or frolic in the tall corn, rocking and waving it back and forth. They turn somersaults and clap their hands; sometimes one can hear them laughing in the woods. Sometimes they sit in the trees and call out to women for a frock, or to girls for a shirt. They sing beautiful, delightful songs, and bewitch passers-by with their beauty and sweet voices—often, their victims are tickled to death. Swimmers who are lured into the depths are drowned, but death at the hands of the Rusalki can be a beautiful thing.

Living with the Rusalki

The Rusalki are especially active around Whitsuntide. During this time, don't go out at night, don't bathe in rivers, don't clap your hands, and don't do any kind of work that might make them angry. To honor them, place bread, cheese, butter, or any other kind of food by the banks of rivers and streams.

If you hear the Rusalki calling for clothes during Whitsuntide, hang a few strips of linen or shreds of an old dress in the trees; this will make them happy.

Children should never shout in the woods while gathering mushrooms, because the Rusalki are likely to punish them. However, if you are quiet, they will show you where the best mushrooms dwell.

To thwart a Rusalka who is negatively inclined, hold in your hand a leaf of the "cursed herb" absinthe.

THE RUSALKI ARE not the only spirits inhabiting the lakes, pools, streams, and rivers. The Water of Life must be balanced by the Water of Death, and the male spirits of the waters, the Vodyanoi, are dangerous and malevolent.

As befits their watery element, the Vodyanoi are marvelous shapeshifters. Some of them have human faces, but sport outlandish big toes, paws, long horns, tails, and eyes like burning coals. Others look like huge men covered with grass and moss or slime. Sometimes they are black with enormous red eyes and noses "as long as a fisherman's boot," while at other times they may look like old men with green hair and beards, save when the moon is waning and their beards turn white. Still other times, they appear as bald-headed old men with fat bellies and puffy cheeks, a tall cap of reeds, and a belt made of rushes. They may also be seen as huge fish covered with moss, or as ordinary tree trunks furnished with small wings and flying along the surface of the water. In addition to being able to transform themselves into fish, the Vodyanoi may take the shape of swans.

When the Vodyanoi enter human towns, they may look like the rest of us, but you can spot them by the water oozing from the left side of their coats. If one of them comes to your town, he will wish to visit a market: if he buys dear, there will be a bad harvest, but if he buys cheap, a good crop may be expected.

The Vodyanoi are immortal, but their age waxes and wanes with the moon. Those whom they drown and carry below the water become their slaves. The peasants of northern Russia believed that they live in logs and branches covered with slime, but in the south and in the Ukraine a different tale was told. It was said that they live in crystal palaces, ornamented with gold and silver from sunken boats, and lighted by a magic stone which shines more brightly than the sun. There they keep numerous horses, cattle, sheep, and pigs, which are driven out at night to graze. During the day they rest in their palaces below the water. They come forth in the evening and amuse themselves by striking the water with their paws, making a noise which can be heard from far away.

The Vodyanoi are family men in their underwater world; they may often marry Rusalki, and it is said that a typical Vodyanik has 111 beautiful daughters who torture and torment the drowned. When the waters of a river or lake overflow, it is said that he is celebrating his wedding and acting in a wildly drunken manner. If his wife is with child, he may enter the human world to obtain a midwife and sponsors, all of whom will be richly rewarded with gold and silver.

In general, however, the Vodyanoi don't like humans; they lie in wait for us, hoping to drag us to the watery depths. Men and women caught bathing after sunset (or at high noon) are summarily seized. If the Vodyanoi become well disposed, however, they may drive the fish into one's nets or guide sailors to safe harbor in stormy weather, though in a bad mood they will upset boats in dangerous places.

Vodyanoi sometimes gather under a mill wheel or sit on top of it, combing their long green hair. They don't like mill-dams; they try to tear them apart so that the water may flow freely. Russian peasants would sometimes toss strangers into the mill-race to appease the Vodyanoi. This un-neighborly practice was said to be a special vice among millers, who often became friends with the Vodyanoi, acquiring occult powers from them and making sacrificial offerings to them—a black rooster beneath the threshold of the mill house was common, while human victims were a bit more rare.

A Vodyanik is powerful in the water, but becomes weak and powerless on dry land. He is very seasonal: he remains underwater in his home during the winter, but wakes in spring feeling cranky and hungry, thus breaking the ice, troubling the waves, and scaring the fish.

Fishermen may wish to know how to appease the Vodyanoi. Three ways to accomplish this are:

- pour some butter into the water, or

- offer your first fish of the day, or

- throw a pinch of tobacco into the water while saying: "Here's some tobacco for you, Grandfather Water! Now give me a fish!"

BY NOW, WE have reached the depths of the forest; we are at our farthest remove from the quiet orderly world of izba and pech, yet we are not altogether in a world of evil. Though the forest is "negative," "yin," or "black," it has its virtues—for as we have seen, the polarities are interdependent. Yin power places may heal, as Vladimir pointed out; and in one sense the entire forest may be regarded as a place of healing. As Polyakov observed, most people are more comfortable with yin energy.

So rather than having stumbled into a realm of darkness and evil, we now find ourselves at rest in the cool green of the forest, in the realm of the Leshy.

As we have seen, the Leshy was once a god—the Neolithic Forest Lord, most ancient of male deities. We have already become acquainted with him, several chapters earlier; now let us learn how to make him our ally.

Some things are obvious: don't make noise in the woods and scare the animals. Be kind to the trees, for the Leshy has a special love for them. Less obvious are a number of folk charms for becoming friends with the Forest Lord, most of which involve reversing your ordinary reality.

Befriending the Leshy

If you want to avoid getting lost in the woods, sit down under a tree trunk, remove your clothes, and put them on again backwards, remembering to put your left shoe on your right foot. Bend down and look between your legs. Now you can move on.

To avoid becoming ill in the woods, wrap a piece of salted bread in some linen and place it in the forest for the Leshy. He also likes kasha and pancakes; wrap these in a clean white cloth tied with red string and place them at a cross-roads in the forest.

If you like to hunt in the woods, leave a piece of salted bread on a tree stump for the Leshy. If he rewards you with success, leave him the first game you take.

If you seriously want the Leshy to befriend you, go into the woods on Midsummer's Eve (June 20) or St. John's Eve (June 23), and cut down an aspen tree so that its tip falls to the east. Stand on the stump facing east, then bend over and peer back through your own legs. Say: "Leshy, Forest Lord, come to me now, not as a gray wolf, not as a black raven, not as a flaming fir tree, but as a man."

If, on the other hand, you are uncomfortable with the wilderness and feel you need protection from the Leshy, let the lady of the house make a magic circle by running around the house naked three times, just before dawn. Leshys can also be warded off by lighting a magic circle of fire in the woods.

We have noted that the Leshy is often said to be a "family man," with a wife called the Leshachika or Lesovikha. Among the Western and Southern Slavs, this archetypal Wild Woman has a powerful hold on the collective mind, for in these lands the female Leshy has a well-defined mythic personality of her own.

Though the Wild Women have long fingers and hairy bodies, they are sometimes said to be attractive, with large squarish heads and long thick hair of black or red. Sometimes they are said to be tall, with thin faces and long disheveled hair. They live in underground burrows, though their houses look much like ours. Sometimes you can smell the baking of their bread in the woods. They also like fish, wild game, and liquorice root.

The Wild Women know the secrets of nature, and may become light or even invisible by anointing themselves with concoctions made from local plants and roots. They like music and singing, and if you hear a storm, it may well be the sound of the Wild Women frolicking. Unlike less friendly beings, they richly reward the young men and women who dance with them. They are very lascivious, and may take young men for lovers, though according to some traditions they are also quite cold-hearted. If you leave food for them, they will clean your house, sweeping all the rooms and the courtyard, cleaning the ashes from the fireplace, taking care of the children, reaping corn, gathering and tying grain (though according to the Slovenians, it is the Wild Women who reap and the Wild Men who tie), spinning hemp, and all manner of useful things. Like other Fairy folk, they sometimes marry mortal men, though once again they will vanish if referred to as Wild Women; however, these creatures hate dirt and might even leave a man because of a dirty hearth or an unscrubbed kneading trough.

Like the Leshys, they love to confuse forest travelers and they will spin you around until you lose your sense of direction. They may substitute their children for yours, in which case your child will grow up noisy and unattractive. They are at their most powerful on Midsummer's Night, but appear often at noon or in the evening, as well. They love to spin hemp, and if you spin or comb it for them, they will reward you with leaves that turn to gold.

According to this same Southern Slavic tradition, there are also Wild Men in the woods. They resemble the Russian Leshys, but are less often seen than the women, and hence less prominent in the folklore. Slovenian tradition tells that they dwell in caves and are very strong. Their bodies are covered with hair or moss, and a tuft of ferns adorns their heads. They can be vicious, kidnapping young women and impregnating them, perhaps even tearing the child to pieces if the woman should happen to escape and run away. A strong wind may announce their presence to the lonesome traveler, who is likely to be led astray. They howl and hoot in the woods, and hunt deer.

THOUGH WE HAVE reached the depths of the forest, at farthest remove from the peace and quiet of village and home, we have not yet reached the realm of those spirits who are most alien to humankind. These are the vampires and werewolves—which, unfortunately, are almost the only aspects of the Slavic Otherworld with which most Westerners are familiar.

Their traditional aspect, however, is not what we would expect; they bear little or no resemblance to their Hollywood portraits. The traditional Slavic vampire, for example, is a criminal or sorcerer whose body, after death, is occupied by an unclean spirit—the life energy of some other sorcerer's soul who has chosen to remain in the half-world of the vampire rather than travel on to the Otherworld proper.

It is all too easy to become a vampire. If an "unclean" shadow falls upon you or a dog or cat jumps over you, this may be the result. One who has been marked as a vampire does not decay after death; his corpse retains the freshness of life. A vampire can even suck the flesh of his own breast or gnaw at his own body, as well as destroying his nearest relations.

At night vampires leave their graves and sit upon wayside crosses, rocking back and forth and wailing. They take other forms when they come to suck the blood of people or, more easily, of animals. Their power ends with the first crow of the cock, as everyone knows.

In Slavic countries, as elsewhere, vampires may be laid to rest with a stake through the heart—in this case a piece of ash, hawthorn, or maple. After being exhumed and "staked," the vampire's body must be burned.

Neither vampires nor werewolves are limited to Slavic folklore; they are a worldwide phenomenon. The Slavic concept of the werewolf, however, is of special interest for it adds a different dimension to the lore of lycanthropy.

Initially, a great deal of the Slavic folklore surrounding werewolves may seem rather typical. It is said that a child born feet first or with teeth may become a werewolf someday, and that one may also become a werewolf by choice, although this is a task involving a great deal of magic. It is also said that such a magical transformation is most likely to happen to a bride and bridegroom who are on their way to be married. A werewolf will run about the village on all fours or in the actual shape of a wolf; he will approach people's houses and gaze longingly at the folk inside, but seldom do any real harm to humans—though were-wolves have been known to beat people up and frighten them half to death. A werewolf may, however, seriously harm other animals, attacking cattle, sucking the milk of cows, mares, and sheep, strangling horses, and causing cattle to die of the plague. He remains in wolf-shape until the sorcerer who witched him undoes the spell.

Quite apart from the notion that werewolves were real people—who did, in fact, run around the village "on all fours" and behave like wolves—there is also some powerful evidence that their original function was shamanic.

The Greeks associated such living, human werewolves with a tribe called the Neuroi, who lived somewhere in what is now Russia, or perhaps in the Baltic. In the Baltic region we find a relatively recent and thoroughly remarkable testimony from a man who believed himself to be a shamanic werewolf.[3]

The man's name was Thiess. He was eighty years old and lived in what is now Latvia or Lithuania; the year was 1692. He had been brought to trial by the local authorities as a werewolf. He did not deny the charge; in fact, the old peasant was fiercely defiant towards his prosecutors, and treated them as if they were insane and he were perfectly normal. He affirmed that he became a werewolf on St. Lucy's Day, on St. John's Eve, and at Pentecost. He and other werewolves, along with certain women (but not young girls, he insisted), crossed into the Underworld, traveling to the end of the sea to do battle with the devil and a troop of evil sorcerers. The wolves carried iron whips, while the sorcerers were armed with broomsticks wrapped in horses' tails. At stake was the fertility of the crops—the sorcerers were always trying to steal the new shoots, and it was the duty of the wolves to get them back. In 1692 they had been successful, said Thiess; it would be a good year.

Though his judges attempted to force him to renounce his ways, Thiess insisted that the werewolves, rather than the priests, were the true foes of evil, and that he himself was bound for Paradise because he had always fought for the good of the people and helped save the crops. He was given ten lashes and sent home, still unrepentant.

Endnotes

1. There were house snakes in rural Greece as well, up until the nineteenth century.

2. In *The Civilization of the Goddess*, passim.

3. See Ginzburg, Carlo, *Night Battles: Witchcraft & Agrarian Cults in the Sixteenth & Seventeenth Centuries* (New York: Penguin, 1985), 29–31.

EIGHT

EARTH MAGIC: WINTERSONG

ORECHOVO WOULD BE MY LAST EXCURSION with Vladimir; the day after, I would begin my journey back to the United States.

The day before we were to go to Orechovo, it snowed. It began in the afternoon, a slow and steady snowfall which, though it did not stop until late that night, never grew heavy or fierce. Rather, the snow came down steadily in large soft flakes, and Petersburgers went outside just to see it. Old women stomped it off their boots with chagrin; young men and women put on new winter sweaters for the first time; children and dogs were delighted, burying their mittens and muzzles in its soft depths.

When morning came, the snow lay lightly over the whole city. Vladimir and I thought nothing of it as we

167

jumped aboard the train headed north to Orechovo. The sun came out; the light was intense, brilliant and frozen. The train was crowded with exuberant Russians carrying cross-country skis, most of them bound for the villages where they maintained their *dachas* or summer homes, hoping for a day of good skiing.

Very soon, we could see why they were all in such good spirits :; the farther north we went, the deeper the snow became. The skiing would be good. We passed a dark-blue lake, its margins iced over, the pines and firs that ringed it listing heavily beneath their snowy coats. We passed another village; smoke curled out of the chimneys of the dachas, and the road leading into the woods was a sheet of ice.

Vladimir nodded toward the road and the forest beyond it. "Down that road," he said, "is where the Rusalki may be found. Perhaps we should visit them rather than go all the way to Orechovo. The snow may be deep there. Here, at least, the road will be passable."

We thought about it, but the station came and went, and we remained sitting, headed for Orechovo.

When we arrived, we could see that the snow was deep. We found a cross-country ski trail that followed the train tracks and led us south of town. After perhaps half a mile, Vladimir stopped.

"Near here is a magnificent fir tree where the dzivot can be awakened. But we must cross the tracks in order to reach it."

We disappeared behind the birches and pissed. We paused to attend to my shoes—I had not anticipated trudging through deep snow during my visit to Russia, and therefore I had brought sturdy hiking shoes but no rubber boots. Climbing the berm to the tracks and going down the other side was going to involve making our way through snow about three feet deep. Vladimir managed to find some ragged plastic bags in his pack and I tied them around my shoes. Then we set off.

There was no ski trail on the other side of the tracks. Vladimir and I stood staring at the deep snow.

"There is another way to get to this special tree," he said. "Just a bit farther south. Let us walk along the tracks."

The snow on either side of the rails was deep, and mushier than the rest of the landscape due to the heat of the trains passing over it again and again. We walked with our feet turned out sideways, like Chaplinesque clowns, trying to stay on the metal rails themselves and avoid sinking in the snowy mush. After another half-mile, we peered down to our right again.

"I was hoping that someone would have skied here by now," said Vladimir. "That would have been helpful. But the snow is deep, too deep even for my rubber boots. We will not be able to reach the tree of dzivot. We shall simply have to go back to our first trail and strike off into the woods, just see what we find."

We walked back along the tracks, still with feet pointed outwards, seeking the original ski trail we had left half a mile to the north. As for our failure to reach the special fir tree, I wrote it off to bad weather—but I could not escape the feeling that there was some kind of intent behind it all, and that I was meant to limit my work to the heart center rather than exploring the dzivot intensively.

We heard a train coming from behind us and jumped to one side. As the train passed, I felt its steam on my face; I felt the shower of ice crystals its passage cast upon us like a string of jewels. We continued, found our old trail, and started into the forest.

"I was hoping for animal tracks," said Vladimir. "There is nothing quite like following tracks through the snow. But you see, the snow came so quickly and unexpectedly that all the animals have retreated to their homes. No tracks."

If there was no animal sign, there was plenty of human sign, in the form of families skiing through the woods. We stepped off the trail to let them pass by. One group passed slowly—there were a number of children and dogs in the crew. As they disappeared down the trail, Vladimir said ,"Let us pause here for a while. Turn around and face the other way."

I turned around.

"Do you feel the wind at your back? It is more than just a wind. There is an energy moving through everything in the universe. Sometimes it feels like a wind, but it is not a wind; sometimes it feels like a wave, but it is not a wave. I call it *pranava*. Sometimes, in certain places, one can feel this energy with great intensity. This is such a place. If you pay attention to the wind at your back and use your powers of imagination, you will feel the pranava, the energy which moves like wind and wave."

The author at a campfire in the woods at Orechovo, during the final apprentice session.

I watched as Vladimir spread his arms, breathed deeply, and waited. Then he rose onto his tiptoes, as if moved by some outside force.

"Like that. Now you."

I spread my arms and waited. I felt the cold but gentle wind at my back, and tried to envision it not as a physical wind but as an energy, a spirit wind. The spirit wind, moving through my back, did in fact lift me onto my toes as well.

"This pranava always comes through our backs. If you learn to feel its presence, you may be aware of it at any time, flowing through you from behind. And when you learn to sense its presence, you can channel it into any object or person. And this, Ken, is a great power, because it is a technique for healing.

"Seize the spirit wind blowing through you, channel it into your hands, then channel it into another person. This is a great secret of energy healing. Galina is very, very good at this. Do it again."

Once again I waited for the physical wind at my back, then focused my imagination on that breeze until it became spirit wind. Once again, I was lifted to my toes.

"In such places, where the spirit wind blows, we may also chant," said Vladimir. "But I do not agree with those Eastern schools where the

A golden glow spreads over the waters of a lake near Orechovo.

sacred syllable AUM is always chanted in a deep low voice. Better to chant like this...."

Vladimir emitted a high, clear AUM in a soprano register.

"Now you."

I tried, but succeeded only in producing a squawk, a squeak, and, finally, a croak.

"No, no," said Vladimir. "Like this."

Again Vladimir AUMed like a coloratura. Again I croaked and squawked.

"You see," he told me, "this proves that you are still centered in your upper chakras. If you continue to practice transferring consciousness into your heart or your dzivot, you will be able to chant like me."

We slogged on through the snow, and at last paused at the crest of a hill overlooking a lake. The lake was frozen around the edges, and the sun gleamed on the ice and water with an Otherworldly glow; the fir trees surrounding the lake were a deep black in the vibrant light.

"Shall we go bathing?" asked Vladimir. I wondered if he was joking, and studied his eyes. I decided he wasn't kidding.

"No," I said. "I don't think I'm ready to swim in it. I just want to look at it."

We stood and watched the lake for some time, the light constantly changing as the sun accentuated first a span of ice, then a snowy hill, then the water itself. Yet the spectacle of light was, in itself, a sad thing, for it was a product of the setting sun, and hence a message that it was time to turn back. My sorcerer's apprenticeship was over.

I looked back as we turned to leave; the water was bathed in gold.

We made our way back to the town. Skiers were gathered on the Orechovo railroad platform, homeward bound. Though weary from a hard day's exercise, their mood was still joyful and exuberant. Vladimir and I sat together on a bench. Our time was almost over, but I was still trying to think of new questions to ask.

"Vladimir," I said, "do you ever concern yourself with the future of the world?"

"Always. We must always work for the benefit of all people, everywhere."

"No, what I mean is...do you ever have visions about the future? How do you think things will go in the next ten years or so?"

"In Russia?"

"Yes. In Russia, or anywhere else."

"I don't need to have visions about such things. Just listening to the news, one can see that there are dark times ahead, at least in Russia. But I don't concern myself with that. Let the darkness descend upon us again; I don't care. And do you know why?"

His last words were delivered in a fierce whisper over the whistle of the approaching train.

"Because it is only during such dark times that true spiritual heroes are produced."

SINCE MY RETURN from Russia, I have puzzled over the energy that Vladimir described as pranava. The word itself is Sanskrit, of course. *Prana* is the "subtle" or "vital" breath, the rhythm of the universe or breathing of the cosmos which, in the human microcosm, has its analogue in our own breathing. On the elemental level, prana is the symbolic equivalent of the wind; in Hindu Ayurvedic medicine, the prana or vital breath within us corresponds to *vayu*, signifying a physical wind or the element of Air; hence Vladimir's description of this energy

Vladimir Antonov in meditation.

as a wind, or, in my own rendering, a Spirit Wind. To breathe consciously, as in yoga, rather than unconsciously is to cultivate prana, or, more precisely, to establish a vital connection between the rhythm of our own breath and that of the universal breath. Most importantly, prana is an energy. Pranava, as the term is used in Tantra Yoga, signifies the sacred syllable AUM,[1] which is the worldly expression or manifestation of that energy.

Does this energy—and the practice associated with it—have an analogue in pre-Christian Slavic tradition? The question is a difficult one. All mystical systems and traditions cohere on a universal level wherein everything is related to everything else—the late Joseph Campbell was a master of this method of interpreting mythology and mysticism. From a strictly historical point of view, various streams of thought have, over the centuries, influenced the practice of ancient Slavic magic: the imagery and terminology of the Eastern Orthodox Church along with its powerful meditative tradition, known as hesychasm; the practices of Siberian shamans and Tantric Mongolian Buddhists from the far reaches of the Russian empire; and, more recently, the Theosophical grab-bag of Eastern and Western traditions (concocted by a Russian) which passes for New Age spirituality throughout the world. Also, Slavic shamans are individualists; though they may share certain cultural assumptions, they operate according to a deeply personal vision and inspiration; in this they are no different from the Lakota, the Inuit, or the Jivaro, all of whom remain highly individualistic even within the boundaries of their respective cultural traditions.

Ultimately, Vladimir's pranava is yet another aspect of that all-pervading universal energy which the Russian magi, borrowing a term from Orthodox Christianity, refer to as "the Holy Spirit." If there ever was a distinct indigenous term for this energy, I have not been able to discover it. In Western Christianity, the concept of the Holy Spirit is remarkable only for its vagueness, its nebulous nature, and for the inability of medieval Catholic theologians to find a place for it in their world-view. As we have noted earlier, the Eastern Orthodox conception of the Holy Spirit is much more highly developed and precisely defined. It refers to a dynamic or active energy, one which may enter rivers and plants on certain special days and fill them with power—and one with which we too may fill and empower ourselves through spiritual practice. Its active nature suggests the positive or yang polarity of cosmic energy, while its link with the dove who descended upon Christ's head in the Jordan suggests a feminine potency—and indeed the Holy Spirit was regarded by early Christian Gnostics as an aspect of the goddess Sophia, symbol of feminine wisdom.

Both masculine and feminine together, the Holy Spirit is akin to the *shakti*, the dynamic or active feminine power of Tantra Yoga. I have suggested that the folkloric Firebird—who is active and fiery, but who is usually regarded as female—is a close symbolic equivalent in Pagan Slavic myth. The difference between Vladimir's pranava or Spirit Wind and the inner fire or Holy Spirit as we have encountered it in earlier chapters is one of form rather than essence. The energy may move in a vertical current, as in our earlier examples or in Russian Orthodox mysticism, or it may move in a horizontal current, as in the present case with the pranava.

I have spent some time digressing on the nature of this energy because of its vital importance: it is one of the foundation stones of magical or energetic healing.

Healing is a necessity in the art of magic. When we practice Earth Magic of the type I have outlined in this book, we accumulate energy and power. This is all well and good, but it is not enough. Energy that doesn't flow is energy that has become detached from the vital interplay of Darkness and Light, the in-breathing and out-breathing of the universe which is the foundation of all rhythm, natural and human. If we accumulate personal power without releasing it, we dam up the natural flow of energy, and must in time fall victim to the grandiosity, the ego inflation (and, at worst, the schizophrenia) that forms the great "occupational hazard" of sorcerers. The natural way to release an accumulation of power is to channel it to others as healing energy.

Having released power for the benefit of others, we are then able once again to accumulate power safely. Most importantly, we use our power for the benefit of other sentient beings rather than for our own self-aggrandizement.

Here, then, is a technique for healing yourself with the Spirit Wind or Holy Spirit. This exercise, far more detailed than the version given to me directly by Vladimir, comes from Olga.

The Spirit Wind

Sit upright, back straight and hands on knees. Try to keep from arching your back or allowing tension to build up in your neck—especially after you begin to access the flow of energy.

Imagine that the space behind your back is infinite. Your chair disappears; you no longer feel its presence. The shape of the room behind you, the windows and walls, all disappear. There is only an endless expanse of stars floating in the vastness of the universe.

In your imagination, float on through the infinity behind you, until you come to its end, the very root of the universe, the origin point of all things. There, at the base of the cosmos, is a river of energy, silver-blue in color. In relation to your physical body which still sits upon its chair, this river of energy is not only behind you, but slightly below you. When it begins to flow, its motion will be primarily horizontal, but somewhat diagonal as well.

Now see the river begin to flow. Through the cosmos it glimmers, moving forward and slightly upwards, rising towards you. When it connects with your body, you feel it against your back, like a wind or a wave. The sensation should be quite tangible.

Let the wave or Spirit Wind flow through you, filling you with a silver-blue radiance as it goes. It flows through your heart center, removing all the blockages and impurities. It flows through your lower centers, your dzivot, again removing blockages and impurities. In fact, it flows through every part of you, purifying you and empowering you with healing energy.

Chant the sacred syllable AUM in a high clear voice, sending it forth to the entire universe. Let the sound roll through you, beginning with the A at a point just behind your heart, then rolling the U up through your chest and the M out through your throat center.

The cultivation of pranava or the Spirit Wind is useful for purifying one's basic energy structures very quickly and at a very high level. The chanting of the syllable AUM—in as high and clear a voice as possible—serves to fine-tune the energy of the Spirit Wind and set up a resonance with the subtle planes of the universe around you. If done properly, you will feel the energy vibrating off the very walls that surround you.

This exercise works exceptionally well when performed in the mountains, especially at altitudes above 10,000 feet. Olga notes that when she practiced this technique with a group in the sacred Altai Mountains of Central Asia, the mountains sang back the AUM with a powerful vibratory frequency for nearly forty minutes.

After one becomes familiar with the Spirit Wind, one may learn how to accumulate its power within one's own body, to channel it into the energy meridians in one's hands, and then to project it into the sphere of other people for healing. But that is a whole different course of study, and one which would lead us far beyond the parameters of the present book.

THE DAY AFTER our excursion to Orechovo, I began my journey back to the United States. I cleared Russian customs and started up the stairs to the departure gates at St. Petersburg International Airport. Just as I reached the top of the stairs, a bird hurried by. Somehow it had come into the airport building and was flying madly around the terminal, looking for a way out. It came to roost in a potted tree at the top of the stairs, then studied me curiously. I remembered the bird in the train at Lisy Nos, and smiled.

THE FIRST LEG of my homeward journey took me to Amsterdam. It was an appropriate stop, for St. Petersburg itself was built in Amsterdam's image. Before he became czar, Peter the Great spent time as a ship-builder in Amsterdam—though royal, he was fascinated by mechanical things. Indeed, he was impressed by all facets of Western science and technology, and tried to turn Russia into a modern Western nation overnight (fortunately without great success, judging from the archaic practices in which I had just participated). In the service of his manic idea, he erected his own Amsterdam in the Baltic swamps and called it St. Petersburg.

Though the architecture and design of the two cities is similar, their scale and temperament are entirely different. Amsterdam is built for ordinary mortals; it is one of the world's great walking cities. St. Petersburg, on the other hand, is gigantic and grandiose; Peter the Great was nearly seven feet tall and built his city in his own outsized image. Where Amsterdam is genial and mellow, Petersburg is driven and intense.

But I had not come to Amsterdam to indulge in historical comparisons. I had come to see my old friend Wim, and to visit some of my old haunts.

Amsterdam was almost my second home. I had lived there on and off for several years during the 1970s. In fact, in many ways I was living there still. Though I was in my early forties now, and the particular bohemian ambience in which I had spent my student years was just history (a whole new generation of bohemians had adopted Amsterdam as its own now), my experience there was still very much alive within me, all the people and colors and sounds existing like some vast carnival in their own spacious room inside my psyche. This was painful. For me, Amsterdam was so vivid with longing that I had never, during the last twenty years, been able to thoroughly enjoy myself in the present; the power of the past was too strong. I couldn't move on. I knew, of course, that we can never recover the past—let alone our youth. Why, then, would my own past not let go of me, or I let go of it?

Wim met me at the airport. Of all my friends from the old days, he was the only one with whom I was still in contact. For all we knew, we were probably the only members of the old crowd who still kept in touch at all. He was no longer the free-wheeling gypsy of his student days, any more than I was. Married with three children, he was an administrator of psychiatric nursing at a hospital in the south of Holland, and had come up to Amsterdam for the night so we could spend some time reminiscing.

We took a taxi downtown to the Leidseplein. In the old days, Damsquare had been the center of hippie life in Amsterdam, and the Leidseplein a rather peaceful square. Now, however, Leidseplein seemed to have become a matrix of counter-cultural Amsterdam, lined with restaurants and clubs; students and other international types loitered around, meeting, talking, smoking, drifting in and out of cafes. We turned off the main square and walked down the Lange Leidsedwarstraat, looking for the apartment we had shared some twenty-three years ago. The address was still intact, and it was still an apartment, but all the shops on the street below had changed; this was no longer a purely residential neighborhood with a few milk stores, but a noisy collection of nightclubs and Greek restaurants.

Wim and I chose a restaurant close to the Leidseplein. The room was filled with Amsterdam's usual mixed collection of straights and freaks, and the usual friendly waitresses pouring the usual good Dutch beer. Seen from this angle, nothing had changed in twenty years, and as I wolfed down my dinner I became more or less ensconced in the Amsterdam of my past, the only difference being that Wim and I now spoke of our children and our work commitments rather than Tim Leary's version of the *Tibetan Book of the Dead*. A young couple came in from the cold, he with a guitar, she with a tambourine. They sang Latin American folk songs and passed the hat. I could feel the door opening on that room in my soul where I still lived in the bohemian world of my twenties; I could feel myself getting pulled in and starting to ache.

We walked southward through the city. I thought that Wim moved more casually than I because he was less driven by the need to either outrun the past or else run fast enough to break the boundaries of time and re-enter it. But as we passed under the vast archway of the Rijksmuseum—so like the one that leads to Palace Square and the Hermitage in St. Petersburg—he began to speak of how he, too, sometimes felt called by that past with a sad, passionate ache.

We drifted aimlessly and ended up on the Apollolaan, going nowhere in particular. We remembered all the people who had been part of our group in those days—people we hadn't seen in twenty years but who were still vivid in our memories. We tried to figure out why that particular time in our lives still held us so strongly, and what made those years so intense that they were still all too alive inside of us. We could, if we wanted to be self-indulgent, call it a spiritual thing, though for the most part we had all just smoked a lot of hash and discussed the hippie mysticism of those times in a rather vague way. Whatever may have held all of us together, it certainly wasn't the quality of our ideas; our utopian social ideals were as vague as our mystical and cosmic ones.

Suddenly, we both stopped in the middle of the sidewalk. Wim said it first: "It was the heart."

"It was an intensity of the heart," I added. "We were all bound to each other by an intensity of shared emotion."

"Right," said Wim. "It wasn't a spiritual acceleration that we experienced together, it was an emotional acceleration."

We paused. Then I said:

"This is what we all live for, isn't it? These moments of emotional intensity, these moments in the heart that are so powerful they make you really feel yourself as part of the life-force."

"Yes. This is what we live for."

We walked on, but now we were silent. I had never really seen my Amsterdam years in this light before—as a burning intensity in the heart. Without even thinking about it, I let my consciousness drop into my heart center and, from that vantage point, I began to study—no, to feel—my own past.

What happened next was not my own doing. I made no attempt to consciously create images or move energy. I saw all my old companions—those with whom I'd shared that "intensity of the heart"—wrapped in a glowing pink light, consumed by it, transported by it. It was as if a great weight inside my heart was wrenched out of me, as strongly and palpably as a tooth being pulled. I could feel, almost see, that interior room full of people take flight and disappear, wrapped in that rose light. And when I took another look inside myself, the Amsterdam of my youth was still there, but now relegated to a quiet place in my memory—where it always should have been. I was released from it. Now there was only a light mist beginning to fall on two old friends strolling down the Apollolaan.

THE NEXT MORNING I parted from Wim at the train station, and went on alone to the airport. I sat upstairs, looking out at the ever-present Dutch rain as it drizzled on the runway. In the waiting area, an Asian couple sat across from me. They were dressed in the most conservative suits imaginable, but the lady, who was in her middle fifties, was sitting with her eyes closed in meditation, a crystal gripped in each hand.

After a while, I saw her open her eyes. She was gazing at the potted tree in front of her, and smiling. I turned my head, looked at the tree. Yet another bird, loose in the terminal, was perched there. It flew around and rested in the tree again, flew around and rested in the tree.

I settled back into my heart center and waited for my plane.

Endnote

1. The Tantric texts insist on the combination AUM rather than the more familiar OM; the two letters, A and U, which may be grammatically combined as O, have a special and distinct magical significance in Tantra and hence must be treated separately. See Arthur Avalon (Sir John Woodroffe), *The Serpent Power: The Secrets of Tantric and Shaktic Yoga* (New York: Dover Publications, 1974).

NINE

Healing the World Tree

FLYING OVER THE SOUTH CAPE OF Greenland on my way from Amsterdam to Minneapolis, I could almost feel the North Pole to my right, drawing me like a magnet. I could envision the World Tree, the axis of the earth, as a slender column between the North Pole and the South, a column of energy extending infinitely into space until it reached the North Star.

In the poetic language of myth, this central axis is sometimes thought of as a mill wheel, forever turning in the sky. This, of course, is precisely what it looks like; anyone who has ever watched the circumpolar constellations such as the Big Dipper revolve slowly around the northern star has looked a ways into the mystery of creation, and seen the mill wheel of the gods in its endless turning. The Pagan Norse called it Amleth's Mill, and the name Amleth changed, through the centuries, into Hamlet—Shakespeare's "melancholy Dane" was originally the miller of the gods.

In that fierce and magical collection of old Finnish tales called *The Kalevala*, the divine smith Ilmarinen forges a mysterious magical object called the Sampo, which is capable of grinding out abundance and beauty for the whole world and is hence a great prize to be won. Although the Sampo is never described in detail in the old poems, it appears to be yet another divine mill wheel.

As we have seen, this endless cycle, this turning wheel, is the wheel of our lives as well as of the seasons and the stars. The unwavering axis around which the wheel of life and time revolves is a highway, a road between the worlds.

The shaman, because of his magical abilities, is able to travel up and down the World Tree. Climbing upward, he visits the heavenly realms. Here he receives transcendent messages or snatches of prophecy. These messages he will communicate to the people. Climbing down toward the roots of the World Tree, the shaman takes the fearsome road to the Underworld where dwell the souls of the dead—who, like the gods above, may also serve as sources of wisdom and knowledge.

Thus the World Tree is of vital importance to the shaman, for it is his road between the worlds. This long road upon which the shaman travels, flies, or climbs is, like the tree itself, to be found everywhere. Though the celestial reflection or correspondence of the "central pivot" is most often said to be the North Star, the World Tree or road that leads us there usually finds its astronomical counterpart in the Milky Way. In Baltic myth, the Milky Way is called Daugava, the great celestial river or "river of souls." The Balts and Slavs, like most ancient European peoples, perceived their natural environment as a microcosm of the great universe; hence the celestial river Daugava was also a real, physical river, now known as the Dvina.

The souls of the dead played a powerful role in all European mythologies—more so, perhaps, than we would care to admit, for we would often choose to understand the spiritual practices of our ancestors in terms of esoteric psychology rather than in terms of something so ostensibly primitive as "ancestor worship." Yet the spirits of the dead permeate most European myth systems—the hosting of the Fairy

Folk in Celtic legend and the Wild Hunt in Germanic lore were essentially processions of souls, dances of the dead around the central axis of the world or along the great road of the Milky Way.

If we wish to understand the continuity between past and present—as well as the contrast between the spiritual certainties of ancient European people and our own restless, hungry seeking—then we must understand something of the concern that traditional peoples feel for the ancestors. Nowhere is this concern for the ancestors more apparent than in Slavic magical lore.

We have spent a good deal of time in the heavenly world of the icons, as well as in the greening world of Earth where nature spirits dance just beyond the borders of our everyday consciousness. Let us now, like shamans, travel down the World Tree and consider the realm of the dead.

IN CLASSICAL SIBERIAN shamanism, as defined by Eliade,[1] the World Tree is a tree of souls; the souls of human beings grow on the branches of the tree like flowers or fruit. After death, we travel either to the base of the World Tree, or, sometimes, to its topmost branches. The dualism implied between the roots and upper branches of the World Tree is not as absolute as the later Christian dualism of Heaven and Hell—sometimes, and especially in European mythologies, the regions at the base of the tree may hold joys such as the Elysian Fields, while sometimes the dreary hosts of the undistinguished dead circle around the North Star at the top of the tree. Whatever the image or metaphor, the old shamanic cosmos includes an Otherworld subject to the same duality which underlies all sentient existence, an Otherworld that is sometimes dark and gloomy, sometimes joyous and beautiful.

In Slavic as in Norse myth, a primordial serpent sleeps in the dark waters at the base of the World Tree. In the Norse version particularly, we are told that serpents and other dark creatures gnaw away at the roots of the tree. This pit of cold darkness is the land beneath the barrows where, as in the Greek Hades, the dead dwell in an undifferentiated host. A vivid portrait of this dark Underworld may be found in the Russian tale of the hero Potok Mikhailo-Ivanovich. His beautiful wife died only a year and a half after the two were married. He had a great tomb built for her and, after she was buried, he himself descended into the tomb fully armed and on horseback. At midnight he was surrounded by a host of monstrous reptiles, and finally by a great serpent who burned with flames. Potok attacked the serpent and cut off its head. With this head he anointed the body of his wife, who was then restored to life—as we might expect, knowing that the Water of Life is hidden in the coils of the primeval serpent. Arising from the tomb, the couple lived to a great age. Potok died first—and his wife was voluntarily buried alive with him.[2]

There was another, more positive side to the world of the dead as well. This happy Otherworld is perhaps best known to us from Celtic mythology, where it is called The Land of Youth and described as a blessed island in the west. So, too, the Greeks believed in a serenely beautiful Otherworld called the Elysian Fields, and, more joyous still, the Fortunate Isles, the happiest quarter of the realms of the dead. In European folklore generally, the happy world of the Elysian Fields was, for the most part, depicted as a meadow of beautiful flowers. The benandanti or "good walkers," members of a shamanic cult which flourished in northeastern Italy as late as the mid-seventeenth century, traveled in the spirit to a wide, large and beautiful meadow they called the "Field of Josaphat," a place which bloomed with fragrant roses and where feasting and frolic took place.[3]

Northeastern Italy is not far from Slovenia, a Slavic-speaking region in the former Yugoslavia, and some Slavic influence on the practices of the benandanti has been suspected. Further afield, but still skirting the boundaries of the Slavic sphere, live the Ossetian people of the Caucasus Mountains. This population, speaking an Indo-European tongue, is believed by some to be descended from the Scythians who once roamed the steppes of the southern Ukraine. Until the end of the nineteenth century, they worshipped the old thunder god Perun in the guise of Elijah the Rainmaker, whose shamans sought visions in sacred caves. The Ossetian shamans, like the benandanti, also journeyed to a land of flowers—though the wise traveler was not allowed to pick these Otherworld blossoms, but must leave them alone.[4]

In all likelihood, the happy Otherworld of the Pagan Slavs was also a field of roses—the dziadys or feasts for the dead in Belarus were called Radunica, which means "meadow of roses." In ancient times it was said that in spring, when the goddess Lada returns to Earth, the spirits of the ancestors come with her from a land called Vyri, a warm, green land which lies in the southeast. The Fortunate Isles also appear in Slavic myth; it was said that the Winds dwelt upon a mystic island in the sea, the Isle of Boyan where heroes feasted perpetually; according to Vladimir, these joyful dead can still be heard laughing and singing in certain places where the wall between the dimensions is sufficiently thin.

We should remember that Volos, the Lord of the Underworld, was also regarded as a god of shepherds and flocks and all things agricultural; in Pagan thinking, the Underworld is not perceived as a place of punishment for human transgressions but as the source of all the life, power, and vegetation which blesses our lives here above. After all, the plants, warmed by the heavenly sun, arise from beneath the Earth, from the Underworld realm. Hence it is there, in the world of our ancestors, that the secret of life itself is to be found. The three worlds are linked together in an endless cycle—the sun shines down from Heaven, coaxing the life-giving plants out of the Underworld and upwards to our Earth. Though the dead, between incarnations, may sometimes occupy "medial space" as Rusalki, Forest Guardians, or other spirits, for the most part they wait between lives amidst that great collectivity which we may simply call "the ancestors." And it is upon their good will and continued benevolence that life, sustenance, and the greening of the Earth depends.

ACCORDING TO THE ancient Slavic concept of the human soul, every one of us has a unique personal identity or "human face," identified with our particular name or appearance, our shadow, our "footstep." After death, this immortal "identity" may continue to function as a Domovoi or guardian of our family home, or it may pass into the world of the nature spirits as the caretaker of a special lake, mountain, or forest. This identity soul may also have its totem or animal counterpart, typically a domestic animal such as a cat, dog, or one of the sacred "house snakes" which, as we have seen, served as tutelary spirits for Pagan Baltic homes.

There is also what may be called an "organic," "vegetative," or "animal soul." This is the component of the soul that occultists call the astral or etheric body, the part of the soul that may "travel." We ordinarily think of the astral body as something that permeates and surrounds our entire physical organism. In pre-Christian European thought, however, the astral body is something that follows us. In Old Norse it was called the *fylgja*, which means "the follower." In Celtic lore, the fylgja is called the "fetch"; if we see our own fetch, it means we may be about to die, for after all, we can only see our "follower" when it detaches itself from its proper station at our backs and drifts in front of us, where we can actually see it. To a shaman or astral traveler, this is just business as usual; but to ordinary folk, such a radical separation of the "follower" from the body may indeed herald the final, ultimate separation of death.

When we are asleep, our astral soul may go wandering, dwelling in trees, or taking the shape of a white bird; it may also leave our bodies when we faint. Slavic folk tradition affirms that we must never go to bed thirsty, for if the astral soul is forced to go hunting for water, our whole body may be weakened. This astral soul forms one of the most important tools or (literally) vehicles of sorcerers and magicians, who are usually astral travelers. They may wander to the Otherworld while their bodies lie in a trance for as long as three days. During such journeys, the soul may travel to the top of a "bald mountain" to fight, whether alone or in troops, against malignant astral forces who might otherwise blight the harvest and the cattle. Great care must be taken for the safety of those who go on such journeys, for if they perish in the astral battle, they will never awaken to this world again. Animals also have this aspect of the soul; like us, they may go wandering on the astral plane.

In ancient times, Slavic funeral rituals began even before death. The dying, preparing to re-enter the bosom of Moist Mother Earth from which they had emerged, confessed their sins to her and called out: "Moist Mother Earth, forgive me and take me." They were placed upon the ground, perhaps on a bed of straw, even as when they were born (which was typically on a bed of straw in the bathhouse); they had to leave the Earth as they had entered it, and in time they would be reincarnated out of the body of the Earth as well. They were washed with water from earthenware pots, for one might not meet Moist Mother Earth in an unclean state; the water was either placed in the coffin or else thrown into the fields.

After the death, a temporary opening might be cut in the inauspicious north side of the house to allow the deceased to pass through. Afterwards, it would be sealed up again so that the spirit of the dead would not return. (This entire process could be accomplished much more simply by opening a window or a door.) The soul most often departed the body in the shape of a bird—a dove, duck, hawk, nightingale, swallow, cuckoo, eagle or raven—or else as a butterfly, snake, white mouse, hare, or small flame.

The first day's mourning represented the farewell to the physical being. The soul, however, was said to remain, fluttering around the house in the shape of a fly and occasionally sitting down on the stove to watch the mourners and the funeral preparations. Or it might hover in the courtyard as a bird.

While the collective psychic imprint of one's ancestors may have taken shape as the Domovoi, it was necessary for the individual souls of the dead to "move on" to the Otherworld, hopefully to Heaven or the "lush green land" of Vyri. Here is a ritual, taught to me by Olga, to persuade the dead to move along on their way:

Persuading the Dead to Move On

Cook a pancake while thinking (or, if with company, speaking) fondly of the deceased. Then open the front door and stand with one foot on either side of the threshold. Still thinking intently and fondly of the deceased, eat the pancake.

On the third day of the funeral, there was laughter, drinking, games and orgies to represent the liberation of the dead person from his or her name, persona, and social ties. Food and drink were placed in the coffin or the grave so that the soul might suffer neither hunger nor thirst. Small coins were also given to the departed, so that he might buy himself a good place in the Otherworld. Part of the ritual meal was set aside for him, and it was said that he was feasting with his friends. A jug of water was left under the icons for him, since it was believed that he would come back that night to see the house one more time and to refresh himself. The water in the jug was always examined the next morning to ascertain whether the expected visit had, in fact, occurred.

It was said that on the ninth day the body "came apart." At this time the astral body departed, separating from the identity soul and dissolving into the elements from which it was fashioned. For forty days after death the identity soul continued to dwell on the earth, seeking out the places it knew while still alive. It might wander far and wide, to the sun, the moon, the stars, or into forests, waters, mountains, clouds and seas; confused souls sometimes troubled the living and caused numerous annoyances.

On the fortieth day, the "heart was extinguished" when the soul tried unsuccessfully to re-enter the body but found it already decayed and decomposing. At this point the life energy, which was associated with the individual's feelings and desires, was said to either leave the body and enter the anonymous realm of the ancestors or else wander as an unquiet upyr, forever trying to fulfill its desires by vampirising the living.

Even after being placed in the Earth, the dead were honored. Ceremonies were held by the family on the third, seventh, twentieth, and fortieth days after the funeral, as well as a year and a half later. At this final service, the family held a feast beside the grave and set aside part of the banquet for the soul of the deceased.

BECAUSE THE WELFARE of the household, the crops, and in some sense of the world itself depended on the ancestors, they were continually honored in a number of rituals which lie at the very heart of Slavic folklife. They were called "guests" or "visitors"; they participated in all the seasonal rites and festivals. As we have seen, the household gods of Slavic myth owe their origin, to a great extent, to the cult of the ancestors.

Vladimir had told me that he knew of a place where the dead were always laughing and feasting like the Fairy Folk of Celtic myth who spend their time in perpetual celebration beneath the barrow mounds. Most Slavic festivals for the dead took the "eternal feast" as their central metaphor. During the spring festivities, feasts were held at cemeteries and food left for the dead. During the Green Holidays associated with Rusalki Week, the ancestors were ritually invited back into one's household and honored with food. During the Winter Solstice the dead were honored with a special food called *kuchiya*, the centerpiece of an elaborate ritual feast.

The most complex of the ancestral rituals, however, were held in Belarus and Bulgaria and were called dziadys.[5] They were celebrated four times a year; some of the ritual details of these Slavic feasts for the dead are echoed in other traditional cultures around the world, notably the Mexican Days of the Dead.

The autumn dziadys were held on St. Demetrius' Eve (October 26 of the Russian calendar). On the preceding Friday, the family's courtyard was swept clean, all tools were put away, and the house set in order. Cattle were slaughtered for the feast, and the women cooked from nine to fifteen separate dishes, scrubbed the tables and benches, and gave special attention to the place behind the oven. Food and a tidy house were believed to attract the spirits of the dead and to make them happy.

On the Eve of St. Demetrius, everyone bathed. A fresh pail of water with a wisp of straw in it was set aside for the dead to bathe in. Family members dressed in their best clothes and assembled. The head of the household lit a candle in one corner of the room, said a prayer, and then blew out the candle. As everyone sat at table, the head of the family asked the holy dziadys to join the living in their meal. He poured water into a cup, allowing it to spill over the brim and stain the tablecloth. Then he emptied the water, and everyone at the table also drank, allowing a bit of water to spill.

Before eating, the householder set aside part of each dish on a separate plate, which was then placed in the window. Whenever a dish was finished, the spoons were set upon the table so that the ancestors might eat. The meal was taken in silence, save for abrupt whispers devoted to remembering the departed. Everything that occurred during the feast was regarded as an omen, whether it was a rustling of air or of leaves, or the appearance of a moth. When dinner was done, the dziadys were bid farewell and requested to fly back to Heaven. The food set aside for them was left on the table and distributed among the poor the following day.

The winter dziadys were almost identical. A fire was kindled in the hearth, and candles were set on either side of it as well as near the door. The oldest woman in the house sacrificed a black hen and cooked it, while other women cooked special flour cakes. The head of the family began the ceremony by pouring half a cup of wine into the fire; then, placing one of the cakes on his head, he cut it into four pieces, hopping around the room the whole time. Then butter and honey were spread on one quarter. This piece, together with three small cups of wine and the left leg of the black hen, were placed in three corners of the loft for the Domovoi. Before beginning to eat, the crone led the family in pouring wine into the fire. The people prayed to the Domovoi for prosperity, health, and so forth. Songs were sung and the household spirit praised. The crone checked the house spirit's food two weeks later; it was a good omen if anything had been eaten.

The spring dziadys were called Radunica, meaning "meadow of roses." The housewife prepared two kinds of dishes, one for the living and one for the dead. The family prayed in front of the icons and went to the churchyard carrying the food and drink. The women chanted special dirges while the men rolled eggs that had been blessed by the priest. A cloth was spread over the family grave and the food was placed upon it, perhaps with a bottle of vodka. The family sat in a circle around the cloth and invited the ancestors to join the banquet. Everyone ate and drank and talked about the dead. The leftovers were given to the poor or else left on the graves.

During the spring dziadys, the women made at least twelve ritual dishes, which one of the men took with him to church. Upon his return, the entire family gathered. The master of the house drank a hot, peppery drink. The wife laid out a clean table, lit a candle, and placed a pile of cakes on the table. Everyone prayed and sat down. As in the Russian Yuletide festivities, the master of the house hid behind the cakes at a corner of the table and asked his wife at the other end, "Can you see me?" She, of course, replied, "No I cannot," and he answered, "I hope you may not see me next year either." Then the master of the house poured a cup of vodka and made the sign of the cross, inviting the dziadys to eat with him. Everyone helped empty the cup, then ate and drank till they could do so no longer.

The summer dziadys were celebrated in much the same way; sometimes the graves were swept clean with sprigs of birch, a practice called "giving the dziadys a steambath."

MOST OF WHAT I learned concerning present-day beliefs about the ancestors in Slavic sorcery was acquired from Natasha Sviridova. I had once asked her if she could "read" people who were absent, perhaps through the medium of a personal object or a photograph. I had heard that Russian psychics were very good at this sort of thing and I suppose, in a way, I was testing her.

I showed her a picture of my current partner. Natasha began impressively enough by describing her back problem, obtained in a work-related accident. She went on to outline, with equal clarity, some other issues in her life. Then she said, "The problem is with her ancestors. Something is out of harmony there."

She held up her pendulum, watched it move from side to side.

"The problem is not too serious. It's only one or two generations deep."

"Hold on a minute," I said. "Tell me about the ancestors."

AS I MENTIONED earlier, Natasha used the terms "Tree of Life" and "Tree of Rod" interchangeably. We have seen that the word rod literally means "kinfolk," but may also mean "the collective," seen from that point of view, the World Tree is the Tree of the Collective, the sum of all human energies past and present.

At the base of the World Tree, said Natasha, the spirits of the dead sleep in what she called "a pool of energy." She drew a diagram that depicted that "well of souls" as a circle surrounding the base of the tree. This pool or circle of energy, she believed, was essentially negative; most of our ancestors left this life in something less than an ideal state of spiritual development, and their suffering and distress is reflected in the negative vortex of energy at the base of the tree. This anger, sadness, and pain has an unhealthy effect on the great World Tree itself; such negative emotions in the ancestral pool eat away at the roots of the tree.

If the roots of a tree are blighted, the branches will suffer as well; the turbulence at the base of the tree has its effect here in our world, and even in the spheres above it, manifesting as a species of "tree blight." We can see this blight all around us, not only in crime, violence, and war, or in the breakdown of families, but also (and perhaps especially) in the form of environmental pollution, the withering away of the greening earth.

The people of Eastern Europe, Natasha went on to say, were in an especially sorry state: for the last few generations, most of them had died as unregenerate atheists, believing in nothing spiritual. The unhappy dead were creating a profound disturbance at the base of the World Tree, and the economic upheaval, political unrest, and extreme pollution problems of that region were evidence of this.

Natasha was not the only practitioner of Slavic magic who held these or similar beliefs. Apart from their negative feelings about grave-yards (and despite the opinion of Vladimir, who scoffed at such feelings as yet another species of "mystical dread"), most of the kolduny believe that the dead continue to play a direct role in the affairs of the living. Natasha's friend Andrei Goroshosky told me: "Lenin still lies in his tomb on Red Square, and this is a big problem for us; until the founder of the Soviet state is properly laid to rest in the Russian earth, we shall never have peace."

According to Olga Luchakova, many of Natasha's ideas about the Tree of Life and the role of the ancestors can be found among Russian thinkers of the 1920s and 30s. While this is undoubtedly true, there is nevertheless a marvelous synchronicity between the modern and shamanic thinking—a synchronicity all the more remarkable when we remember that the cosmology of shamanism, only now becoming well known in the West, was probably quite unknown to thinkers of the early part of this century.

For example, the primordial serpent of myth, coiled at the base of the tree just as the kundalini coils at the base of the human spine, seems clearly to correspond to Natasha's circle of negative energy, an energy that gnaws away at the roots of the Tree of Rod just as those primor-dial serpents gnawed away at the Norse World Tree Yggdrasil. In Natasha's cosmology, then, the mythological serpent at the base of the World Tree, chewing at the roots, is analogous to the unhappy souls of the dead whose energy eats away at the base of the collective tree and blights the physical world above.

As we have seen, the alchemical dragon—yet another archetype of the primordial serpent, the circle of negative energy—guards the Elixir of Life, a deadly poison which, transformed, brings health and joyous immortality. Baba Yaga, too, is a serpent who keeps the Water of Death in her coils, but the Water of Death may be transformed into the Water of Life. Similarly, the pain and suffering of the ancestors may be transformed into joy, and their souls ascend the World Tree to a happier Otherworld, raised out of the gloomy darkness where serpents gnaw in pools of cold water and elevated to the starry crown of the World Tree, a metaphorical lush green south where all is joy and where the air smells of roses.

It is our own responsibility to perform this act of love for those who went before us, and in so doing to assist in the healing of the World Tree itself, and in the continual greening of the world. Like shamans, we must learn to travel to the roots of the World Tree, there to become healers of lost souls.[6]

To make the healing journey to Ancestor Land is not precisely "spiritual work." Rather, it is "soul work," or, in the words of psychologist James Hillman, "soul-making."[7] Most contemporary New Age writers have argued that Western society places too little emphasis on the spiritual dimension of life; Hillman, on the other hand, believes that we suffer from too much spiritual work and not enough soul work. "Spirit," he reminds us, is something "above"; to pursue the spiritual path is to climb the peak of a mountain and reach the heights. Our cultural metaphors describing the spiritual path are typically based on the idea of "ascent," of raising ourselves above common, ordinary reality. To take the spiritual path is to journey along the North Star Road, up the World Tree to the Heavenly palaces where the Gods live. When we are "spiritual," we are aloof, unconcerned with mere material reality. Like contemplative sky gods, we sit on a mountain top where everything is "pure," where the peaks glimmer with eternal snow and ice as in some Tibet of the imagination. "Soul," as Hillman reminds us, was anciently believed to be connected with the Underworld, the depths rather than the heights. Without a proper respect for the depths, he argues, a journey to the heights simply helps us remove ourselves from the hard emotional work of living in the world and relating to others.

Hillman is deeply critical of the cult of spirituality and all doctrines of "ascent"; in the Slavic magical concept, however, spirit and soul, height and depth are linked in an integrated rhythm. The goal of working with the ancestors is to "raise" the collective vibration of their energy to the Upper World; but in order to do so, we must first journey down, there to embrace our ancestors in the darkness of the well of souls. Only when we have reached the bottom may we begin the ecstatic journey to the top. The journey is eternal, back and forth, up and down, for the work is never finished.

As Hillman points out, the New Age movement, following the philosophical lead of India, tends to disdain the messy and emotionally charged regions of the soul. Consequently, the "spiritual" component of Western society has removed itself from the world at large, favoring the upper chakras over the lower, the peaks over the valleys. Looking down from our lofty Himalayas of the mind, we find neither interest nor value in the bungling world below. This detachment will not help us to heal the ancestral stream and participate in the "re-greening" of the World Tree, for to journey down the World Tree and search out the anguished souls of our ancestors demands an absolute immersion in the turbulent waters of soul. Confronting our ancestral karma, seeking out the sludge and darkness which has made so many of our families miserable, is a process that raises all those "lower chakra" issues that "spiritual" people would prefer to avoid—fear, anger, insecurity, sexual wounding, and so on. I do not mean to imply that the concept of ancestral healing as understood in Slavic magic is in any way similar to the contemporary Western psychological practice of "dealing with family issues." It isn't.

In the first place, the magical view of ancestral karma works with levels that are much deeper than most psychologists would care to acknowledge. In order to heal the ancestral tree, and hence assist in the greening of the World Tree, one may sometimes have to travel back over many generations. Western psychology tends to focus on the parental level, the wayward woes of Mommy and Daddy. Natasha told me that the negative energy in my partner's family system was "only one or two generations deep," which implies that the blighting of her collective tree is something that goes back to the time of her grandparents.

It is true that some psychologists are becoming cognizant of the fact that problems in family systems may indeed stretch back for several generations, that unhealthy patterns may have been established long ago. But how far is far? Galina Vaver told me that there was a darkness in my stomach, my dzivot, which was caused by long-ago conflicts between my pioneer ancestors and Native Americans. Her comment had been completely unprompted and unsolicited; nevertheless I knew precisely what she was talking about and who she was talking about. The "conflicts" in question took place between 1813 and 1831, much further back in the "family system" than most psychologists would care to go.

Not only is the Slavic magical concept of family karma much larger than ours in terms of time-depth, it is also much different in terms of attitude. Contemporary Western psychology often focuses on cutting our ties with our family past. Twelve-step programs and other forms of pop psychology assert that we must sometimes divorce our parents and other family members in order to heal our relationship with them. Consequently, we write letters of forgiveness and farewell to estranged or long-dead relatives in order to separate ourselves from them. We learn to "caretake ourselves" and focus on our own, rather than familial or collective, issues. In this sense, contemporary psychology takes us to the top of the mountain, where, fully "spiritualized," we gaze down upon our past with Olympian detachment and unconcern.

In the magical world-view, however, such detachment is inherently selfish, for in order to heal the family collectivity or Rod, to raise the ghosts of the past and send them on their journey up the World Tree, we must reconnect rather than disconnect. The healing of souls is an act of love; to coax the spirits of the ancestors gradually up the World Tree until they reach their place in the Upper World is a time-consuming and frequently painful exercise. It asks us to accept rather than condemn; we cannot exile Grandpa from the emotional ground of our being simply because he was an unregenerate old militarist, or turn away from Mom because she was alternately weak and domineering at the same time. We cannot divorce ourselves from our alcoholic brother, or from the sister who made us feel bad because she was sufficiently "unevolved" as to commit suicide. We cannot deny them; we must embrace them all.

According to Natasha, we do this through continual prayer and meditation. If she had any particular prayer that she used to access the world of the ancestors, she never told me about it. In general, the ability to see into the well of souls, to read one's incarnational or ancestral past, is regarded in Slavic magic as a psychic gift, a species of clairvoyance rather than a learned technique. In the Balkans, the ancestors were contacted (at least until quite recently) by women called *rusalii* (i.e., Rusalki) or "angels" who gathered at night and fell into trances during which they communicated with "angels" and with the dead. In certain areas, these rituals were performed publicly rather than in nighttime secrecy; the dead were offered gifts and their favorite tunes played for them in order to entice them back for conversation. The village men danced around the entranced mediums; when the seance was over and the dead had departed, one of the men sprayed a concoction of river water and herbs into the faces of the women in order to awaken them.

In Russia, a visit to the ancestors bears a close resemblance to a typical seance, sometimes even including the use of a planchette or ouija board (the most talented mediums dispense with such tools, however); a candle flame, upon which the medium concentrates until in a trance state, typically serves as a doorway between the worlds. Some extremely powerful sorcerers use the eyes in their dzivot to gaze into the bodies of other people, locating dark spots in one's psychic centers which are then "cleansed" to reveal a tunnel or doorway leading into karmic and ancestral realms. It was through the use of this or a similar technique that Galina Vaver discovered the blockage in my own ancestral stream.

All that most of us can do, however, is to pray that our ancestors, whoever they may be, will find peace and healing. Little by little, prayer by prayer, we experience their pain, and little by little, prayer by prayer, we try to heal it. Each time we succeed in laying a ghost to rest and accomplishing a healing—and we simply have to keep working at it, even though we may, for the most part, remain unaware of our own accomplishments—the souls of the ancestors move up the tree towards the Upper World; each time we succeed in doing this, there is just a little less gnawing and blight at the roots of the World Tree, and we have played just a little bit of a role in the healing of the world.

I GOT OFF the plane in Minnesota. Though I had never been there before, it was one of my own "ancestor lands," for this was where my great-grandfather, after the long hard journey from Sweden, had settled back in the 1870s.

After dinner, my publisher, Carl Llewellyn Weschcke, drove me to his home. Headlights revealed the skeletal framework of deciduous trees in their winter barrenness. We talked about the ancestors; I was trying to explain, in a few words of conversation, what I have just tried to explain in several pages of print.

Carl nodded. "We are always walking on the bones of our ancestors," he said.

Snow on the fields glowed softly in the dark country night.

Endnotes

1. Eliade, *Shamanism.*
2. Alexinsky, "Slavonic Mythology," *New Larousse Encyclopedia of Mythology*, 297.
3. Carlo Ginzburg. *Night Battles: Witchcraft & Agrarian Cults in the Sixteenth & Seventeenth Centuries.* New York: Penguin, 1985).
4. Carlo Ginzburg, *Ecstasies: Deciphering the Witches' Sabbath* (New York, Patheon, 1991), 162–3.
5. For this portrait of the dziadys, I have drawn upon Machal, "Slavic Mythology," 235–8.
6. Many readers who are acquainted with contemporary metaphysics may wonder at the emphasis on the ancestral stream rather than upon one's incarnational past. In actual practice, Slavic sorcerers are concerned with both: when we take incarnation in a particular family, we enter that ancestral stream and take on all the issues and responsibilities it entails. In fact, we are always dealing with at least two levels of karmic healing: our own past-life karma, and our family or ancestral karma.
7. For an introduction to James Hillman's work, see *Blue Fire* (New York: Harperperennial Library, 1991).

RESOURCE DIRECTORY

THE CONTEMPORARY TRADITION OF SLAVIC SORCERY IS STILL PRIMARILY an oral one; therefore I shall list people rather than books.

It may be noticed that I have not listed Dr. Vadim Polyakov, a very public teacher, in this directory. Nor have I included Natasha Sviridova. I regret to inform my readers of Dr. Polyakov's unexpected death in 1996 and Natasha Sviridova's death in late 1997.

Vladimir Antonov
Russia 197022
St. Petersburg
D.O. Vostebovaniya

As noted in various places throughout the book, Vladimir is a universalist with teachings and opinions about everything from Taoism to esoteric Christianity. Pagan Earth Magic (a label which he himself would not use) is only a part of his opus. At one time a university professor, Vladimir lost his academic position during the Brezhnev years when he became a leader of the Russian spiritual underground. He has been, at various times in his life, a psychologist, an academic, a refugee from the KGB, a pilgrim in Siberia, and a sorcerer.

The reader may wonder why I have given no information as to where Vladimir obtained his deep knowledge of Pagan Earth Magic.

The fact is, Vladimir himself never talks about it. I have managed to learn, from other sources, the identities of some of his teachers, and though I am not at liberty to reveal his lineage I am satisfied that he is part of the genuine oral tradition of Earth Magic and sorcery.

Andrei and Alla Goroshosky
Center for Inner Harmony

Andrei and Alla are quite willing to make contact with Westerners; and though I have lost their address and phone number, it can be found in the St. Petersburg telephone directory. However, neither of them speak any English; some knowledge of Russian or (as in my own case) the services of a translator are required.

Dr. Igor Kungurtsev, M.D.
Dr. Olga Luchakova, M.D., Ph.D.
Hridayam^{SM} School of Transmutational Kundalini Yoga and
    Self Realization
P.O. Box 7009-157
Lafayette, CA 94549
(510) 869-2611
E-mail: 73543.62@compuserv.com

Although Igor and Olga have studied extensively with traditional sorcerers in Russia, their teaching is at present is grounded in the spirituality of India. Nevertheless, they retain an interest in and affection for their native tradition; they lead Earth Magic hikes at various places around the San Francisco Bay Area, and Olga occasionally teaches workshops in the meditative and magical use of icons. Their location in San Francisco area makes them the most accessible resource for interested Westerners.

Kenneth Johnson
c/o Llewellyn Worldwide
P.O. Box 64383, Dept. 374-3
St. Paul, MN 55164-0383, U.S.A.

Though I myself am only a student, I am willing to share what I have learned with anyone who is interested.

GLOSSARY

Baba Yaga: Literally "Old Bony Legs" or "Grandmother Bony Shanks." The archetypal witch of Russian folklore, Baba Yaga lives in a hut (*izba*) in the depths of the woods—a peculiar residence which stands on chicken legs and turns around by itself; indeed, the very dawn and dusk begin their daily circuit from Baba Yaga's hut. The fence around her izba features human skulls on the fenceposts, and when Baba Yaga travels, she rides through the air in a magical mortar and pestle. Sometimes she is said to be the embodiment of evil, a wild witch or *vedma* who likes to catch little children and cook them in her stove (*pech*). But she may also be a wise teacher and a help to those in need: it is she who guards that magical elixir of immortality, the Waters of Life and Death. Baba Yaga may well be a folkloric memory of the old shamanic Bone Goddess, the lady of Life and Death whose stiff white figurine is found carved in stone or bone as far back as the Neolithic era.

Bannik: The spirit of the bathhouse or *banya*. The Bannik, though mischievous, is not really malignant; he may aid us in rites of divination.

banya: The bathhouse. More like a sauna or Native American sweat lodge than a simple bathroom, the banya was a wooden structure placed some distance from the house. A fire was kept burning there to heat water, which was then poured over hot rocks to produce steam.

The banya was thoroughly Pagan; it had its own indwelling spirit, the Bannik, and no Christian icons were ever placed there. Children were sometimes born in the banya; therefore it was also known as the "temple of the Rozhenitsye"—the Mothers or Fates. The banya was—and sometimes still is—a scene of esoteric Pagan ritual. *Kolduny* who practice melting the ice of frozen streams with their own inner fire typically begin this rite of power with a steam session in the banya.

Belobog: Literally "the White God." In old Slavic myth, Belobog is a personification of the masculine or yang principle of Nature, the polar opposite of Chernobog, the Black God.

Bereginy: The Bereginy are mentioned in ancient texts as nymphs or goddesses of river banks, associated with the creation of life. In later times, these female spirits were known as the Rusalki.

Boyan: In Russian legend, Boyan is the archetypal bard or minstrel, a grandson of Stribog, god of the winds. The winds themselves are said to dwell upon the Isle of Boyan, an Otherworldly island where heroes feast and carouse eternally.

Chernobog: Literally "the Black God"; an embodiment of the yin or passive principle in Nature, the polar opposite of Belobog.

Dazhbog: Believed by most scholars to have been a solar god, Dazhbog was also said to be the grandfather of the Russian people.

Domovoi: The Domovoi is "the lord of the house." This household spirit and protector is a family guardian, and may sometimes even appear in the guise of a departed family member. The Domovoi, however, should not be thought of as a mere ghost, which he isn't. Rather, he is the psychic imprint or spiritual essence of the family collectivity (rod) as a whole. In folklore, he is sometimes said to have a wife called the Domania or Domovikha. In other stories, however, his wife is said to be a spirit called the Kikimora.

Dvorovoi: This spirit watches over one's yard; he is a kind of spirit groundsman. He is a great deal trickier and more mischievous than the Domovoi.

dziadys: This festival, celebrated several times a year in Bulgaria and Ukraine, honored the dead. Divination regarding the family's prosperity and agricultural prospects was typically performed during the dziadys.

dzivot, dziz'n: One of the most important concepts in Slavic sorcery or *koldovtsvo*. The word *dziz'n* literally means "life," but should be understood esoterically as the aggregate life-force of all humanity. Furthermore, it is a life-force which is ensouled, for these Russian words are related to the Sanskrit *jiva*, which literally means "soul." In addition to the collective dziz'n, we all have an individual life-force or dzivot. This dzivot is centered in the belly—and hence dzivot is also the common Russian word for "belly." The sorcerer or *koldun* learns to perceive the world with the eyes in his dzivot, for his consciousness lives in the center of the life-force rather than in the mind alone.

gadalky: Literally "guessers." Among the various kinds of sorcerers or kolduny, the gadalky are those who specialize in finding lost objects.

izba: A peasant's hut. Despite its humble status, the izba was frequently a microcosm of the universe, with symbols of the Tree of Life painted above the door, a heavenly six-petaled rose at the top of the building, and a stove, or pech, in the center of the house to symbolize the Otherworldly fire in which the benevolent spirits of the ancestors dwell.

khorovod: A ring dance performed in Pagan times and during folk festivals at least until 1917. The word *khorovod* contains the name of the sun god Khors and was dedicated to the rising of the solar light and power. Ring dances have been found depicted on Balkan and Ukrainian pottery which dates to the Neolithic.

Khors: An old Slavic sun god whose name survives in the khorovod or ring dance.

Kikimora: A female spirit of the household, she spins and does domestic work of all kinds.

koldovtsvo: Literally "sorcery" or "the craft of the wise." A man who practices koldovtsvo is a koldun, while a woman is a koldunya. Collectively they are the kolduny; much of this book is based on the more esoteric side of their magical practice.

kolduny: See koldovtsvo.

Koliada: A Slavic folk festival which occurred during the winter solstice period and was later syncretized with Christmas. The old Koliada festivities, however, were thoroughly Pagan and included groups of people who, representing the spirits of the ancestors, dressed in animal masks and wandered through the village singing songs.

Kostroma: One of several names for the deity I have called "the Young Harvest Lord." Other names were Kupalo and Yarilo. The festivities in honor of the Harvest Lord were sometimes called the Kostroma.

Kuchiya: A special food, dedicated to the ancestors, which was eaten in Slavic countries during the winter holidays. In Belarus it was a pudding made of barley groats and honey, and in the Ukraine of wheat groats, pounded poppy seeds and honey. In Russia proper, kuchiya was a special porridge made of whole grains and pork.

Kupalo: Another name for the deity I call the "Young Harvest Lord." The indwelling spirit of all growing things, his name is also related to an old Slavic word for "healing waters" or "healing springs"; thus he is also the healing power inherent in water. His festival was celebrated at the summer solstice and was characterized by dancing, carousing, and sexual license. This time of year was syncretized with St. John's Day (June 24) during Christian times. Because Ivan is the Russian word for John, the summer solstice period was the Feast of Ivan-Kupalo. Some scholars regard Kupalo as Kupala, a femine deity rather than masculine; others speak of a male-female pair called Kupalo-Kupala. In any event, the myth of the Goddess and the Young Harvest Lord is the pertinent one; like other harvest gods and consorts of the Divine Mother, Kupalo dies and is ritually buried at the end of the festival.

Lada: A goddess of springtime and fertility. A beautiful young woman, Lada returns to the world during the Stritennia festival at the beginning of the spring, bringing with her the birds, who are her totem animals. She also brings the return of many of the souls of the happy dead, who have been dwelling in Vyri, a lush green land in the south. Vyri would seem to have been Lada's special domain.

Leshy: The Leshy is the spirit of the forest. Wild and hairy, he is frequently treacherous and mischievous. Sometimes he is helpful, though he tends to favor society's outlaws and misfits. This spirit of the trees, a descendant of the old Neolithic god I call the Lord of the Forest, is a family man, with a wife called the Leshachika or Lesovikha, and a number of children who are known as Leshonki. Leshys are among the more persistent nature spirits of Slavic folklore, and reports of "sightings" occur even into the present day.

Maslenitsa: A folk festival which fell in the early spring, and which perhaps takes its name from an old Slavic goddess. Like the Mardi Gras (Maslenitsa also falls just before Lent), this festival is a time of general celebration and license. It is characterized by the baking of ceremonial pancakes called *bliny*.

Mati Syra Zemlya: Literally, "Moist Mother Earth." This is one of many titles for the old Slavic Earth Goddess or Earth Mother whose most common name is Mokosh. The association of moisture with earth is reminiscent of the term Bereginy, which signifies the banks of streams. All of this may be taken as evidence that the Slavic Earth Goddess is intimately related to other goddesses of the life-giving, earth-fecundating waters, such as the Iranian Anahita and the Vedic Saraswati. As for the word *zemlya* or "earth," it is cognate with the Greek name Semele, which suggests that this figure, the mother of Dionysus, is also a variant of the great Goddess of the Life-Giving Waters.

Mokosh: The most common name for the Earth Goddess. Mokosh is the earth itself; the rocks are her bones, and the leaves of the trees are her hair. All human life comes out of the earth, and all of it goes back to her; even in Christian times, dying Slavic peasants consigned their souls to Mokosh as often as to Christ. In fact, many of the attributes of Mary Mother of God, as perceived in popular Eastern Orthodoxy, seem to be derived from Mokosh. An obscure Orthodox saint, St. Paraskeva, is even more like Mokosh: a solitary woman with wild gray hair, she watches over spinning and weaving. Mokosh was long remembered in Russian folklore as an old woman with long gray hair and very long fingers who is associated with spinning and with other "women's arts." Peasant women performed rituals (such as plowing the fields by night in their shifts) in honor of Mokosh at least until 1917.

Myesyats: The Slavic deity of the moon. In some folktales, Myesyats is "the Sun's old bald uncle"; in others, the name is applied to a beautiful young maiden, goddess of the moon.

odgatchik: The singular form of gadalky (q.v.).

Perun: The God of Thunder. The name of Perun is linguistically related to that of Thor, and the two deities resemble each other. Perun the Thunder God rides through the sky in a chariot, casting thunderbolts. He is an eminently heroic god, a spiritual warrior, and one of the most popular gods of the ancient Slavs; his name survives in geographical landmarks all over Eastern Europe. Perun was the principal deity of old Kiev—a state founded on Pagan ideals of chivalry and valor. After Christianization—when Perun's statue was dumped in the Dnieper—he survived in legend as Ilya Muromets, the great warrior of the Kievan folk epics. In the icon tradition, Perun becomes St. Elijah, another weather wizard in a flaming chariot. And in the wilder parts of the Carpathians, Perun survives (or at least did survive until about the 1920s) in an almost "pure" form as a magical being known as the Thunder Emperor.

pech: The common Russian word for "stove." In olden times, however, a pech (much like the banya or bathhouse) had a powerful magical aura. The stove was the spiritual center of the peasant's hut or izba (q.v.), which was itself a microcosm of the universe. As a replacement for the old family hearth of Pagan times, the pech was a simulacrum for the ancestral energy which enlivens the base of the World Tree—or which, for that matter, kindles our own inner fire, the dzivot. Hence the ancestors dwell in the flames of the pech, making the family stove a sacred fire, worthy of honor in its own right. An old Russian pech was a very large piece of furniture; in former times, the children and the family's grandmother might curl up and sleep together on top of the pech during winter.

Pokrov: In the Eastern Orthodox Church, this is the Feast of the Intercession of the Mother of God. Pokrov probably replaces the autumn harvest festival of Pagan times, which was dedicated to Mother Mokosh.

Polevik: The spirit of the fields. During harvest times, he hides amid the wheat or barley until the last sheaf is taken; at that time, he is bound up and brought in. Sometimes this all-important last sheaf is identified with the god Volos.

Poludnitsa: The Spirit of Midday. Usually perceived as a beautiful woman, she roams the fields during the noon hour, and may inflict illness upon those who are sufficiently unwary to be out working at this inauspicious hour.

Radunica: The Radunica is a festival celebrated in honor of the dead; it was associated with a "Field of Flowers" because the Happy Otherworld is often imaged in European myth as a flowering meadow (the Greek Elysian Fields, the Celtic Land of Youth, and so on). I believe that this Otherworldly field of flowers is equivalent to the "lush green land" of Vyri.

rod: Literally "a collectivity," this word signifies an extended family, clan, or similar "ancestral stream." Some scholars believe that the rod or collective energy of any given group was once embodied as a god called Rod, focus of the old ancestral cult; the same scholars purport to see a survival of this ancestral deity in the friendly Domovoi or household spirit. One of my sources referred to the old shamanic World Tree or Tree of Life as the Tree of Rod.

Rozhenitsye: A combination of *rod* (q.v.) or "collectivity" and *zhenitsye,* or "women"; hence "clan women." The Rozhenitsye are a group of women—usually dressed in white—who watch over the affairs of the family or household, especially as regards births; they are often called "the Mothers." Usually there are three of them, which suggests that they are a survival of the Old European Triple Goddess, much like the Norns of Teutonic myth or the Parcae in Celtic countries. Their closest relations, however, are the Greek Fates; like them, the Rozhenitsye spin the web of the child's destiny, and one must honor and feed them in order to obtain their good favor and help persuade them to grant the child a happy destiny. Because children were often born in the bathhouse or banya, that structure was sometimes called "the Temple of the Rozhenitsye." Sometimes the Rozhenitsye appear as a single figure named Rozhenitsa.

Rusalki: The tree-and-water nymphs who play such a large role in Slavic folklore, Russian poetry, and so on. The souls of young women who have died, the Rusalki live underwater during the fall and winter, then emerge around Whitsuntide to take up residence as the spirits of the trees. Their return to a silvan abode was celebrated in olden times with a festival called the Rusalye. The Rusalki may be either malevolent or benign. Often, they dance and frolic on the banks of the rivers and lakes—which suggests that they are related to, or perhaps descended from, the Bereginy (q.v.)—but sometimes they lure unwary peasants (especially men) to their deaths. The worship of the tree-and-water nymphs appears to be very old indeed; it often survives (as in Greece) long after the names of the gods have been forgotten. I was shown a road leading to a pond in the woods where the Rusalki are believed to live and to speak—at least to those who can hear them.

Semik: A ceremony for the dead, held during the Rusalye or festival for the Rusalki.

Simargl: A deity worshipped in ancient Kiev. Simargl is probably derived from *simurgh*, the Persian term for a magical bird-deity. Simargl survives in Russian folklore as the Firebird.

Stribog: The god of the winds. The Holy Spirit is said to be his breath; hence the Holy Spirit is itself a kind of wind. Stribog may have yet another folkloric reflex as Grandfather Frost.

Stritennia: A festival held in early spring, the Stritennia is the time of "meeting" between winter and spring. It was dedicated to the goddess Lada, who returns at this time from the land of Vyri, bringing with her the birds and the spirits of the ancestors.

Svarog: A deity worshipped all over the Slavic world, Svarog was the God of Light. A creator spirit, he symbolizes pure enlightened reflection.

Svarovitch: Literally "the Son of Svarog." Svarovitch is usually identified as the indwelling spirit of the sacred fire.

svyato mesto: Literally "power spot." In ancient times, healing wells or springs and the tops of bald mountains were regarded as power spots or sacred spaces. Contemporary kolduny tend to think of power spots in terms of energy vortices. These may occur anywhere; as I was told, you can even find them "in the metro."

upyri: The Russian word for "vampires." These unclean spirits of the dead have been feared and propitiated since the most ancient times. Entirely unlike the elegant aristocrats of Hollywood vampire lore, the Slavic upyri are hideous ghouls, the spirits of dead criminals and sorcerers who have found other bodies to inhabit and/or feed upon.

vedma: Literally "witch." A few words must be said about the emotional color and tone of certain terms. An individual who practices the old Pagan arts may be called (among other things) a znakharka, a koldun, or a vedma. The difference is: a znakharka is specifically a healer, and therefore held in positive regard; vedma is generally a negative term, signifying one who practices black magic and casts curses; a koldun or koldunya is a sorcerer or wizard, and his or her powers may be used for either good or evil, though the words *koldun* and *koldunya* also have the meaning of "wise man" and "wise woman."

vily: Though this word is commonly used to describe the Fairy Folk, its literal meaning connects it with the spirits of the dead. As in other parts of Europe, the Fairy Folk of Slavic countries were associated with the spirits of the departed. The Slavic vily were usually imagined as beautiful young women, and are hence closely related to the Rusalki.

Vodyanoi: The Vodyanoi are water spirits who dwell in ponds and lakes. Surly and occasionally malicious, they may nevertheless be friendly to fishermen and others who enter their domain with the proper offerings and respect. The Vodyanoi like to ruin mill wheels, and hence millers often made sacrifices (occasionally human!) to these spirits in hopes of obtaining their friendship.

volkhvy: This word, of uncertain etymology, was used during Kievan times to describe the priests of the Pagan faith, and was still used up until a few centuries ago to describe magicians and sorcerers of all kinds. The more customary term in contemporary times is kolduny. The old Kievan epic songs feature a character named Volkh Vseslavevich, a sorcerer-hero who may be the eponymous god of the Volga River.

Volos: Though scholars disagree on the nature and functions of this god, he is most often regarded as a god of the dead—his name, in fact, comes from the same root as the word *vily* (q.v.). He is connected with agriculture as well as with death, and has survived in folklore disguised not as one saint but as two—he is St. Vlas, the patron of agriculture, as well as the more familiar St. Nicholas. In Slavic folklore, St. Nicholas is a magical and mysterious wanderer who roams through the world performing miracles—which suggests that Volos was much like his Norse counterpart Odin, who behaves in much the same fashion.

vorozheia: Literally a "fortune-teller," a vorozheia is a koldun or koldunya who specializes in divination.

Vyri: A beautiful, lush, warm green land in the south or southeast where the spirits of the happy dead have their abode. Vyri would seem to be identical with other European conceptions of the Happy Otherworld, such as the Greek Elysian Fields or Celtic Land of Youth. It was probably imagined as a vast, sunlit field of beautiful flowers (see Radunica). Lada was the goddess who ruled in Vyri.

Yarilo: Yet another name for the Young Harvest Lord who is also called Kostroma or Kupalo). Yarilo is the name used for this deity by Stravinsky in his ballet *The Rites of Spring*.

znakhary: Literally "healers." The znakhary are kolduny who specialize in the healing arts.

Zorya: The name of a goddess or pair of goddesses worshipped by the Pagan Slavs. The Morning and Evening Stars are sometimes called Zorya Utrennyaya and Zorya Vechernyaya, respectively; in Kiev, however, there was a goddess called Zorya who was associated with warfare and battle.

BIBLIOGRAPHY

Slavic Mythology and Magic

Alexinsky, G. "Slavonic Mythology." In *New Larousse Encyclopedia of Mythology*. London: Hamlyn Publishing, 1981.

Gieysztor, A. "Slavic Countries: Folk-Lore of the Forests." In *Larousse World Mythology*. Edited by Pierre Grimal. London: Hamlyn Publishing, 1965.

Hubbs, Joanna. *Mother Russia: The Feminine Myth in Russian Culture.* Bloomington: Indiana University Press, 1989.

Ivakhiv, Adrian. "The Cosmos of the Ancient Slavs." *Gnosis*, No. 31, Spring 1994.

Ivanits, Linda J. *Russian Folk Belief.* London: M. E. Sharpe, 1988.

Kungurtsev, Igor, and Olga Luchakova. "The Unknown Russian Mysticism." *Gnosis*, No. 31, Spring 1994.

———. "Earth and Spirit." *Gnosis*, Fall 1994.

Machal, Jan. "Slavic Mythology." In *The Mythology of All Races, Vol. III.* Edited by L. H. Grey. New York: Cooper Square, 1964.

Min'ko, L. I. "Magic Curing." Translated by Wm. Mandel in *Soviet Anthropology and Archaeology*, Vol. 12 No. 1 (Summer 1973), Vol. 12 No. 2 (Fall 1973), and Vol. 12 No. 3 (Winter 1973–4)

Vincenz, Stanislaw (translated by H. C. Stevens). *On the High Uplands: Sagas, Songs, Tales and Legends of the Carpathians.* New York: Roy Publishers, n.d.

Ancient Europe

Eisler, Riane. *The Chalice and the Blade: Our History, Our Future.* San Francisco: Harper and Row, 1987.

Gimbutas Marija. *The Goddesses and Gods of Old Europe: 6500–3500 B.C., Myths and Cult Images.* Berkeley and Los Angeles: University of California Press, 1982.

———. *The Language of the Goddess.* San Francisco: Harper and Row, 1989.

———. *The Civilization of the Goddess: The World of Old Europe.* San Francisco: Harper and Row, 1991.

Mallory, J. P. *In Search of the Indo-Europeans: Language, Archaeology and Myth.* London: Thames and Hudson, 1994.

Metzner, Ralph. *The Well of Remembrance: Rediscovering the Earth Wisdom Myths of Northern Europe.* Boston and London: Shambhala, 1994.

Comparative Religion and Mythology

Avalon, Arthur (Sir John Woodroffe). *The Serpent Power: The Secrets of Tantric and Shaktic Yoga.* New York: Dover Publications, 1974.

Eliade, Mircea. *Patterns in Comparative Religion.* Lincoln: University of Nebraska Press, 1996.

———. *Shamanism: Archaic Techniques of Ecstasy.* Princeton: Princeton-Bollingen, 1972.

———. *Yoga: Immortality and Freedom.* Princeton: Princeton-Bollingen, 1970.

Ginzburg, Carlo. *Night Battles: Witchcraft & Agrarian Cults in the Sixteenth & Seventeenth Centuries.* New York: Penguin, 1985.

———. *Ecstasies: Deciphering the Witches' Sabbath.* New York, Pantheon, 1991.

Puhvel, Jaan. *Comparative Mythology.* Baltimore: Johns Hopkins University Press, date to come.

INDEX

A

Air, 32, 153, 172
alchemy, 28, 95, 99, 117, 143
Amleth's Mill, 182
Amsterdam, 177-179, 181
ancestors, 8-9, 13-15, 22, 38, 41-
  43, 78, 94, 96, 111, 119, 129,
  135, 143, 182-183, 185, 187-
  197, 205, 206, 208, 210
animals (see also fish, serpent,
  snakes), 6, 14, 35, 38, 41-42, 52,
  81-85, 87-88, 91, 99, 128-129,
  131, 138-139, 144, 148, 154, 161,
  164-165, 169, 185-186, 205-206
  bear, 5-6, 12, 77-79, 87, 105,
    115, 164, 196
  beaver, 35
  butterfly, 187
  cat, 144, 148-149, 164, 185
  cattle, 13, 40, 90-91, 149, 154,
    160, 165, 186, 189
  deer, 87, 153-154, 163
  dog, 75, 77, 144, 148-149, 152,
    164, 167, 169, 185
  frog, 52, 149
  hare, 87, 187
  horse, 15, 76-80, 83, 89, 91, 93,
    99, 143, 148, 151, 153, 158,
    160, 165
  mouse, 187
  sheep, 91, 99, 149, 160, 165
  wolf, 87, 153, 162, 165
Antonov, Vladimir, xi, 3, 10-12,
  14-17, 45, 67, 74-75, 79, 81, 90,
  102-116, 118, 120-121, 123-126,
  128-135, 137-142, 152, 161,
  167-175, 185, 188, 192, 199-200
Apollo, 66, 74
Apollolaan, 178-179
Apostles, 29
Aquae Sulis (Bath, England), 21-22
archetypes, 71, 72, 74, 75, 81, 85,
  89, 93, 96, 98
Aredvi, 81
arms, 39, 65, 116, 135-136, 139,
  142
  energy arms, 115-116, 135-136,
    139, 142
Asgard, 90
astral body (see also soul, astral),
  186, 188
astrologers, 35
Asvins (see twins), 76
aura, 59, 64, 66-68, 130, 134
Aurobindo, 28
autumn, 36-37, 40, 98, 132-133,
  137, 189, 208
  autumn equinox, 36
Ayurvedic medicine, 172

B

Baal, 80
Baba Yaga, 8, 19, 28, 82, 93-98, 193, 203
Balkans, 196
Baltic
  region, 14, 35, 45, 97, 101, 124-125, 152, 165, 177, 182, 185
  sea, 124-125, 137, 165
Balts, Pagan, 14, 45, 90-91, 185
Bannik, 110-111, 149-150, 203-204
bardos, 142
Barn Spirit (see Ovinnik), 149
barrow mounds, 188
Basil, St., 79
bathhouse, 23, 52, 110-111, 143, 149-150, 186, 203, 208-209
bathing in ice water, 22, 23, 33, 88, 111
Bay of Finland, 125
beeswax, 13, 49-50, 52, 54-56, 59-60, 65
Belarus, 13, 24, 41, 79, 83, 89, 128, 184, 189, 206
Belobog, 24, 30, 204
Belun, 24
benandanti, 184
Bereginy (see also nymphs, Rusalki), 13, 102, 157, 204, 207, 209
Big Dipper, 181
birds, 38, 85, 87, 88, 96, 109, 125-126, 151, 153, 206, 210
  chicken, 42, 93, 145, 148, 203
  cockerel, 34
  cuckoo, 187
  dove, 29, 34, 174, 187
  duck, 6, 24, 187
  eagle, 51, 153, 187
  falcon, 34
  hawk, 153, 187
  hen, 42, 189-190
  kedrovkia (also orechovkia), 126
  mallard, 6, 24
  nightingale, 187
  raven, 99, 162, 187
  swallow, 187
  swan, 153, 159
  water birds, 24
Black God (see Chernobog), 24-25, 30, 204
Blaise, St. (see Vlas, St.), 91, 211
Boann (Celtic river goddess), 21
Bohemia, 102, 144, 147
Bone Goddess or Bone Mother (see Goddesses), 6, 92-95, 203
Bosnia, 13, 78
Brigid, 21
British Isles, 128
Buddhism, Buddhists, 173
  Tibetan Buddhism, 142
Bulgaria, 13, 78, 147, 189, 204
Byzantium, Byzantines, 3, 13, 55, 71-72, 78, 82, 91, 99

C

Campbell, Joseph, 9, 173
Cappadocia, 91
Castaneda, Carlos, 128
cauldron, 143
  in Chinese alchemy, 117
caves, 148, 153-154, 163, 184
Celts, Celtic, 21, 85, 129, 142, 147, 183-184, 186, 188, 209, 211
cemeteries, 38, 106-107, 109, 188
Central Asia, 5, 176
Cernunnos, 85
chakras, 16-17, 28, 57, 60, 65, 69, 117, 121, 171, 194
  heart, 65
  root, 117
  sexual, 117
  solar plexus, 57, 117
Chernobog, 24, 30, 204
Chernyshevskaya, 102
China, Chinese, 3, 8, 25-27, 35, 45, 117, 128
Christ, 29, 33, 40, 174, 207
Christianity, Christians, 8, 13-15, 25, 29, 31, 33, 37-40, 66, 71-74, 79, 82, 86, 89, 111, 127, 142, 144, 173-174, 183, 199, 204, 206-208

Byzantine Church, 72, 82, 99
Catholics, 14, 55, 174
Eastern Orthodox Church, 14,
    173-174, 208
Greek Orthodox Church, 14, 72,
    75, 81, 85, 89, 147, 152, 157,
    178, 183, 207, 209, 211
Protestants, 8, 14
Russian Orthodox Church, 14,
    174
Western, 14, 55, 174
Church of the Resurrection, 10
circumpolar tradition, 23
Communism, 16
Cosmas and Damian, Sts. (see also
    twins), 76
cosmology, 192
Croatia, 13, 78, 147, 153
Cross of the Four Directions, 74,
    95-96
crystals, 28, 30-31, 107, 155, 160
curanderas, 55, 67
Czech Republic, 13

D
Dalmatia, 78
Damsquare, 178
dance, dancing, 4-6, 9, 15, 34-35,
    38-39, 43, 74, 81-83, 88-89, 95,
    98, 115-116, 140, 153-155, 157-
    158, 163, 183, 196, 205-206, 209
Dawn Maidens, 76-77
Days of the Dead, 189
Dazhbog, 13-14, 74-76, 143, 204
Devil, 31, 52-53, 149, 165
Diaghilev, Sergei, 5
Dionysus, 5, 81, 89, 125, 207
divination, 16, 39, 41, 90, 96, 107,
    110-111, 149, 157-158, 203-204,
    211
Domania (see Domovoi), 144, 204
Domovikha (see Domovoi), 144,
    204
Domovoi, 143-149, 185, 187, 190,
    204, 209
Don Juan, xii, 128

dowsing, 20, 47, 58
Dr. Zhivago, 62
dragon, 28, 35, 66, 85, 95, 192
Druids, 129
dualism, dualities, 3, 23-28, 30-31,
    95, 142, 183
Christian, 25, 31, 183
Pagan, 23, 142
Zoroastrian, 25, 26
Dvorovoi, 148-149, 204
dziadys (see feasts and festivals),
    184, 189-190, 197, 204
dzivot, dziz'n, 57, 116-120, 124,
    126, 132-134, 136, 143, 168-
    169, 171, 175, 195-196, 205, 208

E
earth, 6, 8, 15, 24, 26-28, 30, 32,
    34, 38, 40, 43-44, 53, 65, 72,
    75, 80-85, 89-93, 97, 103, 125,
    127-129, 139, 153, 181, 183,
    185-186, 188, 192
Earth Magic, 5, 10, 16, 102, 107,
    118, 174, 199-200
Earth Mother (see Goddesses), 6,
    14-15, 81-82, 84, 207
east (direction), 35-36, 76-77, 84,
    162
East Prussia, 144
Easter, 33, 38, 144
egg(s), 24, 38, 54-55, 112, 151,
    157-158, 190
cosmic, 24
Easter, 38
of life, 24
Eisler, Riane, 6
Eleusis, 125
Eliade, Mircea, 65, 76, 183
Elijah, St., 40, 72, 80, 208
Elijah the Rainmaker, 184
Elijah, Feast of, 80
Elixir of Life, 28, 66, 192
Elysian Fields (see also Other-
    world), 183-184, 209, 211
energy, 1-3, 11, 20, 22, 28-32, 40-
    41, 51, 56-60, 65-68, 95, 103-
    106, 109, 112, 114-121, 123,

125, 128-136, 139, 142, 161,
164, 169-170, 172-176, 179,
181, 188, 191-192, 194, 208-210
energy massage, 56, 66-67
England, 21-22
Europe:
Eastern, 5-6, 11-12, 72, 85, 89,
91, 128-129, 192, 208
Neolithic, 6-7, 92
Pagan, 7, 13
Slavic, 72, 211
Western, ix, 5, 13, 72, 85
Evening Star, 77

F

Fairies, 147, 152-154
Fates (see Rozhenitsye), 111, 147-
148, 204, 209
feasts and festivals, 8, 15, 24, 33,
35, 37-40, 45, 53, 74, 80, 85, 87,
89, 96, 126, 129, 138, 148, 155-
157, 184-185, 187-189, 204-210
Birth of the Mother of God, 40
Christmas, 41-43, 80, 205
dziadys, 184, 189-190, 197, 204
Feast of Elijah, 80
Feast of Ivan-Kupalo, 39, 89, 206
Feast of the Baptism of Christ, 33
Feast of the Intercession of the
Mother of God (Pokrov), 40
folk festivals, 15, 37, 155, 205,
207
Green Holidays, 38, 188
Koliada, 42-43, 96, 205
Kupalo's Night, 88, 127-128
Maslenitsa, 37, 207
New Year's, 41
Orthodox Feasts, 33, 40, 208
Radunica, 184, 190, 208, 212
Rusalye (Rusalki Week), 155-
158, 188, 209-210
seasonal festivals, 15, 45, 74
Semik, 157-158, 210
St. John's Eve, 39, 127, 162, 165
Stritennia, 38, 206, 210
Yuletide, 110, 190
feminine principle, 31, 85, 96
feminism, feminists, 7, 31

fetch (see also soul, astral), 95, 186
Field of Josaphat, 184
fields of roses (see also Otherworld), 184
Finland, 105, 112, 125, 129
Fire (element and principle), 13, 23,
28-30, 32, 38, 39, 51, 56, 64-67,
76, 95, 97
Firebird, 14, 24, 29, 75, 109-110,
174, 210
fish, 64, 66, 83, 159-161, 163
Fjorgynn, 78
Flor and Lavr, Sts. (see also twins),
76
folk art, 34
folklore, xi, 8, 24, 29, 34-35, 71,
75, 79-80, 82, 90-91, 94, 96,
109, 129, 138, 143, 155, 163-
164, 184, 203-204, 206-207,
209-211
Russian, 8, 29, 35, 75, 91, 109,
143, 203, 207, 210
Slavic, xi, 34, 80, 94, 138, 155,
164, 206, 209, 211
forest, 8, 13, 34, 39, 42, 52, 81-82,
85-88, 93, 95, 102, 105, 108-
109, 112, 114, 116, 124-133,
137-139, 147, 149, 153, 155,
157, 161-164, 168-169, 185, 206
hardwood, 128
evergreen, 128-129
Forest Guardian, 137-138
Forest Lord (see Gods), 52, 85-86,
88, 138, 161-162
Fortunate Isles, 184-185
fortune-tellers (see vorozheia), 54,
211
Frazer, James, 88
Freyr, 90, 97
funeral rites, 43, 89, 158, 186-188
of Kupalo, 40-41, 89
of Slavic peoples, 186
fylgja (see also soul, astral), 186

G

gadalky, 54, 205, 207
gemstones, 61
George, St. , 72-73, 85, 88

ghosts, 11, 90, 111, 195-196, 204
Gimbutas, Marija, 17, 37, 45, 144
Gnostics, Gnosticism, 62, 174
Goddess of Heaven (see Goddesses), 83
Goddesses (see also indvidual goddesses, e.g. Mokosh, Lada, etc.),
6-8, 14, 17, 21, 24, 29, 35, 38,
42, 45, 71, 74-75, 77, 81-83, 89,
92-96, 98, 143-144, 147, 155,
166, 174, 185, 203-204, 206-
207, 209-210, 212
    Bone Mother, 6, 92-93, 95
    Bone Goddess, 94-95, 203
    Death Crone, 92
    Earth Mother, 6, 14-15, 81-82,
        84, 207
    Goddess of Heaven, 83
    Great Mother, 89
    Horse Goddess, 83, 143
    Mistress of the Waters of
        Heaven, 6
    Mistress of Animals, 6
    Mother Earth, 8, 55, 81, 83-85,
        89, 186, 207
    Snake Goddess, 144
    Snake Mother, 6
    Tree Goddess, 83
    Triple Goddess, 96, 209
    White Lady, 6, 8, 92
Gods (see also individual gods, e.g.,
Perun, Kupalo, etc.), 0, 5-9, 13-
15, 17, 21-22, 24-26, 28-31, 35,
39-40, 42, 45, 55-56, 66, 71-72,
74-76, 78-81, 83, 85-86, 88-92,
95-99, 101-102, 125-126, 129,
135, 139, 142-143, 152, 161,
181-182, 184-185, 188, 193,
204-211
    Forest Lord, 52, 85-86, 88, 138,
        161-162
    Lord of the Wildwood, 6, 8
    Master of the Forest, 85, 88, 102
    Thunder God, 7-8, 13-15, 28,
        66, 78-80, 129, 184, 207
    Underworld Lord, 90-92
    Young Harvest God, 6, 8

Golden Bough, The, 88
Goroshosky, Alla, 31, 200
Goroshosky, Andrei, 192, 200
Grandfather Frost, 75, 210
graves, 56, 105, 153, 164, 187-
    188, 190
Great Mother (see Goddesses), 89
Greenland, 181
guessers (see gadalky), 54, 205

H

Hades, 183
Hansel and Gretel, 93-94
Hatha Yoga, 128
healers, healing, 2, 10, 12, 16, 22,
    48, 52, 54, 56, 59-61, 63, 67-68,
    73, 193, 210, 212
    with water, 22, 28, 39, 60, 88,
        206
heart center, 103, 114-116, 123-
    124, 126, 130, 136, 139, 141-
    142, 169, 175, 179-180
Heaven, 6-7, 24, 27, 30-31, 34, 62-
    66, 69, 72-73, 75-76, 80, 83, 90,
    93, 99, 129, 142, 153, 183, 185,
    187, 189
Hell, 11, 27, 30-31, 72-73, 92-93,
    183
Hephaestus, 75
herbs (see plants and herbs), 54,
    61, 88, 126-128, 159, 196
Hermitage Museum, 1-3, 20, 72,
    178
hesychasm, 173
hills, sacred, 4, 101
Hinduism, 12, 29-30, 32, 69, 95,
    117, 142, 172
Holland, 178
Holy Thursday, 38
Holy Spirit, 29, 33, 109, 173-175,
    210
Horse Goddess (see Goddesses), 83,
    143
house spirit (see Domovoi), 143-
    144, 190
Hutsuls, 42, 76

I

Ice Age, 5, 8, 33
icons, 3, 40-41, 49, 51-53, 55, 71-75, 77, 79-83, 85, 87, 89, 91-93, 95, 97-99, 111, 127, 149, 183, 187, 190, 200, 204, 208
  meditation with, 3, 72, 200
  saints and gods, 71, 73, 98
iconoclasts, 72
Igor of Kiev, 79
illness, illnesses, 59, 77, 142
Ilmarinen, 182
Ilya Muromets, 66, 79-80, 208
Inanna, 29
incantations, 62
India, 8-9, 57, 62, 76, 82, 99, 125, 128, 194, 200
Indo-Europeans, 7-8, 13, 17, 45, 78, 99, 184
Indra, 28, 66, 78, 80, 99
Iran, 25
Ireland, 21-22, 129
Isis, 62
Isle of Boyan (see also Otherworld), 185, 204
Istria, 78
Italy, 184
Ivan the Terrible (Czar Ivan IV), 82
Ivanov, Porphyry, 22, 27, 33
izba, 93, 143, 161, 203, 205, 208

J

jiva (see also dzivot), 116, 205
John the Baptist, St., 39, 72, 89
Jung, Carl, 9
Jupiter, 78

K

Kabbalah, 29
Kalevala, The, 182
Kali, 95
karma, 16, 66, 152, 194-195, 197
  ancestral, 66, 194, 197
  collective, 66
khorovod, 35, 39, 74, 158, 205
Khors, 35, 74, 143, 205
Kiev, 14, 74-79, 81, 90, 143, 208, 210, 212

Kikimora, 144-145, 147, 204-205
Kirtchik, Dr. Ina, xii, 10, 68
Kol'tsova, Arina, xii, 63, 199
koldovtsvo, 205
kolduny (koldun, koldunya), 10-11, 16, 48, 54, 62, 107, 192, 204-205, 210-212
Koliada (see feasts and festivals), 42-43, 96, 205
Kostroma, 15, 39, 89, 206, 212
kozuli, 38
Kubarikha (fictional character), 62
Kuchiya, 41, 188, 206
kundalini, 16, 28, 93, 192
Kungurtsev, Dr. Igor, 0, 16, 45, 69, 117, 119, 133, 200
Kupalo: Kupalo's Night (see feasts and festivals), 8, 15, 39-40, 88-89, 96-98, 126-128, 206, 212
Kupalo's Night, 88, 127-128

L

Lada, 8, 38, 42-43, 45, 81, 96-98, 185, 206, 210, 212
lakes, 21-22, 33, 38, 101, 125, 153, 157, 159-160, 168, 171-172, 185, 209, 211
Land of Youth, 184, 209, 211
Lange Leidsedwarstraat, 178
languages, 7, 12, 24
  Slavic, 12, 24
  Indo-European, 7, 13, 78
lares, 143
Latvia, 165
Lay of Igor's Campaign, The, 76
Leary, Timothy, 178
Leidseplein, 178
Lemminkainen, 62
Lenin, Vladimir, 192
Leningrad (see St. Petersburg), 11
Leshy, 8, 52, 86-89, 138, 150, 161-163, 206
Leshachika, 87, 162, 206
Lesovikha, 87, 162, 206
Leshonki, 87, 206
life-force (see dzivot, dziz'n), 39, 88-89, 99, 116-118, 179, 205
Lithuania, 78, 144, 165

Little Russia (see Ukraine), 78
Little Bear, 77
lokas, 142
Lord of the Wildwood (see Gods),
    6, 8
Lubeck, 101
Luchakova, Dr. Olga, ix, xii, 16,
    45, 69, 117, 133-135, 192, 200
lycanthropy, 164

M

Macedon, 13
magi, 107, 117, 119, 173
    Russian, 107, 117, 173
magic, 5, 16, 20, 23, 31, 52-53, 57,
    62-63, 66, 71, 74, 76, 80, 91-92,
    97, 107, 110, 117, 118, 121,
    129, 152, 157, 162, 164, 173-
    174, 192, 194, 196, 199
malachite, 61
mandalas, 37, 43, 72, 95-96
Marduk, 28, 66
Mary Theotokos, 83
masculine principle, 31
Master of the Forest (see Gods), 85,
    88, 102
Mater Verborum, 78
Mayakovskogo Street, 27
mental imagery, 56, 61
Michael the Archangel, St., 76
Midday Spirit (see Poludnitsa),
    151-152
Midgard Serpent, 66
Milky Way: as , 182-183
Min'ko, L. I., 16, 18
Minneapolis, 181
Minsk, 16
Mistress of the Waters of Heaven
    (see Goddesses), 6
Mistress of Animals (see God-
    desses), 6
Moist Mother Earth (see Mokosh),
    8, 81, 83-85, 186, 207
Mokosh: as Moist Mother Earth, 8,
    14-15, 74, 81-83, 96-98, 143,
    207-208
Moldavia, 37
Moon, 9, 25, 27, 30, 32, 35, 77,

82, 155, 159-160, 188, 207
Moreskaya, 124, 132
Morning Star, 77
Mother Earth (see Goddesses), 8,
    55, 81, 83-85, 89, 186, 207
Mother of God (see Mary
    Theotokos), 40, 55-56, 81, 83,
    96, 207-208
Mothers (see Rozhenitsye), 143,
    147, 150, 204
mountains, 78-79, 101-102, 153,
    176, 184, 188, 210
    Alps, 128
    Altai, 176
    bald, 77, 101-102, 186, 207, 210
    Carpathian, 79
Mt. Perun, 78
Muromets, Ilya (see Ilya
    Muromets), 66, 79-80, 208
mushrooms, 87, 112-113, 124-125,
    137-138, 159
    fly agaric, 125
Mussorgsky, Modest, 101
Myesyats, 77, 207
Myra (Anatolia), 91
myth, mythology, 5-7, 9, 13, 17-18,
    24-26, 28, 35, 37, 45, 62, 66, 72,
    76-77, 81, 85, 88, 90, 96-97, 99,
    121, 128-129, 140, 162, 173-
    174, 181-185, 188, 192, 197,
    199, 204, 206, 209
    Babylonian, 28
    Celtic, 129, 184, 188, 209
    Egyptian, 62
    European, 66, 182-183, 209
    Norse, 35, 90, 183
    Slavic, 13, 25, 45, 66, 85, 96-97,
        129, 174, 183, 185, 188, 197,
        199, 204
    Teutonic, 66, 129, 209
    Native Americans, 23, 33, 110,
        117, 195, 203
    Amazonian, 128
    Inuit, 173
    Jivaro, 173
    Lakota, 173
    Maya, 66

N

Nature (see also spirits: of Nature),
13, 15, 19, 25-26, 32, 53, 57, 61,
74, 79, 86, 88, 93, 102, 108, 119,
121, 137, 142, 152, 157, 163,
174, 183, 185, 204, 206, 211
Neolithic, 6-8, 13, 15, 24, 35, 37,
81, 85, 88, 92, 144, 161, 203,
205-206
Neuroi, 165
Nevsky Prospect, 124
Nicaea, Council of, 29
Nicholas (author's son), 5, 91, 108
Nicholas, St., 40, 53, 72, 91-92,
99, 211
Nijinsky, 5
Nodens (Celtic river god), 21
Norns (see also Rozhenitsye), 147,
209
north (direction), 26, 36, 84
North American Indians (see
Native Americans), 66
North Pole, 91, 181
North Star, 33-34, 181-183, 193
Novgorod: icons of, 80
nymphs (see also Rusalki, Bereginy),
9, 13, 93, 99, 102, 138, 142, 152-
153, 155, 157, 204, 209
tree, 93
water, 138, 157

O

Odin, 90-92, 97, 211
Ogham alphabet, 129
Olga, Princess of Kiev, 78
Orechovo, 126, 167-168, 170-172,
176
Osiris, 62
Ossetians, 184
Otherworld
geography of, 142
Slavic, 82, 90, 115, 134, 136-
139, 141-143, 145, 147, 149,
151-153, 155, 157, 159, 161,
163-165, 183-184, 186-187,
193, 211
Ovinnik, 149

P

Paganism, Pagans, 3, 5, 7, 9, 12-16,
22-23, 25-27, 29, 33-35, 38-39,
44-45, 55, 57, 72, 75-76, 78, 82-
83, 89-91, 96-97, 102, 107, 111,
127, 129, 142, 149, 174, 182,
184-185, 199-200, 204-205, 208,
210-212
Kievan, 14, 90, 208
Slavic, 3, 5, 12, 22-23, 25-27,
33-34, 44-45, 55, 57, 75, 78,
102, 127, 142, 174, 184, 200,
212
Pan, 49, 85, 146
Paraskeva, St., 72, 82-83, 207
Parcae (see also Rozhenitsye), 147,
209
Parjanya, 78
Pasternak, Boris, 62, 69
Patollus, 91, 97
pendulums, 20-21, 30, 103, 107,
191
Pentecost, 29, 165
Perkunas, 78, 91, 97
Peron (see Perun), 78
Perun: places names associated with
(i.e. Perin Planina, Peruna
Dubrava, Perunja Ves, Perunji
Ort, Perunov Dub, Peruny,
Piorunow), 13-15, 66, 74-75, 77-
80, 89-90, 97-99, 129, 143, 184,
207-208
Peter the Great, 177
photographs, 108, 191
planets, 16, 33, 75, 77, 139
plants and herbs, 54, 61, 81, 88,
125-130, 138-140, 159, 163,
174, 185, 196
absinthe, 159
dreopteris fern, 125, 128, 130
fire-fern, 127-128
liquorice root, 163
nettles, 124
purple loose-strife (tear weed), 127
rose hips, 124
saxifrage, 127
Plato, 72

poison, 28, 66, 192
Pokrov (see feasts and festivals), 40, 96, 208
Poland, 13, 77-78, 128, 152
polarities, 20-21, 25-33, 35-38, 41, 45, 56, 58-59, 72, 80, 82, 98, 109-111, 128, 142, 161, 174
   cosmic, 20, 25, 27, 29, 33, 37, 45, 109, 174
   Chaos and Order, 24, 27-28, 30, 32-33, 56, 66, 142
   Fire and Water, 23, 28, 30, 32, 38-39, 56, 95, 97
   Light and Darkness, 24-27, 35-37, 39, 43, 66, 95-96, 174
   yin and yang, 3, 25-26
Polevik, 150-151, 208
Poludnitsa, 151-152, 208
Polyakov, Dr. Vadim, xii, 2-3, 10-11, 20, 22, 27-30, 32, 35, 47-52, 54, 56-59, 61-63, 65-67, 71-73, 117, 161, 199
Potok Mikhailo-Ivanovich, 183-184
Potrympus, 91, 97
power spots, 103-104, 106, 112, 114, 120-121, 131-132, 139, 210
pranava, 169-170, 172-174, 176
prayer(s), 20-21, 29, 41, 56, 84, 92, 121, 148, 189, 195-196
   Orthodox, 29, 121
Procopius, 13, 78, 99, 152, 157
Proto-Indo-European (language), 7, 26
Pushkin, Alexander, 3, 155
Python, 66

R

rain, 48, 72, 80, 82-84, 142, 153, 180
Rasputin, 62
Red Square, 192
Rig Veda, 28, 80, 99
Rijksmuseum, 178
ring dance (see khorovod), 6, 15, 39, 205
Rites of Spring, The, 5, 74, 212
Ritual Exorcism, 63-65

rivers, 13, 21, 39-40, 81, 101-102, 153, 155-157, 159, 174, 209
   as mothers, 81
   Boyne, 21
   Danube, 21, 155
   Daugava, 182
   Dnieper, 13-14, 155, 208
   Dvina, 182
   Jordan, 29, 174
   Neva, 10-12
   of souls, 182
   Severn, 21
   Vistula, 13
Rod (see also ancestors), 13, 15, 20, 40, 143, 191-192, 195, 204, 209
Rozhenitsye, 143, 147, 150, 153, 204, 209
Roerich, Nicholas, 5
Romuva, 91, 97, 129
rose, six-petaled, 143, 205
Rudra, 91
Rugen (island), 14, 45, 101
Rusalki (see also Bereginy, Fairies, nymphs), 21, 38, 93, 99, 129, 138, 142, 155-160, 168, 185, 188, 196, 204, 209-211
Russia, Russians, 2-5, 8, 10-18, 22-27, 29, 31-32, 35, 39, 41-42, 45, 48, 51-55, 62-63, 67, 69, 71-72, 75-76, 78-81, 83-85, 89-91, 98-99, 102, 105, 107, 109-110, 116-118, 121, 126, 128-129, 142-143, 147, 152-153, 155, 157, 160, 163, 165, 168, 172-174, 176-177, 183, 189-192, 196, 199-200, 203-210
Russian (language), 2-3, 5, 8, 10-12, 14-15, 17, 22-27, 29, 31-32, 35, 39, 45, 48, 51-52, 62-63, 67, 69, 71, 75-76, 79, 81, 83, 85, 89-91, 98, 107, 109-110, 116-117, 121, 129, 142-143, 152, 155, 160, 163, 173-174, 176, 183, 189-192, 200, 203-210

S

saints, 22, 29, 55, 71-72, 76, 98, 109
Sampo, 182
Sanskrit (language), 7, 11, 26, 62, 95, 116, 172, 205
Santa Claus, 91
Santeria, 55
Saraswati, 81, 207
sauna, 23, 110, 150, 203
Scandinavia, 82, 128
Scythians, 184
seashells, 28, 30
Secret Life of Plants (book), 129, 140
Seine River, 21
Semele, 81, 207
Sequana (Celtic river goddess), 21
Serbia, 13, 153
Serbs, Serbians, 13, 42, 77, 80, 152-153
    Lusatian, 152
serpents, 8, 19, 35, 66, 95, 180, 183-184, 192-193
shakti, 93, 174
Shpalernaya Street, 12
Siberia, 125-126, 152, 200
Simargl, 14, 75, 210
simurgh, 75, 210
sky, 7, 13, 26-27, 30, 32-34, 75-76, 78-80, 82, 90-91, 105, 142, 181, 193, 207
Slavs, 12-14, 25, 40, 45, 55, 76, 78, 80, 127, 142, 152-153, 162, 182, 184, 208, 212
    Eastern, 13, 72, 170
    of the Elbe, 78
    Southern, 13, 80, 153, 162-163
    Western, 13, 162
Sleeping Beauty, 147
Slovakia, 13, 78
Slovenia, Slovenes or Slovenians, 13, 42, 78, 147-148, 153-154, 163, 184
snakes (see also Godesses: Snake Goddess, Snake Mother), 6, 19, 24, 91, 144, 153, 166, 185, 187
    as house spirits, 144
    house snakes, 144

soma, 125
Sonora Desert, 128
Sophia, 174
sorcery, sorcerers, sorceresses (see also kolduny, etc.), 10, 16, 20, 22-23, 25-29, 52-54, 56-57, 62-63, 90, 102, 111, 116-119, 127-130, 132, 143, 164-165, 172, 174, 186, 191-192, 196-197, 200, 205, 210-211
soul, 57, 63, 68, 105, 116, 164, 178, 185-188, 193-194, 205
    animal, 185
    astral, 186
    identity, 185, 188
    organic, 185
    souls of the dead, 41, 135, 182-183, 187, 192, 206
    vegetable, 185
south (direction), 26, 35-36, 38, 84
Soviet Union, 10-11
Spirit Wind, 170, 173-176
spirits, 8, 13, 15, 21, 29, 33, 38, 40, 42, 52, 55, 64-65, 69, 79, 82-86, 88-91, 94, 96, 99, 109-111, 117-118, 127, 129, 135-139, 141-166, 168, 170, 173-176, 182-185, 187, 189-191, 193, 195, 203-206, 208-211
    ancestral, 15, 40, 42, 90-91, 142, 153
    of Otherworld, 82, 139
    evil, 142, 150, 155
    of Nature, 8, 13, 15, 21, 38
    of the dead, 42, 83, 143, 152, 155, 182, 187, 189, 191-192, 210-211
spring, 8, 36-40, 42, 77, 85, 88-89, 96, 131, 185, 188, 206, 210
spring equinox, 4-5, 36-40
springs: sacred, healing, 21-22, 82-83, 154, 206
St. Demetrius' Eve, 189
St. Lucy's Day, 165
St. Petersburg, 2, 4, 11, 27, 102-103, 124, 128, 139, 176-178, 199-200

Stargard, 101
stove (pich), 6, 34, 54, 94, 143-144, 146, 187, 203, 205, 208
Stravinsky, Igor, 5-6, 35, 74, 212
Stribog, 14, 74-75, 204, 210
Sumer, 29
summer, 24, 32, 36-39, 76-77, 88-89, 96, 155-157, 190
summer solstice, 8, 36, 88-89, 96, 126
Sun, 7, 13-14, 25, 27, 30, 32, 35, 38-39, 45, 65, 74-77, 82, 93, 155, 160, 185, 188, 205, 207
Svarog, 13, 75-76, 80, 210
Svarovitch, 13, 75-76, 210
Sviridova, Natasha, xii, 20-21, 143, 191, 200
svyato mesto (see power spots), 103, 114, 210
Svyatoslav, Prince, 90
sweat lodge, 23, 110-111, 203
Sweden, 90, 129, 196
    Pagan, 14, 90

T

T'ai Ch'i, 128
Tantra, 29-30, 32, 45, 173-174, 180
temples, 13-14, 45, 111, 143, 149, 204, 209
Thiess, 165
Thor, 66, 78, 90, 97, 207
Thunder Emperor (see also Perun; Elijah, St.), 79-80, 99, 143, 207
Thunder God: (see Gods), 7-8, 13-15, 28, 66, 78-80, 129, 143, 184, 207-208
Tiamat, 28, 66
Tibet, Tibetans, 23, 142, 178, 193
Tibetan Book of the Dead, 178
Tompkins, Peter, 129, 140
towels, ritual, 6, 34
trees, 13, 38-39, 42, 65, 79, 81-83, 87-88, 91-93, 101-102, 106, 111, 123-139, 144, 152-159, 161-162, 169, 185, 191, 206, 207
    alder, 131
    aspen, 131, 133, 162
    as teachers, 133-134

birch, 39, 82, 112, 129, 131, 133, 135, 139, 157, 190
elm, 128
fir, 107, 124, 132-133, 144, 162, 168-169, 171
hazel, 126
oaks, 79, 128-129
pine, 112, 131, 133, 137-138, 144, 153
sacred groves, 101-102
tree alphabet, 129
Tree Goddess (see Goddesses), 83
Tree of Life, 82, 93, 143, 191-192, 205, 209
Tree of Rod, 143, 191-192, 209
walnut, 128
willow (see also World Tree), 158
Triple Goddess (see Goddesses), 96, 209
tumo, 23
twins: Asvins; Castor and Pollux; Divine, 26, 76

U

Udelnaya, 102
Ukraine, Ukrainians, 5, 13, 24, 37, 41, 153, 160, 184, 204-206
Underworld, 8, 24, 26, 29, 31-32, 34-36, 39-41, 62, 64-66, 69, 74-75, 90-97, 99, 129, 152, 165, 182-183, 185, 193
Underworld Lord (see Gods), 90-92
United States, 3, 132, 167, 176
Upper World, 32, 34-36, 64, 69, 75, 81, 90, 97, 110, 194-196
Uppsala, 90, 97
upyr (see vampires), 188

V

Valhalla, 90
vampires, 13, 142, 164, 210
Vassilisa the Wise, 93, 95
Vaver, Galina, xii, 12, 67-68, 194, 196
vedma, 93, 203, 210
Velikoretskaya (Vyatka region), 92
Velinas, 90-92, 152

Venus (planet), 77
Vikings, 13-14
vily (see Fairies), 152, 211
Vladimir of Kiev, Prince, 0, 14, 74-75, 79
Vlas, St., 91, 211
Vodyanoi, 21, 52, 159-161, 211
volkhvy, volkhv, 16, 211
Volos, 40, 74, 90-92, 96-98, 152, 185, 208, 211
vorozheia, 54, 211
Vritra, 28, 66
Vseslavich, Volkh, 21
Vulcan, 75
Vyri, 38, 81, 96, 185, 187, 206, 209-212

W

Water, 19-25, 28-30, 32-33, 38-39, 49-50, 52-56, 58-61, 64-66, 88-89, 92, 96, 99, 109, 111, 128, 138, 142, 149, 155-161, 184, 186-187, 189, 193, 196, 206, 211
    healing, 22, 28, 39, 60, 88, 206
    of Life and Death, 8, 19, 29, 92, 95
water spirits (see Vodyanoi, Rusalki), 21, 52, 99, 211
wells, 22
werewolves, 142, 164-165
Weschcke, Carl Llewellyn, 197
west (direction), 35-36, 84
whisperers, 62
White God (see Belobog), 24, 30, 204
White Lady (see Goddesses), 6, 8, 92
Whitsuntide, 38, 155, 157, 159, 209
Whitsun Monday, 157
Whitsunday, 157
Wild Hunt, 90-92, 183
Wild Man, 88
Wild Men, 163
Wild Women, 162-163
Wim (author's friend), 177-180
wind(s), 14, 53, 75, 84, 88, 169-170, 172-176, 185, 204, 210
winter, 22, 25, 32, 36-38

winter solstice, 32-33, 36-42, 77, 85, 96, 124, 143, 157, 161, 167, 188-189, 197, 205-206, 208-210
witchcraft, 14, 64, 66, 111, 166, 197
World Tree, 9, 34-35, 39, 44, 64-66, 75, 91-93, 95, 97, 129, 135, 181-183, 185, 187, 189, 191-197, 208-209

Y

Yahweh, 80
yang (see polarities), 3, 25-27, 29, 33, 59, 103-104, 109, 121, 174, 204
Yard Spirit (see Dvorovoi), 148
Yarilo, 5, 15, 39, 89, 206, 212
Yekaterinsky Canal, 10
Yggdrasil, 192
yin (see polarities), 3, 25-27, 58-59, 103-104, 117, 121, 161, 204
Yoga, 12, 16, 57, 65, 69, 128, 173-174, 180
Young Harvest God (see Gods), 6, 8
Yugoslavia, 184

Z

Zbruch (village), 34, 81
Zelinogorsk, 105, 110-111, 113
Zhirinovsky, Vladimir, 10
znakhary (see also healing, healers), 54, 212
Zoroastrians, Zoroastrianism, 25-26
Zorya
    as Kieven Goddess, 77, 212
    as Zohra, 77
    as Zorya Vechernyaya, 77, 212
    as Zorya Utrennyaya, 77, 212

☾ LOOK FOR THE CRESCENT MOON

Llewellyn publishes hundreds of books on your favorite subjects! To get these exciting books, including the ones on the following pages, check your local bookstore or order them directly from Llewellyn.

ORDER BY PHONE
- Call toll-free within the U.S. and Canada, 1-800-THE MOON
- In Minnesota, call (612) 291-1970
- We accept VISA, MasterCard, and American Express

ORDER BY MAIL
- Send the full price of your order (MN residents add 7% sales tax) in U.S. funds, plus postage & handling to:

  Llewellyn Worldwide
  P.O. Box 64383, Dept. (K-374-3)
  St. Paul, MN 55164–0383, U.S.A.

POSTAGE & HANDLING
(For the U.S., Canada, and Mexico)
- $4.00 for orders $15.00 and under
- $5.00 for orders over $15.00
- No charge for orders over $100.00

We ship UPS in the continental United States. We ship standard mail to P.O. boxes. Orders shipped to Alaska, Hawaii, The Virgin Islands, and Puerto Rico are sent first-class mail. Orders shipped to Canada and Mexico are sent surface mail.

International orders: Airmail—add freight equal to price of each book to the total price of order, plus $5.00 for each non-book item (audio tapes, etc.).

Surface mail—Add $1.00 per item.

Allow 4–6 weeks for delivery on all orders.
Postage and handling rates subject to change.

DISCOUNTS
We offer a 20% discount to group leaders or agents. You must order a minimum of 5 copies of the same book to get our special quantity price.

FREE CATALOG
Get a free copy of our color catalog, *New Worlds of Mind and Spirit*. Subscribe for just $10.00 in the United States and Canada ($30.00 overseas, airmail). Many bookstores carry *New Worlds*— ask for it!

Visit our website at www.llewellyn.com for more information.

Jaguar Wisdom
Mayan Calendar Magic

Kenneth Johnson

The Mayan people and their Sacred Calendar continue to be a subject of fascination and speculation. *Jaguar Wisdom* presents, for the first time, an accessible introduction to the spiritual teachings and practices of the ancient *and* contemporary Mayan people. Since the Sacred Calendar remains the foundation of the Mayan spiritual tradition, *Jaguar Wisdom* introduces its complete magical system including correspondences, ritual, astrology and divination.

Make your own Mayan altar, celebrate the Day of the Dead, create a traditional Mayan amulet for protection, concoct Mayan herbal remedies, observe the five major Calendar ceremonies, find your own personal Mayan birth sign, and create your own "Tree of Life" astrological reading. In addition, you will learn how to make a typical Calendar diviner's medicine bag and practice divination with seeds and crystals.

1-56718-372-7, 6 x 9, 264 pp., illus., softcover $14.95

The Grail Castle
Male Myths and Mysteries in the Celtic Tradition

Kenneth Johnson and Marguerite Elsbeth

Explore the mysteries which lie at the core of being male when you take a quest into the most powerful myth of Western civilization: the Celtic-Teutonic-Christian myth of the Grail Castle.

The Pagan Celtic culture's world view—which stressed an intense involvement with the magical world of nature—strongly resonates for men today because it offers a direct experience with the spirit often lacking in their lives. This book describes the four primary male archetypes—the King or Father, the Hero or Warrior, the Magician or Wise Man, and the Lover—which the authors exemplify with stories from the Welsh Mabinogion, the Ulster Cycle, and other old Pagan sources. Exercises and meditations designed to activate these inner myths will awaken men to how myths—as they live on today in the collective unconscious and popular culture— shape their lives. Finally, men will learn how to heal the Fisher King—who lies at the heart of the Grail Castle myth—to achieve integration of the four archetypal paths.

1–56718–369–7, 224 pp., 6 x 9, illus., index $14.95

To order, call 1–800–THE MOON
Prices subject to change without notice

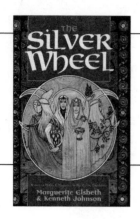

The Silver Wheel
Women's Myths and Mysteries in the Celtic Tradition

Marguerite Elsbeth and Kenneth Johnson

Myth is one of the foundations of the spiritual path. For those who are disillusioned with their own religious history, myth has become the cornerstone of Western wisdom.

For today's women, the old Celtic stories have genuine relevance. Celtic heroines come to us full of fire and spirit, fresh from the Otherworld and part of wild Nature. Their stories speak the eternal truths about power, self-identity, relationships, love, creativity, passion and death.

The Silver Wheel is a direct exploration of women's mythic past, and it offers exercises aimed at awakening and integrating the archetypes within the female personality. Revel in your own transformation as you resonate with the goddess Rhiannon and her everspiraling life-path to the heart of the Silver Wheel, wherein lies the Lady of the Otherworld, the primal Wild Woman within us all.

1-56718-371-9, 224 pp., 6 x 9, illus., softcover $14.95